Maladies
OF THE
Soul

ALSO BY JAMES SWEARINGEN

Fiction

Black Sheep (2011)

The Prodigals (2013)

In the Hollow of Time, Galatea Saga, I (2021)

Starship Galatea: A Sacred and Profane Time Machine, Galatea Saga, II (2021)

Nonfiction

Reflexivity in Tristram Shandy (Yale, 1977)

Maladies
OF THE
Soul

James Swearingen

"What did they live on," said Alice, who always took a
great interest in questions of eating and drinking.

"They lived on treacle," said the Dormouse, after thinking
a minute or two.

"They couldn't have done that, you know," Alice gently
remarked. "They'd have been ill."

"So they were," said the Dormouse; "very ill."

—*Alice in Wonderland*

Preface

א You may call me Nuntius, a messenger without a message from a world behind the world. Little more than a witness "breathing-in" whatever may be on offer and a voice "breathing-out" as in giving names.

We have been here before, we immortals, though the word—being negative—conveys little. Even the words "we" and "I" don't apply where there is neither one nor plurality. More a cloud of witnesses or just a voice located between before and after, in the moment between the beatings of the heart.

These observations were underway long before the fur traders built huts against tempest and sun and called this place La Nouvelle-Orléans;

. . . before the ribbons of concrete bridged the stagnant waters, binding the ridges of silt into an illusion of land;

. . . before the seawalls and the levees prohibited the creative zigzag of the river;

. . . before the Ojibwe even named the great river Misi-ziibi, "long river"—or the river found its long bed, or the ice melted and made a bed for the river to fid—before all these we were here.

What is striking in returning to this place of water and silt is the city itself—begotten by the river but, like it, always resisting definition and measure. The sheer adventure of the place! Observation post for a thousand experiments in living. They say *Laissez les bon temps roulez*, but the heart of the matter is *laissez* in a city that has always been willing "to let."

A century ago, just yesterday, the pleasure palaces of Storyville rivaled the flesh pots of Carthage. For some a canker—Sin City, Babylon, Gomorrah—awaiting death by water rather than fire. For others, a jewel at the mouth of the great River, as magnificent in suffering as in pleasure when the plagues of yellow fever and cholera killed as horribly as old-world black death.

The city was always precarious in its long and languid motion toward order and propriety. But beneath the surface, in street music, in carnival, even in vice, the old spirit throbs on. Vitality rekindled between law and breach. Not tolerance or pleasure. Not these only. But the daring to live and the will *to let*.

Here, in the Garden District, there is an old monastery, now called The Valmont, where a solitary writer gives his nights and days to diagnosing modern ills from a babble of voices. But the mystery is why, amidst all the tainted glory of this city, he should choose an old nunnery as his observation post. Surely not for the incongruity of the thing. Unless its present iteration is especially suitable for eavesdropping on the modern soul, if there is such a thing.

For a while there was a soul, the function at least. We watched the Greeks invent it and the religious develop it. For a while they had an easy time of it. Its maladies could still be diagnosed by consulting a set of rules, until the soul itself was lost and the maladies were relegated to the medical faculty.

This scribe, this scribbler, seems to think the world has fallen away from its old ideals and come to ruin. So, as he writes, Nuntius, the messenger without message, watches unseen over his shoulder to find what he makes of it all and why he bothers. Among the transitory desires and restless pursuits of his neighbors, the Scribe detects seven ancient vices that blight the very walls of this building. It's unclear what profit he expects from his efforts to understand and correct an errant world. Is he building himself an ark against the once and future deluge? Searching for a cure for his own riven being? Not knowing that the search for a cure may be the disease itself?

The Valmont

How I, Alejandro ("Alex") Dupin, an Arcadian Creole writer, came to be sitting here in New Orleans in an old monastery like one of god's spies might be story enough, but first you must know how a convent slowly dwindled into a posh residential establishment on St. Charles Avenue. I'll give you the bare bones of the place for now. For the muscle and nerve, you'll have to wait. As for myself, the scribbler of the tales that follow . . . well, that can wait till the moment after next.

Originally The Valmont was an Ursuline convent in the Garden District, a quiet but prominent institution, until the sisters died out or got too old to carry on. After closing, it was abandoned for years then desecrated by a restoration in which nothing was restored but the lumber and mortar. Yet it's still possible to see how life was once organized in the four wings of the rectangular building with its central garden enclosed by the pointed arches of a still-older cloister.

In the center of that sun-drenched green space, ancient flagstone paths outline patches of lawn and cross in the middle. In each quadrant, tropical plants and flowers wave softly in the afternoon breeze, but the most unusual surviving feature rests in the northeast corner behind a little fence where the nuns remain, "buried" above ground because of the water table and left undisturbed by progress. So little marble on the outside; so many shades within!

To understand the significance of this place, you must linger in the quiet cloister or sit in the garden and learn to be still. But you must also hold in mind that it was once a school. In those days "educate" still meant to "educe" and "draw out" beyond bare life into the uniquely human potential for living-well. Though no longer. And that's only one of the historical details that are forgotten here.

Another detail that perhaps should not matter, strangely does. It goads me during my late-night vigils and leaves me searching for words I cannot find, for a thought I cannot think: There are no children at The Valmont!

After the convent school closed, the building stood abandoned and decaying for years until the real estate tycoon Lester King bought it and "developed" it. Aren't words curious things? You'd think "de-velopment" of a monastery would open its "en-velope" and reveal its true content! As, in a way, I'm trying to do here, perhaps because during several of its years of abandon I had the place to myself as the only resident. That happened like this:

After college while deciding what I would do with my life, I, Alejandro ("Alex") Dupin, seeking a place to read my books and lay my head, was allowed to live rent-free in the derelict building in exchange for the minimal service of keeping watch and taking care, though no one else cared about the place so long as the façade on the famous Avenue remained tidy. During the renovations Mr. King extended the arrangement, since my two small rooms in a third-floor corner—once the convent library—had no market value anyway. And that's the history of how I came to occupy this observation post for keeping tabs on the modern world.

It's ironic that Lester renamed the building "The Valmont," since there are no valleys to sound and no mountains to scale. In the remodeling, the classrooms on the second floor were turned into spacious condominiums with wide decks extending over the cloister below. The third floor, the old dormitory, became smaller units with Juliet balconies that overlook the garden. They, the balconies, are an oddity: French doors and a few inches of overhang enclosed by iron railings may expand the sense of space on the inside, but otherwise they're artifacts stuck on walls where they don't belong. No memory here of the mythic love of Romeo and Juliet, even less of a different love that was once the heart and soul of the convent.

What you can't see from the garden is the old refectory, now a party room; or the kitchen, used for storage; or the chapel, which isn't a chapel anymore. After the lamp was blown out and the holy water drained from the stoup and the altar stone removed, the two-story sanctuary became a nondescript, empty space whose reality is now expressed in the extraordinary word "real estate." In a world where space is on sale by the square foot and human beings by the hour, the room is kept locked up and useless until Lester King can think of a way to turn it into a profit.

At least the monastery garden remains unchanged. Though the residents might prefer a garden of earthly delights to a nuns' cemetery, it's much as it ever was except that the residents call it "the Quad," another "useful" space going unused in the high-rent center of the modern city. At one time Mr. King thought of tearing it out and building a swimming pool, but the residents opposed the ravage, and Lester's title deed even forbade it. It's used, the Quad, as a pretty passageway and otherwise avoided or ignored. Yet whatever Mary Bourdieu, the caretaker, does with the flowers or the hedges the residents notice and approve as "atmospheric."

There's an untold story concealed somewhere in this relation of the well-heeled secularists to the once-sacred space of the nuns' quiet house. You might think these moderns would want to obliterate the traces of the religious life.

As for the caretaker, Mary Bourdieu, she lives on the garden level southwest where she can monitor the entrance from St. Charles Avenue. She's a fixture here, always tending her roses. A large, cheerful woman with a short bob of greying hair, in a blue apron and straw hat, like a working-class eccentric among the affluent middle classes. A good-hearted soul—middle-aged now, simple, a bit tiresome—but she's the continuity, perhaps the soul of the place, the one surviving principle of cohesion and the only person with a connection to The Valmont that can't be measured in dollars.

Mary grew up in New Orleans and attended the convent school as a child. She lived with her parents in a shotgun down on Constantinople Street and never married. Eventually she became a practical nurse and cared for Mr. King's elderly aunt until the aunt died.

Later still, when Mary's mother passed and Mr. Bourdieu had a stroke, Lester King offered her the job as caretaker. That's "King Lester," as the satirical Mr. Bourdieu enjoys calling him. Since the offer was generous, Mary and Mr. B moved into the unit by the gate where she serves as concierge, though she probably doesn't know that the word means "fellow-slave." Gardener too. By choice.

She loves this garden and is determined to preserve the nuns' memory—as in the columbines that, she's glad to tell you, stand for the Holy Spirit, or in the red roses she keeps on the base of the statue of the Virgin in the cloister. She calls the roses "the tears of the Madonna." I wonder if it's nostalgia for the sisters going their silent way, or whether she really feels the lost spirit of the place.

The residents take Mary for granted as one of the amenities collecting their deliveries, admitting their guests, and generally looking out for their property. For them, The Valmont is much like any other residence where the social status and the price are right and the rooms comfortable. Only Mary remembers what it all means.

✗ Monastery garden, once open to the heavens, now enclosed. Community forbidden by walls and gates. In the empty center where once a "we" celebrated a nameless "You," now insular "I's" coexist.

My odd task as scribe, meanwhile, is to fill in the blanks of the residents' lives, trying to understand their modern maladies and imagine cures. But interruption, like the one above about the garden, brings me to the most mysterious thing of all. Perhaps one who's concerned with *modern* diseases should have the good taste not to bring it up, but I can't resist. It's so odd. The fact is, The Valmont is haunted. By voices! Sometimes unheard but felt as alert "presences" even by people who know exactly what's real and what's not. Sometimes worse! Not goblins or spooks under the table, mind you. More like familiar spirits who speak and even converse.

Mr. B, for example, the sanest person in the place, hears such a sympathetic voice in his room. Still more alarming, when I leave my writing desk, I often return to find *these* messages written across the empty white spaces of my notebooks by an interloper who could only have intruded on my narrow third-floor cell with Mary's passkey!

Still more alarming, the messages respond to my words at just the point where I can't go on! Nothing mystical about it. No voodoo priestess from Congo Square. No tempting demon. Yet an invisible commentator who somehow gathers up what I can't find words for or reveals thoughts that are not mine in words I could not have found. And they come without author or authority. So let's you and I keep the mystery to ourselves. After all, at the moment, you, reader, don't quite exist for me, and, to you, I'm nothing but words.

—

"I don't see you, but I know you're here."

An old man in an empty room watches the vacant garden for clues. His words, blurred at the edges, still resonate like words received and understood. Snappishly, his good hand spins the wheelchair back with the pent-up fury of one trapped in a body that no longer does his bidding.

"I can feel you're here. The way a blind man feels. The way a dog knows his master, by smell."

He expects no answer and receives none, but gradually relaxes into his chair and grows calm.

Mr. Bourdieu—Mr. B to others, "Papa" to Mary—is a short, stocky man with a deeply tanned face creased by years in the sun, working on the riverfront. He's partially withered by two strokes, but anyone who gives more than passing attention to the squarish face detects the glint of shrewdly observant eyes, though few at The Valmont are inclined to gaze so closely at another being.

The skin on the neck is loose and leathery where old-man hairs grow randomly from the wrinkles. The arms are weathered, with curly reddish hair standing out along swells of muscle going slack. Hands, likewise, rugged and calloused and square. As for the clothes, he wears what he's always worn: high-water pants with suspenders, laced-up workman's shoes, and brown socks.

Mr. B's speech may be a little slurred, but there is no slurring in the clarity of his mind. By force of character, he refuses to be defeated by age and illness. The sad tendency of the mouth to sag downward on one side is countered and dominated by a cheerful upward slant on the left. It's a face that has tasted the joys and the sorrows of life without surrendering to the vagaries of fortune.

His room is nondescript. Minimal furniture so the chair can move about freely. On the wall above the hospital bed, a crucifix and, over the table covered in a white lace cloth and family pictures, a monthly calendar with a winter scene in the Rockies. Opposite, a monstrous TV with foil-wrapped rabbit ears stares blindly back at the bed and an overstuffed chair.

"Mary's gone to a party in the refectory so we can have a gossip while I keep watch." He turns his chair back to the French doors that open into the cloister and continues quietly, unselfconsciously, taking his time, in communion with the empty room that doesn't feel quite empty.

He grins. "Mary says I'm a snoop like that man in the Jimmy Stewart movie. The one about the photographer who watches his neighbors from his wheelchair. Says she'll end up having to call the vice squad. Not that she'd know a vice if she saw one." He raises the grizzled eyebrows and chuckles.

"I shouldn't be so hard on her. She's a good girl. A bit gullible. *Loves* everybody, for Christ's sake! But a good girl. Helps others without needing to give herself credit." He pauses for a moment then brightens at some further development of the thought. "If you needed her old coat, she'd say to the coat, 'This is your lucky day, coat. You'll have a better future with her. She needs you more than I do.'"

It must be hard for a man who has lived an active life to see his world shrink to the frame of a single window. Reduced hour after hour, day after day to looking out on a rectangle of less than half an acre where fewer than two dozen people pass and most of them rarely. Anyone else might wallow in idleness and self-pity, but Mr. B spends his solitary days and nights examining life, looking for consistency, and keeping tabs on people who lack the leisure to think things over and think them through.

Having always faced unpleasant truths about himself, he expects no less of others. Anything else, he says, leads to hypocrisy and Mary's "nice people." A life of physical labor where things done have clear consequences makes a man hard-headed and rational. Hence the bare-knuckled moralist has no truck with fine sensibilities and subtle distinctions. Just clear judgment and plain speaking.

He chuckles again. "The truth is, the nice, successful people in this place are crazies. With two exceptions. As it happens, the only residents of color. One is a successful engineer and businessman named Fabien Bergeron whose name is legendary on the docks. He built a large company downtown then suddenly quit, so they say. Divorced his wife and family and moved here, where he lives a sort of half-life with his camera, of all things!

"The second more or less sane resident is another loner"—he points up and across the garden—"on the third floor where a light always burns in the window at night. Name's Alex, though others call him The Hermit. I know him as a kind of resident handyman who sometimes works tugs on the river. I like talking with him about old times, but I keep that to myself to protect him from curiosity.

"Anyway, one morning not long-ago when he wasn't there, Mary had to let a workman into his unit. When she came back, her eyes were like saucers. 'You wouldn't believe it,' she said. 'So orderly! Like nobody really lives there, except for a table in front of the balcony doors where the lamp is, and neat stacks of books around the room. He must be a writer of some kind, like Robinson Crusoe on his island. There's a notebook on the table and an open pen, like he just left off. I couldn't help glancing at the pages. Not that I could make much sense of them. But you'd never guess! It was all about Mr. Basson!'

"Basson, you must know, is the federal prosecutor who's been making such a stir in the city in recent years. Anyway, Mary continued her story: 'It's like we've got a handyman who's really a spy living right here under our noses, spying on the spy.'

"Then she lightened up a bit and said, 'Looks like you and George Basson aren't the only ones watching people, Papa.'"

After his brief account of Mary, Mr. B falls silent, staring into the dimly lit garden, now empty, as though considering the mystery. Eventually he adds, to the absent person in the room, "What I see from this window is a parade of vices. You'd think it was Purgatory, and we're all here for the treatment."

—

It's time for me, Alex, the Scribe, to begin introducing the residents who constitute the heart, if not the soul, of these tales. Now imagine, if you will, that you're sharing my perspective from the third-floor window of my small room in the northeast corner of the Quad. If you look for the two men at a wrought-iron table in the opposite corner of the cloister, you will see from the cassock that one is a priest. Actually, both are. Not a type I normally take much interest in, but these two are curious enough. The one in the dapper civilian clothes, sitting rigidly upright in his wrought-iron chair, is Fr. Joseph Barthes, a geologist on sabbatical from his college up East. He's house-sitting for his sister and brother-in-law while he assembles his research into a book.

Even sitting, the angular dignity of his tall figure suggests that he's at that table under duress and withholding himself. His physical presence—the clothes; the dark, full head of well-coifed hair, greying at the temples and parted almost in the middle; the sculpted head and commanding eyes—all contribute to his authority and Olympian bearing. There is nothing fussy or studied in his appearance. But precisely ordered as though once for all and maintained by habit. Even the way he occupies a chair—pushed well back from the table, he holds himself in reserve from the man opposite—makes him appear aloof even from the cloister and the garden.

Fr. Barthes' character is expressed in the rigor and solemnity of his attention to everything around him, missing nothing, judging everything. Not self-consciously perhaps, but instinctively taking dominion everywhere, even over Mary's perfectly tended garden. He's clearly accustomed to the world standing at attention in his presence. Not arrogance exactly, as when, intermittently, he glances at the man opposite, but rather as one born to rule by the power of a rigorous and well-furnished mind.

The other man, the stocky Irishman with the shock of prematurely white hair, wears a slightly shabby cassock often lightly sprinkled with dandruff and always with the tell-tale Roman collar. He's Mary Bourdieu's parish priest, Mark Maloney. He sits relaxed and quiet, exuding an air of inner stillness, breathing-in the contemplative mood of the garden. It's not new to him as it is to the other priest. He, like Mary, was here in its earlier incarnations, a quiet green space defined by yellowish cobblestones in the shape of a cross below and open to the heavens above.

It is he who eventually breaks the silence by asking the proud Jesuit, "So what's the topic of your research? Mary mentioned that you're working on a book. What's your field?"

The answer is curt and formal. "Geology." Then a pause. "Of the Mississippi Valley. Academic stuff." He, though the younger of the two, seems disinclined to speak of his science, as though it might be lost on a simple parish priest.

Fr. Maloney, unintimidated by the other, is more interested in discerning the life well-lived than collecting bits of learned information. He sits patiently, listening with a sort of vocational detachment, smiling benignly, taking no notice of the dismissive remark, listening through chatter to the spirit of the words.

To keep the topic going, he remarks, "I don't know much about the geology, but I guess the situation of New Orleans has always been precarious." Then, patiently, he waits for a response.

Eventually Fr. Barthes, the scientist, yields and speaks again, reluctantly at first, expressionless and without gesture, but with slowly gathering energy. "An unstable place. Until recently, not really a place at all. To get it in perspective you must imagine the Ice Age meltdown creating the river that divides the continent and expands the Delta along the Gulf from the runoff."

He stops as though to measure whether the other's interest is up to the topic then, finding it plausible, at least, resumes more energetically. "The northern half of the river goes back 70 million years to the dinosaurs. By 60 million years it had crossed the Mississippi Delta and expanded to the size of the Amazon. By contrast, Lake Pontchartrain to the north of the city is a mere 5,000 years old, while the long tail of swamps to the south and the sickle of mud and silt we're sitting on—one of the few spots above sea level—is still more recent. Thrown up by the floods after the river changed its course in the eleventh century, the era of the Norman Conquest."

Launched on his favorite subject, Joseph quickly relaxes into the topic without softening toward his audience, speaking with the enthusiasm and seriousness of a man for whom truth is a lifelong challenge. He strokes his salt-and-pepper mustache as his face alternates between an impersonal but knowing smile and a rather disagreeable frown.

"For the European traders the River was all-important. Wherever there was a harbor, there had to be a town. Even in these marshes and bayous with no place to build."

Fr. Mark, sitting meanwhile at ease and at home in this place of reflection, hears more in these sentences than may be intended. "It's an old story," he replies lightly. "What we do to nature, we do first to ourselves."

The remark clearly annoys the other and raises another frown, but there's more of Fr. Mark's affable philosophy still to come: "Mechanism makes cadavers of us all. Even of nature herself. Enslave the one and we enslave the other."

A shadow of belligerence passes over Fr. Barthes' face. However detached he may be from others, in conversation his face is an open book on his own states of mind. This time he visually dismisses the obscure reference to mechanism as irrelevant, even presumptuous, and shrugs off the interruption to resume his own story: "In the eighteenth century, against the advice of his engineers, Bienville built his trading post in the middle of the swamp on this trembling ridge of silt and sand and clay."

Maloney, more concerned with the character of his brother priest than with geology, casually lights a cigarette and replies with a chuckle, "New Orleans has always been a city in need of foundations."

The other pauses, conspicuously listening away from these words, and concentrates instead on a distant rumble. "Feel that streetcar passing out on the Avenue? Feel the earth tremble? After the flood of 1927 when the levees and concrete barriers were built, the sediment was channeled downstream to the Gulf. Now the whole river is mainly an industrial barge canal, and its floodplains have been engineered out of existence. Meanwhile the residue compacts under our feet, the city sinks, the coastal wetlands dry up, and the land slides slowly south toward a sea that, all the while, is rising!"

The earnestness in his voice and the rigidity of his face suggest a man who bears responsibility for holding the earth and the city in place. "An endodermis of sand. An epidermis of swamp. Water everywhere." He grins sardonically. "The sheer incongruity of it all! And below the thin skin, the lake of liquid fire."

Mark considers even these contingencies with equanimity. "I suppose human building has always been precarious."

Joseph glares as if to show that the last remark is too otherworldly for comment, then continues. "A city of tall buildings at the bottom of the continent rising from this saucer of mud! All these lovely houses riding on top at sea level and sliding south as they wait for the perfect storm or the next melting of the ice. Just a century from now."

The intensity of his gaze insists on the urgency of the point against this man who seems to have the leisure, or the indifference, to enjoy the garden from the edge of impending disaster. "One day the storm will come and dump the lake onto the city. The disaster will be unspeakable. Death by water. The sheer incongruity of it all!"

Fr. Mark's eyes meet Joseph's in calm appreciation of transience, as though disintegration might not be all bad nor building always good. "According to His inscrutable will."

"Huh!"

The Agent
Lust

On Monday morning a tan Jaguar zips along I-10 into the city from Metairie where Lester King and his latest wife live in a gated community on the edge of a golf course. The car and an expensive suit give him a sense of distinction many steps above the streaming multitudes whom he passes in the streets and along the sidewalks of the city.

Aside from Lester's prominence as Real Estate Broker of the Year and ranking member of the Krewe of Proteus, New Orleans' second-oldest Mardi Gras social club, he is reassured of his consequence in the city by the valet's glance of admiration when, at a hotel or restaurant, he hands over the key to the Jaguar, and by the glance of a pretty woman admiring his good taste in clothes.

Lester is an ebullient man, tall, big boned, with broad shoulders and a full head of brown hair. A tad stiff, as if his natural comportment and gestures have been forfeited to some conscious image of himself. Without being especially handsome in his blue business suit and conservative tie, appealing nonetheless to women. Perhaps what they like is the confident look of success and the carefree air of the man-about-town who knows, and is known by, everyone.

Or is it the everlasting cheerfulness of the born salesman whose Rotarian good humor shows even in the spring of his stride? And the smile: If it were a mask, Lester wouldn't let himself know it, though the careful observer might see as much in the agate-colored eyes without depth. Eyes, inclined to avoid a steady gaze and to shift at moments of truth. Behind the public mask, alone in the car, the sharp edges of his features seem rubbed out by long confinement inside himself.

As he saunters through the outer office of the thriving real estate agency in the Vieux Carré, a bright young voice calls out, "Morning, Les." Not even his secretary remembers why his name is truncated at work.

"Morning, Jo," he sings and runs his hand over the back of his head, smoothing the well-coifed hair for the benefit of the clerks and salespeople at the desks behind. Jo is a tall, slender blond with flashing blue eyes and a bubbly disposition. He smiles down on her with the not-quite-leer of the tired hedonist. "Good weekend? What calls do you have for me?"

"Jake Barnes. Says he can be *in* about one thirty this afternoon."

"Good." Lester raises a brow and looks askance without adjusting the insolent grin. "In" does not refer to an office but to the Bottoms Up Club on Bourbon Street, a kind of safe house for business of a discreet character.

After Jo takes another call, he continues the predatory game that, lacking conviction, lacks danger—danger to her at least. "When are you going to leave your husband and come away with me, Jo?" He holds up a finger and grins. "Remember, Les is always more." Only *he* finds the remark amusing.

"Hmm," she casually replies. The scene has been repeated a hundred times. She knows it's mainly habit, a living cliché, though he doesn't know, as he doesn't know that—or why—the intensity is gone.

But to business. "This morning I'll be out checking the inspector's report on that Algiers property. You can reach me on the car phone. After lunch I'll meet Barnes."

The piece of morning business done, he returns by the Pontchartrain Expressway and up the high bridge over the river back into town, but slowly, to survey the scene from on high. Who better than a real estate agent to look out across a city and see it with an eye of possession: to his right the office towers of the thriving downtown, the Vieux Carré and New Orleans East; to his left the warehouse district along the River and along the crescent to the elegant Garden District; and to the north the wide, flat expanse of residential neighborhoods all the way to the Lakefront. All of it, his realm.

Next stop Manoni's Muffaletta Shop on Decatur Street, where he has been going for years and enjoys knowing and being known. A crowded, noisy place with a long mahogany bar down one side, tiled walls, Lincrusta ceiling, and a line of fans along the center of the room, turning slowly. He weaves his way through the crowded space, shaking hands and shouting greetings.

"How's tricks, Lester?"

"Hey, Marty." Marty Berenson, manager of Channel 3 across the street from the real estate office in the Quarter. "Got rid of your silly weatherman yet?" The reference is to one of Lester's residents.

Berenson rolls his eyes facetiously as near to heaven as the character of either man or the gold metal ceiling allows.

Lester passes on. A waitress calls, "Hi, honey." She points him to a table in the back next the courtyard. "The usual?"

"Yes ma'am, unless you're available." She throws an ironic grin over her shoulder and keeps moving.

✗ Neither pagan sensualist without surplus yearnings nor Casanova sinning deliciously. A diminished existence beyond the era of law and desire, promising what?

—

With time on his hands, Lester leaves the car in the lot at the French Market and heads toward the club. More strip joint than lounge, a dive really, but he knows the vulgar face of the city as well as its glamour and the traces of revels past: the dried, half-eaten hotel meals littering tablecloths rumpled and soiled, lipstick-stained bar glasses, cigarette butts floating in the dregs of wine along street curbs, the Monday-morning street smells of restaurant waste and urine. Knows the drunken leers and bacchanalian faces broadened by coarse laughter no less than the elegant restaurants, the carnival balls, and the prestigious gentlemen's club on Canal Street. He's an amphibious social creature who keeps up a broad network of convenient "contacts."

Casually he strolls through Jackson Square in the suit that makes him pleasingly conspicuous in the crowds. In the plaza in front of St. Louis Cathedral, a few people have gathered around a mime playing Jesus as the beneficent shepherd, arms extended, scarred palms out in the come-unto-me gesture. The mime is good at it. So realistic you're tempted to touch the wounds to see if they bleed.

Suddenly the Jesus-eyes-without-motion come into focus on something or someone at Lester's side. He, Lester, turns and finds no one there—though the Jesus-eyes continue looking at the spot and unmistakably answering the gaze of another.

Lester recalls his aunt Helene's saying that animals and children and artists see things other folks don't. "Like God," she said. He shrugs and passes incuriously on. Taking Pirates Alley beside the church to Royal Street, that sensation passes into the next and he thinks of Jake Barnes and the building inspection rules.

"Hey, Mister Lester. How ya'll been doin'?" The greeting comes from the all-purpose porter leaning against the wall outside the club, smoking.

"Hello Emmett. Anybody at home in the cat house?"

"Jus' Madame, and she ain't in no mood for trouble today. I cain't stand it in there. Have to come out for air. Guess the money ain't been comin' in so fast." He flicks the stub of his cigarette into a rancid gutter.

Passing on into the club that shows glitzy by night, sordid and worn by day, Lester stops at the bar where Blanche, the proprietor, sits behind the cash register. She looks up and coughs. "So, Lester. Slumming today, are we?" The voice gravelly from decades of tobacco smoke. Lethargically, she scratches the creases in her wrinkled neck, climbs off the bar stool, and approaches.

He answers her idle question. "Just busy trying to make ends meet, Blanche."

"You might bring some of them high-toned 'ends' in here once in a while." She shrugs. "Oh well." And nods toward the other side of the dingy room. "What'll it be?"

"Nothing today, dear," as he passes a bill across the bar with a facetious smile. "On my account."

Turning away, he looks around, not seeing what tourists see: seeing instead a place as the phantom of its former self—unpainted floors worn into paths by shuffling feet; patches of bare wall where plaster has peeled, the mortar between the bricks in ruin; a scruffy platform, at night the stage; booths and chairs, shabby and moth-eaten; the air fouled by smoke and stale beer.

In a dimly lit corner a man sits at a table with his back turned, nursing a bottle of Dixie.

Lester takes the seat opposite and greets Barnes in a low voice. "How's it going, Jake?"

"Not good. The feds breathing down our necks. Undercover agents everywhere. Can't even use the telephone."

Lester removes a thick envelope from inside his jacket and slips it across the stained table.

Jake pockets the envelope unexamined, then passes a slip of paper back across. "If you need me, call this number. Say you're my doctor. I'll call back from a pay phone."

"Or leave a message with Blanche. We can trust her."

—

To understand the real estate agent, begin with a well-known contrivance for socializing the young: the Lester Box. Incubator for souls and guide to life. Sufficient for living, though less for living-well. The purpose of the box is to imprint on the child a conventional paradigm of the world as a fixed system and the firm boundaries of his own identity. The point is to preclude infection by anything abnormal or unfamiliar that might disrupt the integrity and conservation of the same. Thus endowed at a tender age with a strong ego and an image of his place in the world of goods and services, Lester is armed for the pursuit of serial satisfactions and a life without ideas.

The Lester-code, though not as simple as the visual image, is easily formulated. It frames happiness in five simple commandments:

1. Always subordinate thinking to interests and opinions;
2. Act without wondering why and without asking questions—especially questions about the kind of being who *can* ask a question or have an interest;
3. Never, ever raise the lid of the box and speculate on what-might-be;
4. From box to grave, let nothing change and feel no remorse;
5. Since life is about being well-adjusted and successful, enjoy yourself and die.

Thus Lester, well-imbued with the passion for unthinking and deprived in advance of what makes us human, entered life with the door firmly shut where the human world begins.

Or put the whole process in the less precise terms of biography, and it would go like this: For much of Lester's childhood, his father was absent. The older King returned from the army and found a job as a door-to-door salesman then, when the boy was eight, died, leaving him to the care of a neurotic mother. Mother and son might have been destitute had not a benevolent Aunt Helene provided each with a small room at the top of her boarding house on Prytania Street. She then encouraged the mother to take a course at the Institute of Cosmetology and helped set her up in a beauty parlor.

These three adults—two more or less living, one more or less dead—were the models in Lester's box. From his father he learned the three keys to success: a pair of well-polished shoes; a clean, well-pressed suit; and a knack for "shooting the breeze." This humble initiation into the realities of the human condition was the first key to becoming a man of property and influence.

From his mother he learned a darker truth: that while it might be easy to make other men like him for his "gift of gab," winning a woman's affection was more difficult. The third influence was Aunt Helene and her establishment, where life came prepackaged and clearly labeled in the clichés of nameless people passing through.

His mother was what was called "high strung." Whether she resented being trapped with responsibility for the boy by the death of the father, or whether she fretted indiscriminately from the daily edge of hysteria, she kept Lester at arm's length and dealt with him, when dealing was unavoidable, through a fog of irritation.

If he failed to win *her* affection, he fared better elsewhere. As an attractive boy, polite, charming even, well able to ingratiate himself with others, he learned quickly to get what he wanted from women, with a minimum of effort. When he became the pet of the regulars in the beauty shop, the mother didn't like it, but she was too busy to interfere, especially since he was good for business. As a child he was fondled by the women, held on their laps, given candy and coins, and generally fussed over, so that, one way or another, he never lacked some substitute for scarce maternal affection.

Then with adolescence, the game became consciously erotic. Once in particular: A woman well-known at the shop—married and in her mid-forties—asked him to come to her house for some odd job in exchange for money. The young entrepreneur went eagerly, did the work, and collected his pay. Then she seduced him. Successfully one might say, for he went away from that first sexual encounter with a fuller sense of the rewards life had to offer.

If there was a connection between the desire for money and for women, he discovered it slowly, but the art of benign hustling he learned more quickly. He had a little cart that he took into the Quarter to sell Cokes and candy bars to tourists. They were charmed by the smooth-talking boy with the open face and engaging manner. As a result, he always had enough pocket money to keep himself looking respectable at school, where he was mainly on the lookout for practical information, "practical" being the reliable unit of measure in the Lester Box.

Eventually he got a job in a real estate office and quickly learned that selling a house was not so different from selling candy. It was all about selling himself and pleasing the customer. He had a talent for matching house to client and boasted that anyone who couldn't show people exactly what they wanted in ten tries should have his license revoked. Thus, the complete Lester King: born and bred for success.

N Deprivation of the man of property: incomplete weaning from the mother displaced into fetishism of the female body and further invested in houses and lands. Why no stake in crossing-over toward unforeseeable modes of being? Omitted. "What is a man / If his chief good and market of his time / Be but to sleep and feed?—a beast, no more."

—

The real estate agent's social conditioning makes it doubtful that he would allow himself to be shaken to the foundations and awakened to alternative ways of living. But a day was to come when an incident would casually, thoughtlessly break through Lester King's defenses and threaten all his complacencies. On that day, here's what happened:

It was the afternoon when he put the "Model Open" sign in front of The Valmont. That task completed, he sat alone in his counting-house counting up his money and his female conquests, the only essential difference between the two being the number of zeros on the bottom line. Since counting abstracts from reality, even he eventually got bored and drifted to the living room window overlooking St. Charles, where he stood randomly watching as a streetcar stopped in the median and a young woman got off.

As she stepped to the ground, her shopping bag caught in the carriage door, and an impatient snatch ripped the bag. Several articles of clothing scattered on the ground along with pieces of tissue paper that blew under the streetcar out of reach. Having recovered her treasures and abandoned the trash, the moment of frustration quickly passed, and she resumed a statuesque dignity that belied her small frame.

As she waited for the traffic light, Lester studied her with the eye of a connoisseur, cataloging the female attributes: *age*—mid-twenties; *figure*—average height and shapely; *dress*—grey business suit and white blouse, consciously or not prepared for the eye of the male. His judgment gained strength from one "consumer response," as a well-dressed man on the other side of the tracks turned back for a second glance in the woman's direction. Then came confirmation by the gods, for as she crossed the avenue, a ray of sunlight descended through the oak trees and turned a cascade of blond curls into a golden halo.

Lester might have looked away had he also detected a hint of romantic tradition at odds with her vaguely resentful spirit, but that possibility was superseded by her next move as she paused in front of The Valmont to read the "Model Open" sign and pick up a brochure with his picture on it.

So it happened that he was still watching from the living room when the bell rang and, the door being open, she entered. She stopped, looked about alertly—at the unit, not him—and the full lips involuntarily curved upward, making a dimple in one cheek. She examined the unit with a lively curiosity that revealed practical intelligence and energy, until Lester's vaguely carnivorous grin caused the smile to vanish. Her left hand passed across her brow as though to wipe away his gaze, and from that moment, cold blue and defiant eyes evaded him.

In whatever obscure part of his being it was that passed for a soul, he must have felt the imprint of the hand on that brow and the telltale ring on the fourth finger. The scene lasted only a few seconds, but it registered on him as a brush with new reality, the stronger because where he wanted recognition, he was stung by contempt.

"I'm the developer," he said, offering a hand that was ignored. "Would you sign the register please?" He pushed a sheet of paper across the table in front of her.

She winced and replied indignantly, "Is the model open for inspection or is there an entrance fee?" Then turned and walked into the dining room. That did nothing to reduce the pressure of his gaze, and when next her glance chanced to cross his—because he was standing in her way—the lips tightened and curled into a glower that bluntly said, "And you can keep your eyes to yourself!"

He was an old hand at the game—both games, the commercial and the erotic—but her strange mixture of intensity and coldness made her hard to classify. As she moved through the rooms satisfying curiosity, he followed like a dog on a leash. The more attentive he was, the stiffer her back and the more annoyed her demeanor. She lingered, almost defiantly, exploring the floor plan, the view through the live oaks over the avenue, the plethora of labor-saving devices—everything a person hungry for comfort and prestige might desire. Then when she turned to enter the bedroom, he stepped in her path with another bid for attention. She responded with a frigid "Excuse me," as though he were an inanimate object, and passed him by.

Without entirely giving up the chase, the connoisseur of female types busied himself studying this specimen from such proximity as her contempt and perpetual motion allowed. Judging from the intensity of her interest in The Valmont, she would likely be from a poor family upstate; Protestant in background, economically inferior to her school friends, conceivably embarrassed by hand-me-down dresses, a small shabby house, and a coarse family—in short, a parvenue ambitious to live on the fashionable Avenue that might give her social substance enough to cast a respectable shadow.

After fifteen minutes of scarcely veiled tension, Lester stands chattering in the kitchen about counter tops and appliances while she, still ignoring him, opens doors and drawers, examining materials and workmanship, visibly imagining herself in the model unit. Having heard none of Lester's sales pitch, she wheels around, confronts him, and interrupts: "What's the asking price?"

Instead of mentioning a figure, he launches into a prefabricated and condescending speech on financing and interest rates. She snaps to attention and, without a word, silences him in midsentence by simply standing before him, hands on her hips, feet apart with the weight on one foot, like one who might spring into flight at any moment. The business chatter ceases, and he mentions a number. Promptly, she turns away and marches once more through the apartment while he waits patiently in the kitchen.

When she returns, the situation has changed. Something among the anonymous furnishings and nondescript accoutrements, something has shifted on the horizon of her thwarted life.

Lester sees the spark of imagination in her eyes and forgets the chase. On the objective scale, where he lives, it should be nothing, but one of those nothings that, in the blink of an eye, can turn a life around. The light passing across her face makes a small chink in the fortress of his selfhood and causes some element in his equation of pleasure and pain to slip into a new place. But, as a will-o'-the-wisp escapes being fixed by the eye, so this epiphany—should it turn out to have been one—vanishes before it arrives. Yet for perhaps the first time he has received an impression that the being of another person might *not* be summed up in inches on a tape measure or digits in a bank account. However charged the impression, the effect did not include the recognition that a lifetime is not enough for measuring the immeasurable.

The result was that the woman's husband, Richard Perdue, bought a unit on the third-floor unit they could ill afford, where she at least began enjoying the mortgaged life that starves the spirit. During the period when she spent her free hours shopping for proper furnishings, Lester—who knew a thing or two about money and desire—watched as she drove them to the edge of insolvency.

To Gwendolyn it may not have felt like starvation. She may even have called herself happy for a while, until Richard spoiled it all and Lester got his chance.

—

"**W**here have you been?" Mr. Bourdieu's face is flushed and his hands tremble with the alarm of having been left alone. "You disappeared."

"I told you I had to help Lester this morning, Papa. Don't you remember?"

Mary's bright soprano voice forbids his anxiety. "He's moving more of his stuff into the model unit. All kinds of souvenirs from when he was a child. Pictures of his mother and daddy and of his Aunt Helene. But—this is really cute! —sweatshirts and caps, a box full of baseball cards, his daddy's old uniform and army hat, even the sign that used to hang in front of the boarding house on Prytania. Shows he's really sweet."

Mr. B contemptuously jerks his chair around to face the cloister. "Shows he's a sentimental ass living in the rearview mirror!"

Mary smiles again, ignoring the gesture and sour remark. "His wife has filed for divorce, you know. The second, or is this the third wife?" Her face conveys a frankness incapable of imagining anything to Lester's discredit.

At the news that another wife is divorcing Lester, the energy of Mr. B's aversion intersects the stream of her gossip, and his eyes open wide. The full text appears in the lines of his forehead and cheeks. "Huh! No wonder she divorced him! He's always bringing some tart in 'to show his condo.' One of your nice, good people! That reporter boy"—he means Gwendolyn's husband Richard—"better keep a leash on his wife or he'll be showing his 'condo' to her."

Mary runs her fingers across her forehead to brush aside a wayward lock of greying hair and responds more thoughtfully than the topic requires. "Lester seems changed somehow." She stops in the middle of the floor to consider the change.

"Changed? Him? Like the leopard's spots!"

"I don't know. Quieter. Something has happened. Not the old Lester who thought he owned the world. What he needs is a level-headed girl to shape him up."

"Then why don't you marry The King yourself since you're so proud of him?"

"Papa!"

"Well . . . You're the caretaker in this loony bin. Get Gwendolyn a divorce and marry him to her." He stops as though pondering something. "When you see that girl going out to work in the morning so dolled up, why does it make you think that under her clothes she's naked?"

The question astonishes the innocent daughter in her fiftieth year. "Is that so bad?" she asks. "She's a very pretty girl, but it doesn't give dirty old men the right to undress her."

"I don't like it. She makes a nuisance of herself attracting attention she only wants because it makes her feel powerful."

"You sound like an old Arab who wants to keep his women hidden under a veil."

"I do not! But she ought to be responsible. Not start fires where she doesn't want the heat."

"You're getting to be a regular Peeping Tom, Papa, as well as a crank."

Then in a grumble somewhere between a sigh and a moan, "Well. I want to go home. Honest simple people don't belong here."

"Poor Papa. Did you mention it to Fr. Mark yesterday?"

"Hell no! He always says the same thing, like a broken record." He repeats in a high-pitched whining voice, 'Give us this day our daily bread.' Humph!" He looks down to find his handkerchief in his lap and grows thoughtful again. "I know what he means, but this is harder than happy people think."

"I know." Singing to him, she goes over to the table by his bed and straightens the pictures and magazines, keeping up the chatter.

———

For Lester King, turning the old monastery into The Valmont may have been a hardheaded financial calculation at first, but the energy behind the project flowed from a different source. That, too, may have had to do with the mother-proxy for the missing father and a frustrated pleasure in violating rules where there were none to violate. Not that he needed a special place for his liaisons. The real estate agent had access all over New Orleans to houses furnished and unfurnished where there had been many afternoon adventures with bored housewives, frustrated office workers, and visitors from out of town willing to "let the good times roll."

Taking up residence fifty yards across a garden from one's obsession may not be the most effective means of conquest or of shaking off the influence. It might not even have been Lester's motive in moving into the model condominium. And yet . . .

One day when Mary was otherwise engaged and Lester happened to be on the premises, he supervised a delivery at the Perdues' unit while both owners were at work and passed the time in Gwendolyn's living room examining her collection of interesting objects.

Much of her character was legible in a collection that fit none of the usual categories. Not attachment to the things themselves, since she obviously knew little about them. Not prestige where no one came to look. Not aesthetic in a collection so random. And certainly not for use, since here they were good-*for* nothing. If there was a purpose, it must have been of a peculiar kind: like making her nest one twig at a time because that was what home meant. Consequently the whole collection was indiscriminate and the space overfilled.

Is it possible that Lester's care in examining her treasures betrays an unexpected coinciding of his character and hers? How different is the impulse of the collector from the darker forces at work in him? How far is his handling her things from stalking the woman herself? Doesn't the attachment to objects in them both reveal a hole at the bottom of their worlds? A yearning that must be fed perpetually lest they lose themselves in the maelstrom of desire?

It had become habitual with Lester to spend his solitary hours in the model condo amusing himself—though it was also torture—by watching for "Gwen": Gwen waiting for the streetcar in the morning or returning in the afternoon; Gwen crossing the Quad, dressed for success; Gwen in jeans and shirt, gazing idly into the garden from her Juliet balcony. As this fixation took root, he began surreptitiously photographing her.

It's barely credible that the man of random pleasures could have become obsessed with finding again a face that had, just once, brought him to life. But it's what happened. It might be called "per-verse" since that word says "turned away from" his own intrinsic concerns by turning toward his image of her. And the obsession flourished. When he chanced to meet Gwendolyn in the Quad, she snubbed him so conspicuously that a sensible person would have taken the message and given up, but he could not. He had become religious. An idolater, captured by the image of a goddess in a world without gods, and this restless self-betrayal kept him on the move until he was weary.

So back to his old ways. Or not: For when he tried to reignite the old pleasure of the chase, he felt at odds with himself. The zest had gone out of the game and his cheerfulness had become an act. Leering was no longer leering exactly. It was something sadder, like nostalgia in a man whose pleasures have been spoiled. Nostalgia for what had been or might have been but would never be again.

—

The object that indirectly brought the Perdues' history—hence Lester's—to an early crisis was an empress writing table. It seems that Gwendolyn spotted the table during a treasure hunt on Magazine Street, and, chancing to find it on sale later, bought it, then had a fight with Richard over the "extravagance that is bankrupting us."

It was the same way she had gotten him to look at The Valmont, then to borrow the money from his parents for a down payment. Except that this time Richard ruined it by announcing that they had to move.

The afternoon after this ultimatum, Gwendolyn arrived home from the law office, slammed the apartment door, and threw the shopping bags and the mail at the table with a vengeance that sent accusing envelopes flying across the room. A tabby cat came to the rescue, rubbing against her legs and purring, but she pushed it away, threw her jacket aside, and aggressively pulled her curls into a ponytail. Then she reached for the telephone.

"Mr. King, this is Gwendolyn Perdue."

He passed over the peremptory tone. "Hello, Gwen!"

With a shudder of indignation at his presumption, her head snapped back, the full lips drew inward to a thin straight line, and the lively eyes turned hard as her onyx earrings.

Well might she resent the cheerfulness that he took for friendly, but the full measure of his insolence came in the familiarity of "Gwen."

She spoke into the receiver more loudly than usual. "I'm calling to ask if you can sell our unit." The request was cool. "We're relocating."

He sensed opportunity. "Maybe I can help. I'll stop over and take a look."

"Not now! Richard isn't here now. He'll want to discuss it. He won't be home tonight. Tomorrow night."

Then a chuckle on the other end. "OK. I'll call."

Dropping into a chair without looking at the handful of bills on the floor, she muttered, "He thinks he can use me because I'm beneath him. Well, we'll see about that!"

Taking her cat Artemis on her lap—the one living thing she could trust—she petted its luxuriant fur, then slipped off her heels for the thick, at-home sensation of the pile carpet. Then, just as she settled down in her nest, there came a startling knock at the door.

Lester King, grinning with confidence! "Gwen, I have an idea. We need to talk."

She stared, then backed away from the door. He accepted her retreat as a gesture of admittance. Momentarily off guard, she swept up bills and all from the table and floor and threw them frantically into a pile in the front coat closet. Only pretending not to notice her confusion, Lester marched through to the living room, took a chair uninvited, and sat audaciously staring at her.

Even to her he was not unattractive. Heavyset but well-dressed in suit, tie, and polished shoes. What disgusted her more than his physical presence was the lack of respect. Yet she found strength in the fact that if she must face the enemy, it was on her own ground, and the return to composure brought another dash of native defiance.

Choosing the chair farthest from him, she sat with ankles crossed to one side and arms folded across her breast, returning his stare, unblinking, as though there was nothing in it worth her regard.

He was forced to speak awkwardly across the room and did, undaunted. "I may be able to turn this place for you quickly," he began. "So I thought I'd have a brief look around, if you don't mind." He craned his neck to one side then the other as though examining the condition of the property, then got up, walked to the French doors and the little balcony over the garden, and pulled back the drape with the gesture of one who enjoys proprietary rights.

Next, pausing beside a console to observe several items that he was more familiar with than she could know, added flattery. "You keep the place up nicely. Have such nice things." He didn't miss the involuntary brightening of her eyes at the compliment and saw it as a chink in her armor.

Instead of examining the condition of the condo as she expected, he chose what was most personal, professing admiration of the furnishings and accessories, seeing only what looked expensive. As he moved systematically from object to object with an attention that flattened each in turn, she followed jealously behind, restoring to its proper position whatever he touched. All the while Artemis rubbed consolingly against her legs.

Without comment he observed a pair of grasping hands. Not hands gracefully clasped and certainly not praying hands. Hands with fingers finely wrought but firmly intertwined as though straining to capture and to hold.

"I admire your taste. You have a good eye. You've made this one of the most attractive units at The Valmont. Now, why don't you show me the rest."

She frowned with disgust at having to pretend docility yet became more animated despite herself. Each contact of his hand with one of her possessions made her flesh creep. Still, his admiration pleased and, as she gave names to her things, reluctance waned, returned, and waned again.

Lester moved on to where a violin and bow rested on a mahogany tray table with a bronzed top. "A violin still life. What a happy thought! Do you play?" he asked, seeming surprised.

"No," she replied defiantly, "but I enjoy having it there." Though the remark was followed by a self-conscious laugh.

She knew very well where his real interest lay and, when she wasn't looking, felt the defiling eyes caressing her body.

By now Lester had forgotten the unfamiliar complexity he had felt on the day when she first turned up at The Valmont. The condo might be hers, but he made it his ground by remarking ambiguously, "All very appealing! Your order is sexy."

She registered the inappropriate note, and in haughty disdain led the way mutely to the next room.

He, turning back as though to gather an impression of the two front rooms, smoothed the social surface with another wily compliment—"This could be a showroom for a design catalog"—which somehow managed to leave the impression that she might be the model hired to show it.

Like the rest, the kitchen was arranged perfectly, too perfect for use. There were market baskets and artificial vegetables, countertop appliances and, since Gwendolyn did not cook, a dozen other pointless things. Soon enough he moved on toward the closed door of a bedroom where she stepped in front to block the way. "I think we've seen enough."

"Now Gwen, if I'm to help you, I must see everything." He touched her arm with one hand and reached with the other for the doorknob.

"Don't touch me! I can't bear it when people touch me!" Her gesture of retreat left his way open to the door. "No! You can't go in there!"

Without interrupting his forward motion, he smiled confidently and opened the door. "I don't mean you any harm. I'm on your side, you know."

Once in the bedroom she sat down on the bench at the foot of the bed and held an ivory cushion like a shield as he satisfied his curiosity elsewhere.

After a brief glance into the bathroom, he remarked lightly, as though it was a joke. "There's no trace of the man in the house. Have you thrown him out?"

Instead of replying she turned her head toward the large bed, covered in an acre of pearl-grey satin fine enough for a wedding dress. He approached and ran a finger along the material, leaving a wrinkle in the fabric, which required her to get up and wipe the desecration away.

✗ Something sinister in a hoard of treasures? Will a birdcage, a piece of glass, a yard of satin capture Gwendolyn's desire and bring her joy? Who better to see her illusion than the predator who understands just enough of Eros to detect her blindness and use it?

Back in the living room, she sits down on the sofa, which allows him to park on the other end and prepare, with a chest-swelling breath, to say whatever he has come to say. "Well, Gwen, I think we might get you a good price for this place, though the market is not strong just now. Are you leaving New Orleans? Hubby got a new job?"

Artemis jumps on her lap and purrs reassuringly. It's very irritating being even temporarily dependent on this hulk of a man who squats like a toad on her furniture and regards her with insulting familiarity. The ponytail exaggerates the motion of the head thrown back as she replies dryly, "Let's say we have made other arrangements and leave it at that."

But as he doesn't answer, she can't very well leave it at that. "How long will it take to turn the property? We're pressed for time."

He studies her. "If you don't mind me saying so, I don't believe in your other arrangements."

She snaps, "I do mind. We want to sell. What can we get?"

"Gwen, I have something to say to you, and I want you to hear me out before you reply." He pauses. Then, accepting silence for acquiescence, proceeds with the most outrageous speech she has ever heard, delivered as casually as so many remarks on the weather.

"You don't like me, do you? I know you don't like me. But that doesn't matter. I've always liked you, and I want to help you."

She shudders and averts her eyes.

"I can see that you've decided to divorce Richard—I knew you would in time. He's a nice enough fellow, but you can do better. Unless it's financial trouble."

He makes a casual gesture around the room as though citing evidence. "You're a successful woman of the world and you know the ways of the world, so I have a proposal that will benefit both of us."

She doesn't move and hardly breathes.

As though to allay her fears, he interrupts himself. "This may be a little shocking, but only at first. You're a sensible person, and you'll think it through sensibly. The point is, I'd like you to stay on for the time being on a rental basis. We'll forgive a portion of the cost. It'll be a private arrangement just between the two of us. A kind of social contract. Meaningless, really."

She interrupts, "If it's meaningless, I don't see why you bother."

"Call it a whim," he answers and continues as from a script. "You go to that office in town and spend every day, five days a week, doing whatever those lawyers want. That's exchange. Forty, maybe fifty hours of your life every week for a paycheck that we know isn't enough."

The fresh outrage of the "we"—the sheer impudence of it! She knows very well that the marketplace prostitutes everyone, that however voluntary the exchange, unexpected consequences always follow. And she loathes the sparkle in this man's eyes as she refuses to concede his point.

"Here's my proposal." Lester goes on to describe the arrangement: He will buy the condo back, and she and Richard can rent it until they find a buyer. Half the rent will be deposited in a private bank account in her name as insurance against hard times. "In exchange you'll spend one night a month with me when Richard is out of town."

At those astonishing words delivered in *such* a tone, Gwendolyn goes rigid, causing Artemis to leap to the floor with a yowl and seek refuge under the sofa. Holding to the cushion beneath her with both hands for balance as though it were a lifeboat in a storm, she stares wide-eyed and open-mouthed into the empty room.

Lester ignores the response and continues in a smooth voice without drama. "It'll be a business arrangement just between us. No one will ever know. I won't come here or call or interfere with you in any way."

When this speech elicits from her neither motion nor sound, he continues in the same matter-of-fact tone. "I know this is a little unusual and may come as a shock." Not leering now. Speaking rather as though it's the idea of the thing and not sex that seduces him. "It's really quite conventional. It's only money, after all. And what is money? Money's nothing. It's just a better rate of return than you get at the office. And you get both! Anyway, don't answer me. Just think about it and we'll talk again. Now I have an appointment and must run."

And with that he walks out as brazenly as he had walked in, leaving behind words that, far from being meaningless to Gwendolyn, can never be unspoken.

א Pretense of truth betraying the truth of the lie, to himself no less than to Gwendolyn. Misrepresentation that only works in a livable world held together by words. When words are arbitrary or deceitful, nothing can be true or false, and no genuine act can follow.

—

As you see, the uninvited intrusions into the empty margins of my manuscript continue, but there's a new development. I have begun to have conversations in my dreams with a voice that offers cryptic comments that I only half understand. Otherwise, the dream exchanges feel normal, rather like imaginatively completing interrupted conversations with a friend, except that this voice adds new depths to my understanding of my neighbors' damaged lives.

I never wondered if my ghostly interlocutor might have horns or a halo, but what's frustrating is that by morning the substance of these nocturnal exchanges has drifted away like a puff of air, and I'm left with inarticulate echoes of irretrievable ideas.

The sense of loss becoming acute, I have begun taking notes, as though by writing to the moment I may preserve what I would never be able to recreate on my own. Yet the notes also intensify a question about the anonymous voice: Is it imaginary or real? Can such experiences be trusted without knowing the source?

Now the dreams are slowly evolving into daylight conversations with someone who isn't here: philosophical ghost, demon, angel, phantom muse? Has The Valmont, this place without depths or heights, this haunt of dead nuns, become a place for madness? The beatific Mary has a distinct sense of the continuing spiritual presence of the Dominican sisters, while Mr. B, the most sensible person here, has told with a mischievous glint in his eye that he is occasionally visited by an attendant spirit. Those two even watch old movies together!

And I can tell you, there are other voices we haven't even come to yet!

I think the issue is realism and imagination. We don't simply see, feel, hear, or smell what's in front of us. There's an exchange. The gourmet tastes more flavors in a dish and more layers in a sip of wine than I do. The conductor, the psychoanalyst, or the poet hears more in music or in language because these are unique exchanges that depend on experience, proficiency, and especially the habit of close attention—the way Fr. Mark listens to Joseph Barthes.

Meanwhile, my provisional theory is that I can hardly be sinking into madness as long as my revelations remain coherent to me and communicable to others, since all kinds of intelligible ideas appear in the world and alter it without being verifiably "there." As for the disruption to my tranquility, I've begun to suspect that what has changed is that instead of indulging a comfortable drowsiness of mind to the hard work of understanding, I am growing to love the invisible muse who carries a lantern behind him to light my way.

——

When Lester made his bizarre proposal then walked out, he left Gwendolyn sitting alone, devoid of thought. And so, sometime later, she remains staring at a room left unaccountably empty by his departure. Eventually she rouses and goes to the kitchen. The physical motion of laying out food from the deli helps break the spell so thinking can begin the task of backing and filling. She had called him on impulse, but it hadn't taken him five minutes to turn the situation his way and take her by surprise. More than surprised. Amazed. Shocked. But by what exactly?

As she eats alone at the kitchen counter, stocking feet perched on a rung of the bar stool, she hardly thinks of him—or of Richard. Her eye passes vacantly from the photographs on the cooktop to the prints of herbs on the wall. The shock is that she isn't shocked! More like exhilaration. Not because Lester interests her but because something at last has happened. Something has broken in on the deadening sameness of life and roused her, something other than searching for herself in the pages of *Southern Living*. An eruption of evil perhaps, but the evil, being ordinary, is negligible—isn't it?

She might simply have said, "I'm not for sale." But that wouldn't have been the point. He wasn't proposing to *buy* her. He was simply proposing one satisfaction in exchange for another. So how different would it be from sleeping with Richard? That didn't mean much either. Besides, why, beyond the power of it, all the fuss about sex?

"It *is* only about money," she tells herself aloud. And yet the thing she hates most is Lester's presumption that she wouldn't be shocked. She hates him for being right, exposing her to herself! But what's the real difference between using her body to file papers or answer a phone and sleeping with a man in exchange for the rent? It has nothing to do with her feelings or her ideals. Nothing to do with who she is. It only proves her value and lets her feel as free as if she had won the lottery. It would mean nothing whatever except being able to stay in her apartment and have the things she wants. Not that she will accept, of course. That isn't the point. The idea itself is intoxicating.

In the restless night that follows, Gwendolyn has a dream she's had before. While shopping, she tries on clothes, sometimes dresses, sometimes suits, sometimes blouses. In each case she looks in the mirror and finds no face. The store clothes are visible, but above the clothes, nothing! As if the fault lay with the dress, she tries one after another, searching for herself in each. Finally in a panic, convinced that she has lost herself and become a gap in the world, she tears off the clothes and runs from the store naked. She's perfectly aware of the stares of the curious along the streets but contemptuous because they don't know she's not there. On and on she runs, searching for the lost thing, knowing somehow she will never find it.

She wakes, gets up and paces the rooms, rearranging things that aren't out of place, absently touching one object after another to absorb their solidity and steady herself. Picking up a silver cross that stands, secular and bereft on its pedestal, she says aloud, "Don't I belong to myself? My body's mine! I can do with it as I choose."

✗ And why not? Where life has become exchange and human beings calculators, everyone gains. Lend me the part of your body I wish to use, and I lend you the part of mine you want. Fair exchange. Unless "consuming" is the word. A brothel of commodities begetting insatiable desire. The empty place of consumption where desire begins . . . and ends. Consumer, consume thyself!

—

The week following Lester's proposal, the three came to terms on the sale of the condo. When they met to sign papers, Lester betrayed nothing, and Gwendolyn discovered—or further lost—herself in silent conspiracy with him. That at least made a boring process interesting. For another week nothing happened. When he didn't call or arrange to cross her path, she grew curious about what would happen next.

Every time the topic came to mind she felt a surge of vitality as though monotony had been replaced by a reason to live, however empty the life. Lester hardly figured in these speculations and Richard not at all. Though occasionally late at night, when she was tired, it did cross her mind that she might be denying something in herself, that perhaps she couldn't dispose of herself without consequences. But such doubts were pushed aside. Doubt was weakness, and she was not weak.

More time passed, then one morning as she was crossing the Quad bound for work, she met Lester. He stopped in his tracks. So, she stopped.

"Morning Gwenda." At least he had picked up Richard's name for her! "I hope you and Richard are feeling a bit more comfortable." His smile was friendly, not insolent. "I may have a client in to look at your unit next week."

He spoke casually, in the neutral language of settling a matter that had already been agreed. Then half-turning to pass on, he paused in midstride. "What do you think?"

The topic might have been the weather or the streetcar schedule, and her mood didn't change instantly as it usually did when something unpleasant turned up. Without lowering her gaze, she readjusted a lock of golden hair that wasn't out of place. She had come to no decision and was startled into a sense of how far she had moved by not moving at all.

So, what *did* she think, standing there facing him in the old monastery garden? She did not think. There was a dead space where thinking begins. In a moment available for choice, she let what had already been decided stand, enjoying the sense of being on the threshold of a new world. Keen on being her own master, she declined responsibility and pretended that defection was freedom. When she spoke, it was as though fate, not she, had decided: "Wednesday evening. At seven. Unless I call."

Still under the illusion of doing nothing, she did not call. She came home from work, took a luxurious bath, and began preparing for … she hardly let herself think what. Out of the bath and in front of the mirror she examined her naked body, enumerating the attributes and adding up the available capital, a bit puzzled by the sum. What was it that men saw and wanted? What *she* chose to see was everlasting youth.

At the dressing table, she took no special pains for effect, and yet the procedure was not routine. The face in the mirror defied her calculations by refusing to see what was underway, but when she happened to catch the eyes seeing her, concealment failed, and the mirror returned a mocking gaze.

As for clothes, something modest. She tried several things, but the body refused to cooperate as though the fabric wouldn't rest comfortably against it. The garments either revealed her figure as usual, which she didn't want, or called attention to the disguise—which was worse. Eventually she chose a simple skirt and a blouse with flowing sleeves that buttoned to the chin.

By the time Lester arrived with a bottle of Champagne in hand, she was feeling quite defeated. He opened the wine, and suggested they go out to dinner. Then when she accepted the first and declined the second, he proposed calling out for Chinese.

He was good at it. Considerate and gentle, chattering away about himself until the food arrived and they retreated to the kitchen. In the physical motion of laying things out on the counter, her sense of defeat gradually passed, and she relaxed into the informality of chopsticks and spring rolls.

They lingered over the food and wine and the atmosphere slowly mellowed. Then as they were clearing up and restoring order, she bent down to put something in the fridge and felt his eye tracing the line of her body. She straightened. He touched her elbow; she went rigid.

"Easy, Gwenda. Nothing will happen that you don't let happen. You can still back out, but I hope you won't."

The remark relieved the tension, but it didn't deceive. It wasn't generous. It was tactical. And yet the signs of his desire were reassuring. His remark was a challenge to her command of herself and to the pride of independence.

"Give me five minutes." She went to the bedroom and closed the door.

On the minute, measured by a grandfather clock in the hall, she heard him enter the darkened room where she stood at the window barely visible in an indistinct gown. He approached, took her shoulders in his hands, and drew her to him, unhurried, even gentle. And while she took no particular pleasure in his touch, she didn't hate it either.

Later, staring over a bare shoulder at the ceiling, she ran a finger along the fringe of a pillow, trying not to feel the weight pressing against her, thinking: "I am not here. This is not me."

✗ Not lover's words: "Here I am, open and exposed to you, the beloved." Here, no mutual welcome into the permeable flesh of the other in desire. Only the wish to be an object without flesh, refusing to feel herself feel.

Afterward Lester snuggled down and fell asleep while she remained awake in the dark, empty and forsaken. Yet she had been right: It was easy. Nothing to it. So if it *was* nothing, why did that nothing feel like lead? Why was she preoccupied with the sense that something unknown and inconceivable had been missed? But such questions, not being useful, were promptly squelched.

As he apparently intended to stay the night, she moved away to one edge of the bed and eventually slept. Early, she awoke to the sensation of his body against her back, the pulse of his breath on her shoulder, and the right arm over her side across her breast. Exposed, except for the sheet wrapped tightly around her, a butterfly in its chrysalis.

She gently freed herself from the arm, got up, took her clothes to the bathroom, and dressed. After making coffee, she stood for a while motionless at the French doors, looking out into rain so heavy it blurred the opposite wing of the building. She cracked the door a little to let the sound in, but the drumming on the deck one story below and the gurgling of gutters somewhere above did nothing to cleanse the tainted air.

Since there was nowhere to go, the impulse to escape was futile, so she took her cup downstairs and sat on one of the stone benches along the back wall of the cloister. Across the garden Mr. Bourdieu was barely visible at his window, too indistinct to disturb her solitude. No pain. No guilt. Just the silence and the emptiness of being under her own command. No damage done.

Thus reassured, she stood up, squared her shoulders, and marched back upstairs.

—

That was a beginning. If not the beginning of life renewed, then of a relationship between two isolated individuals pretending to be lovers. Two beetles in a box where all that was to happen would be repetition of what had already happened—and not happened. Except for one thing: a supply of new money.

To conceal the fact from Richard, Gwendolyn bought mainly jewelry and hoarded it in a concealed place. When alone, she would lay the pieces out on the dressing table, put them on one after another and feel bedazzled by the image in the mirror.

And Lester? Equally ignorant of himself, will he continue under the illusion that he's making progress in her affections?

✘ Among the silent cries of desperation, an uninvited guest, having heard it all before in Sodom or Carthage or Thebes, "predicts the rest." Bodies fondled and tasted and felt—without touch. Implements of pleasure—less than objects. Will the Agent stop at the voluptuous body, knowing that this one will also fail him and leave him empty? Not daring to know what he wants, will he see that this is not it?

Meanwhile Richard returned from his overnight trips, tired and dispirited. One morning over coffee, he made an abrupt announcement: "Gwenda, I'm leaving you. I know all about the affair, and I've decided to go."

She stared and said nothing.

He added casually, almost carelessly, "I've had you watched."

The blond head sprang up, arch and defiant. "What do you think you know?"

"I know that Lester King has been visiting you when I'm out of town, but I don't want to quarrel. I'm just moving out and filing for divorce." And so he did. Moved out of The Valmont that day.

The divorce did not upset the order of things. Richard had not figured so largely in her life that his departure constituted a major event, nor did the divorce materially alter her circumstances since on top of the arrangement with Lester she got a promotion at the law firm. And so she set about refilling the few corners of the condo left bare by Richard's exit.

Lester was quick to profit. "Now you're not to think of moving, Gwenda. I would like you to stay on, rent free, until I find a buyer. Otherwise, everything will remain unchanged."

"You'll lose money."

His chest swelled with pride, "If you knew how much money I made last year, you'd see that the money means nothing to me." He chuckled smugly. "Didn't I once tell you that money is nothing?"

For a while at least he seemed happy with the arrangement, but dissatisfaction, when it began to stir, as eventually it must, stirred first in bed. Where they had once "made love" and gone off more or less complacently, if not peacefully, to sleep, she felt him becoming dissatisfied and peevish. Each time a bit less gentle, a bit more insistent, greedier for the unwanted kisses and caresses, like a man frustrated in his search for something deserved but not provided.

He said little, but Gwendolyn saw that he felt cheated, as though she weren't keeping up her side of the bargain when, in fact, she found the price higher than agreed. Her role in the affair was to conceal herself, even to conceal herself from herself in order not to be affected. Beyond *assuming* indifference, it required her to *be* indifferent, and yet the more she succeeded, the more dissatisfied he became.

His state of mind was palpable in dwindling good humor and conversation: curt remarks and increasing impatience, as though time were ticking wastefully away. There was subtle pressure to go straight off to bed, where his hands became harsh and hungry. He wanted the light on before sex so he could gaze possessively at her naked and explore the body with a touch that felt like assault.

Her efforts to conceal herself from that gaze and the insistent hands only increased the pressure. During the act itself, as he searched compulsively for some nameless thing he couldn't find, she felt her body held in a vise, not violent but too ruthless for a human embrace. Instinctively she knew what he wanted: He wanted—or thought he wanted—her to want him with the same hunger that drove his search for oblivion in her arms. But all she had to offer was passivity, so that even at the climax she gave proof of his failure to rouse her to the measure of his need.

—

One afternoon Mary saw Gwendolyn approaching across the garden, coming in from work. The first thing she noticed was the clothes. Smartly dressed, but in clothes that didn't look like her. A business suit of a straighter cut, more linear and severe, as though she was hiding in it. Femininity become a fortress. Grace devolved into cold perfectionism. The hair, which used to float freely, had been shortened and looked stiff. The high polish of nails had estranged the hands and feet from air and earth. Whatever had happened had left the face strained beneath heavier makeup that didn't quite cover hardening lines around the mouth. Shallow blue eyes, once warm and friendly, grown older and sadder without growing wiser.

"Why, Gwendolyn dear! You don't look at all well," Mary exclaims, glancing up from the rose bed. Somehow Mary always knows when other people are unhappy. Her gift. The charitable radiance of her face, attentive without judgment, makes them feel loved and disposed to trust her. But Gwendolyn no longer responds. The lonely face pretends it's not at war with itself and, worse, the fabricated face only pretends to be pretending.

"You're not sick?"

"No, no." The voice is cold and flat. "Nothing's wrong." She quickly looks away as though suspicious of confidence.

Mary sees and thinks, but doesn't say, "She's hiding from something. Disguised like a missing person!" But, as it's not Mary's way to urge confidence or search a face for clues, she stands there without curiosity, ready to hear what, if anything, Gwendolyn might want to say.

"You should get out more. Mustn't sit up there in that apartment night after night brooding."

The only response is a thin, fixed smile that shows a wish to escape. So Mary nods sweetly and turns back to her work.

—

In October during the monthly transaction that Gwendolyn thinks of as "paying the rent," a critical moment arrives. After dinner out and the usual ritual of bodily sacrifice, Lester is especially restless, and she feels the pressure.

The long-gathering storm begins with her remark, "I don't know what you want. I've done what you asked! What more do you want?"

"I don't know. You just aren't there. There's ice water instead of blood in your veins."

Then months of provocation erupt into a screaming rage in which all is gathered up and thrown in his face at once. "I see what you think. You think I've cheated you. Go! You've had your piece. Just leave!"

In this final explosion, she who never cries breaks into tears and sinks to the bedroom floor in a fit of hysteria.

Lester stands by aghast, helpless. It's one thing to rouse a woman's desire—her vanity, at least—and shape it toward eventual possession, another to deal with a woman at the end of her rope. At that he is not at all good. He fidgets helplessly, then begs, and finally orders her to stop crying. When that's no good, he collects his things and skulks away.

✗ Malignant calculation: the hard utility of desire! Cruel in their very souls. Cruel to themselves first, then cruel to each other.

As soon as the door shuts, she stops crying, sits up, and begins assessing her situation, lining up the debits and credits. Any way she turns it, she lives *on* credit with nothing to *her* credit. She has money for the easy, affluent life but remains encumbered by debt; she has her independence except for one night a month when she's bound in servitude to the loathsome Lester King.

Somewhere in that long night she reaches a point of resolve. Even if it means moving out and reducing her expectations, she will sell her jewelry and return the money she's had from him since the divorce.

The next day she calls in sick and spends hours in the grim business of raising funds and diminishing her being. At five in the afternoon, she knocks on Lester's door. As soon as it opens, she draws a wad of money from her purse and throws it at him. "You'll have your condo back by the end of the month!"

A flood of relief lasts as long as it takes to cross the Quad and get back upstairs. Once inside she collapses. She hasn't the heart to go into the bedroom, where the empty jewelry box stands open on the vanity, a black hole sucking her inexorably back toward her mother's empty world. In time she partially recovers and undertakes to fill the hole by reordering other familiar objects at random. In vain.

Meanwhile in the opposite wing of The Valmont, things have been left even more unsettled. Lester, the practical man, disinclined to stop and wonder or to search and feel baffled, sits bewildered with a roll of bills in his lap. He stares down at it helplessly, then leafs through as though counting and recounting. The gesture is absentminded and random. Thousands of dollars in large bills should interest a man who spends his life accumulating signs of success, but the paper and the printed quantities are no longer bits of paper with numbers.

He, who says that money is nothing but a sign, discovers that *this* money is more than a sign. It's a singular and sinister reality, weighing *him* in *its* finely equated scales. Without knowing it, he has bound himself by lying words and put his life at risk. Then, at the outer edge of meaninglessness, he has been struck by reality. The bills in his lap, suddenly transformed, have become the "sacred," or its negative facsimile.

He climbs out of this web by pacing the floor. In another moment— as close as he may ever come to thought—he realizes that in all this fretting he's overlooking the essential thing: She's moving out, and he'll lose her completely. What to do? Propose marriage? If it's hell to desire her and not be able to reach her now, it would be greater hell to have her always there and always inaccessible.

✘ Defeated again. *Ubi sunt?* Where are they, those pagan innocents for whom all things were permitted? Where are the moralists for whom some things were permitted because others were not?

—

The month of Gwendolyn's repudiation ended in paralysis or renewed passivity: nothing done about the money or the condo. By the next month, numbed by indecision, the two have drifted into the old routine.

Then some weeks into the new year, her phone rings. "How would you like to go to a ball on Saturday night before Mardi Gras? Our night out."

The offer is attractive but she answers carefully, keeping the enthusiasm out of her voice, waiting for the price.

"That's all. No strings attached . . . unless you'd like to ride on a float in a parade."

She responds without hearing the animation in her own voice. "Are you serious? What would I have to do? How would I dress?"

He hears all and promptly enlarges on the topic. "Aside from the costume—there are designers for that—you only have to look beautiful. My krewe, the Krewe of Proteus, needs another pretty woman. I thought you might like it."

Anyone who knows the kind of things that Gwendolyn knows, knows she will always be an outsider in New Orleans society, but that only makes the offer more delicious.

For a month, all the resources of an active imagination go into preparations, while Lester looks on and quietly pays the bills. Having gotten a genuine response at last, he can hope for change in a relationship that has died without having been born.

Before the Sunday-night ball there is a private cocktail party in the reception rooms of the Napoleon House. For the men, mask and white tie *de rigueur*. For her, a straight gown that flows like a scarf with an uneven hem composed of mesh-like material in black. Around the forehead of her painted mask, a sequined black headband with plumes on one side that wave theatrically as she moves: a flapper from the twenties.

She and Lester make their way through the press of revelers to the corner of Chartres and St. Louis streets. In the city where time stands still and misrule drowns care, the bacchanal is nowhere more riotous. Crowds flow in and out of posh hotels and strip joints, restaurants and jazz clubs, bars and head shops. In the narrow, densely crowded streets, where the only movement is a collective drunken sway, couples in fancy dress make their way to the entrances of elegant apartments above the street.

The mood of the two is sociable. Gwendolyn, basking in public adoration, leans on his arm and smiles at him through her mask. Lester is as pleased by her pleasure as a man of his ilk can be, as though, at last, he has found a path, if not to her heart, at least to her ambition.

She relishes the anonymity of noncoinciding persons in the assembly rooms, without the need to think about what she's doing, who with, or even admit that acts have meanings. He, reduced by the mask of the Venetian Plague Doctor to an accidental dance partner, is equally free to enjoy the illusion of triumph. All goes by plan and, happiness being out of the question, the night passes as their most enjoyable.

Eventually the party moves from Napoleon House to the ballroom of the Roosevelt Hotel and more dancing into the early hours of the morning. Then on to an equally anonymous breakfast at a mansion uptown before they crash, separately, at The Valmont.

Gwendolyn awakes late in the morning brimming with excitement and begins preparing for her role in the evening parade. Much time passes at her dressing table, where the purpose is to fascinate and distract.

During all stages of the day-long preparation—donning the costume, being positioned on the float, waiting for the evening parade to begin—the banalities of everyday life fall away, and she lives in intense expectation.

Lester, meanwhile, is to watch the parade from the apartment of an acquaintance on Royal Street. The costumes and floats are kept from public view until they appear on the streets, and Gwendolyn won't see him until afterward. So he puts on his best gregarious face and, in genuine holiday mood, parks himself an hour early at his observation post on the balcony.

The narrow passage below amplifies the noise of revelers who fill the Quarter. The restless scene glows with a thousand lights accompanied by the sound of police motorcycles like swarming wasps, pushing the crowds back onto narrow sidewalks under wrought-iron balconies.

At long last two riders on horseback appear in the distance, carrying a banner that announces the theme of the parade: "Mythic Monsters and Mythic Disasters." This much Lester knows, and he also knows that each float will be a masque from mythology with krewe members in costume enacting the characters. He has no idea which one will be Gwendolyn's, or what the scene will be, or how she will be dressed. Not to miss her entirely, he must study each tableau closely as the approaching floats tower above the crowds and fill the street from side to side as high as his second-floor perch.

The spectators welcome each scene with surprise and cries of genuine excitement. First the ship of restless Odysseus, headed for destruction beyond the Pillars of Hercules. The rear of the float is a half length of the ship deck, crowded with the Greek sailors unaware of impending disaster as they throw treats to the crowd and to sirens on the balconies. Beyond the bow, a whirlwind spins in the air above a wine-dark sea, forming a vortex that dooms the ship to destruction. But no Gwendolyn.

The next reveals the human face and triple papier-mâché body of a giant, the deceiving dragon Geryon. The giant reptile, killed by Hercules, lies sprawled on the earth, head on a rock. The only moving part is the cruel scorpion's tail that thrashes about flinging beads instead of people as in the myth. And again, no Gwendolyn.

Another apparition shows Menelaus, instigator of the Trojan War, struggling to overcome Proteus, the sea-god of infinite changes. The monster emerges repeatedly from Styrofoam waves, where he rises then sinks to rise again as lion, dragon, leopard, or boar—even as a tree of many branches. But no Gwendolyn.

Then King Midas, sitting at his table in a rose garden where, behind him, Pan and Apollo play the pipes and the lyre. Midas' woes began by judging feminine beauty truly while badly misjudging feminine vanity and revenge. Here, as punishment, he sits surrounded by food, doomed to starve. As he reaches for one delicacy after another, each at his touch is struck by light and turned to gold. In disgust he throws all to the cheering crowd in the form of golden doubloons and beads.

Finally, a block away, at the very end of the parade, Lester spots a brightly lit float with a simple crescent of Ionic columns against a painted night sky. So dramatic is the effect that a hush spreads over the crowd. On a plinth in the middle of the scene a young woman, radiant in white wig and Greek tunic, mimes the statue of a goddess. At her side the sculptor Pygmalion, mallet and chisel in hand, stands admiring his just-completed masterpiece. It's the instant when Venus transforms the perfect figure of the woman into flesh and blood as Galatea.

There, within thirty feet of Lester, Gwendolyn lies motionless. Her unmasked face as remote and empty as stone. The Pygmalion myth reversed: living flesh transmuted into cold marble with a gaze that crosses Lester's without seeing. Eyes blank in the mist as the float slowly passes—more funereal than festive—and the goddess wafts off into the night without a flicker of recognition.

And Lester? What does he see in the moment when Gwendolyn passes into the twilight? He misses the point and mutters, "Betrayed again!"

𝒳 The Scribe, in his ambition to repair the damaged lives of his neighbors, tries to preserve what in their counting up gets counted out. He would remake Lester by changing his ways, as though if he stopped chasing women and selling his life in the marketplace, he would be made whole. But wouldn't he remain imprisoned by the banal resources of the commonplace? So what if—turning things around—sentiment, possession, and frustrated desire were transformed into loving? Then might Gwendolyn be transmuted from an object of impossible possession into a moving figure of infinite variety? Thanks to his love of words, the Scribe begins to see a difference between a finite object and infinite potentiality.

Meanwhile, an inexistent messenger listens differently. Instead of trying moralistically to improve things, he listens for possibilities scattered among the flotsam and jetsam of everyday life, waiting for the person who might, by a leap into the unknown, see the same world but see it differently. A messenger with no message might be another fantasy except for one difference: Ideas can lie dormant for centuries awaiting the timely moment, the right word, and the attentive ear.

Once upon a time there was another such witness, armed with neither questions nor answers. He was described centuries ago by one Cassiodorus, who explored the maladies of the soul. Cassiodorus tells of a "patron demon of scribes" named Titivillus whose task was to collect the mistakes the monks made in copying manuscripts and plagiarizing the morning prayers. Titivillus' assignment was to gather evidence by the sacksful for impeaching the monks at the Last Judgment.

So the messenger and scribe persist, together and apart, the one gathering evidence of lives spent in evasion, the other turned toward infinity. And not among the residents of The Valmont only. It's the same along every street of the city: creatures suffering the loneliness of frustrated desire. Marooned in self-consciousness, not daring to discover that the inside and the outside of the Lester Box are the same, seen differently.

Legions of them, all strangers to themselves: lawyers and shopkeepers, society women and clerks, prostitutes and priests, street sweepers and teachers. They radiate anxiety and possibility, thinking only: "not enough" or "too much"; "not-yet" or "already-lost." Limited to the horizon of money, celebrity, family goods. But doesn't the effort to find and cure only energize the malady?

The policeman on his beat, not seeing that in all he remembers, something essential has dropped away. Trapped in the machine of practicality,
calling it freedom as he tugs on an alley door along St. Peter Street:
"Shoulda took the bribe. There'd be money for Davy, some shoes, and
Molly, a dress and schoolbooks. Oh God, what'll I do?"

The old woman sitting on the steps of a shotgun, irritably scraping
the sidewalk with worn slippers: "Where can I get the money to have my
teeth fixed? Can't think about anything else. Always thinking. If I could
only stop thinking."

The nanny sitting in the square, not-watching a child in Mary Janes
hopscotching on the chalk-marked walk: "Why don't I love children? Because
they've stolen my youth and my beauty?"

The judge turning in at the church door before lunch to kneel before
the altar: "If they don't come across with the ten grand, I'll see that son-
of-a-bitch rot in Angola. Hail Mary, full of grace . . ."

Lost to any good beyond themselves. Numb to the scent of frying
beignets at Café du Monde as to the sparkle of triple cathedral spires and
a single bell striking, three times three, the notes of the Angelus at noon.

The Dancer
Gluttony

"**V**on, two, three, nice, five, good, seven, eight." Hands clapping. "Ok. Now, *tendu* close fifth with *demi-plié*. Ready? And . . . von, and two, and three, and four, *tendu*, von, *plié*, two, and close, and up; *tendu*, von, and two. Toes on center line! Weight on foot balls! Good. Don't stop. Make nice."

Tanya Marianenko conducting class at the barre, dark eyes snapping with discipline and intelligence. "Enough. Is good. OK. Class dismissed for holiday. Remember ven moonlighting for pay rent, eat fish. Eat salad. No hamburger, no fries. Eat noting."

She moves to the center of the practice room, "Now pleeese, I want see *Apollo*. Domingo, Christy, Ashley, Susanne." Looking coyly at the one closest, thinking of the three Greek muses, "*How* you say Calliope in New Orleans?" She always asks and never remembers how Greek passes through French and into Cajun.

"Ca'-li-ōp," Ashley answers for the tenth time and Tanya laughs as if it's the first.

"OK. We start from *rond de jambe* for first lift. Places please. Ready? Music. "Five, six, seven, and, von, good. . . *Nyet. Nyet. Nyet!* Domingo, dear. Count! You dance like elephant. Sometime I tell you story about Balanchine and Barnum Bailey. Ballet for elephant. You vant be elephant?"

He thumps his chest. "I just don't feel it in here."

"Don't feel like. Do steps! We don't see inside. You god Apollo. Apollo not feel. Apollo do." The criticisms are severe, but in her Russian accent they raise a snigger. "Just dance! You not vorking! You slump like lazy. Think string from head to ceiling like puppet."

Domingo responds in disgust, "I'm not a robot!"

"This dance rehearsal, not encounter group. You not dancing jazz. Not Bourbon Street. Must know where floor, where legs. Control, control, always control!"

Tanya has been at the new New Orleans Ballet four years demanding seriousness and formality. Each morning she appears impeccably dressed, as clearly "on" in the studio as on stage. Her example demands perfection even exercising at the barre or observing from the sidelines. Not amusement or a job. Vocation. Homage to the grand tradition of dance—Russian, of course.

She had arrived in New York from Europe trailing clouds of glory and political scandal. Then after five seasons dancing to the acclaim of audiences and critics across America, her career in the city came to a halt with a series of fluttering *entrechats-quatre* during a rehearsal for *Swan Lake.*

She wasn't even doing the role. The director asked her to demonstrate for a younger dancer who was bouncing rather than pushing off the floor. From fifth position *plié* she pushed off, straightened, opened the legs to the side, scissored, and landed. But landed hard, and the left foot turned with a snap heard across the stage. A tendon. Sabotaged by the body! As she was carried off, she glared ironically at her coach in mock protest, "I forty. *Jetéz, jetez, jetez.* Is bit much."

For the rest of that season she was sidelined. So when her husband George Basson was appointed U.S. attorney in New Orleans, she made a fresh and cheerful start in the local company teaching as well as performing. It put her career on the line in new ways and helped postpone the slow artistic death of the aging dancer. Saved for a while having to watch from the wings as younger, lesser talents basked in glory that belonged to her.

The years under Balanchine had made her a good teacher, and she thrived as guru to a young company where she could choose her roles and still perform. Now, preparing a new production of *Apollo,* she faced what Balanchine had faced in the early days in New York and what his disciples had faced all over this big, dance-empty country: young

Americans lacking the grammar of classical dance and the harmony of the parts of the body. At the Vaganova Academy in Leningrad she had absorbed the same culture as Balanchine, only later. Now, like him, she insisted on formal, mechanical execution—"Do steps, feel later. You vant grow into dance body, not spill out feeling, like mush. Control. Is all control." The aim of her art, her deepest hunger, was to make body say spirit, though in the studio there were only bodies.

The events in the history, known and unknown, that lay behind her anxiety can be mentioned in a few lines. When she arrived here, her story was recounted in a magazine article in the Sunday paper accompanied by flattering pictures from her own files. With the performer's instinct for publicity, she carefully encouraged and shaped the story, complaining all the while of the intrusion: "*Nyet.* Is too much!"

In fact, though she spent a happy afternoon repeating it all to the reporter, the secret pulse of a person does not pass into slick stories of glamour and success. In reality Tanya may be the saddest resident at The Valmont and a bundle of contradictions: earthbound discipline punctuated by moments of inspiration, self-absorption alternating with flights of transcendence, abstinence followed by fits of bulimia. An artist who has known greatness, an artist compromised, diminished by the struggle against herself, knowing she is less than she might be and not even *that* for long.

Her history began in a small town in Ukraine, where she grew up loving the folk dancers of the Dnieper River valley. At age five a single event shaped her life: a performance by a troupe of dancers in traditional costume, the men in billowy white shirts richly embroidered in red and black, loose riding trousers with red sashes at the waist, red boots and swords; the women in similar colors and the flowery headpiece called the *Vinok*.

From the flowing, vertical motion of the ancient Cossack sword dance, Tanya caught the enthusiasm for life, but it was the syncopated dances from the western mountains that fired her imagination. The precise footwork, the sharp movements, and the leaps that hung in the air revealed the joy of the disciplined body. Afterward she imitated them with childish abandon and a profusion of feeling that delighted her family and neighbors.

Her mother took her into Kiev to see a performance by the Kirov on tour. It was her first ballet, but there she heard about a famous school in faraway Leningrad where talented children went to study. It became her consuming passion to go to that school, which she imagined to be filled with the energy and joy of the Ukrainian troupe.

For this and for darker reasons, at the age of nine she and her mother made the thousand-mile trip by train for an audition at the Vaganova Academy where, miraculously, she was accepted. The darker forces that led to the painful separation from her family and transplanted her to the distant city were to haunt her forever after. The unspoken had to do with an uncle, an older brother of Tanya's father, who lived with the family. Her mother had caught him with the child on his lap, fondling her under her clothes.

The whole event—the fondling, the shock of the discovery, the commotion in the family when her mother's rage was answered by her father's refusal to forbid his brother the house—the whole upheaval and the final separation left scars. Whether it was the abuse itself, the shame of exposure, or the consuming dark mood, the event affected her relation to her body in demonic parallel with the discipline of the famous school.

School, however, was not the place of freedom and play she had imagined. It was a system of labor that set her in single combat with a body she had already learned to hate. When it was recalcitrant under the ascetic routine of training, she took pleasure in punishing it. Day by day she confronted the enemy in the studio mirror, commanding it into shape, forcing it to perform with machine-like efficiency. Instead of being encouraged to grow into the dance, her body was compelled to become light and airy and, for the beauty of the line, thin but strong. Thus began a lifelong preoccupation with the body as alien object and the image of the enemy on the wall.

Tanya Pavlivna had never known real deprivation before. At home, the family had land and was largely self-sustaining, but in her first winter in that northern city everyone suffered from brutal cold and poor diet. Not perhaps to the degree of the war generations who fought for crusts of bread. Still, during these post-war years of drudgery, there was never enough. A potato was a delicacy, and much of what was available otherwise—mostly coarse bread and salt herring—she declined as unfit for human consumption.

That winter her fastidiousness, combined with the arduous training, led to a dangerous illness. One morning she fainted at the barre and was taken unconscious to her cot in the cold garret she shared with other students. There she lay for days unattended except when, morning and night, she was fed a little gruel. The pale, thin face with the big, sunken eyes extended a few inches from beneath an old quilt that barely traced the outline of the skeletal form. Beyond interest in herself or the world, she stared like a wasted Buddha at the patterns in a peeled yellow ceiling and made no sound.

She was expected to die, but she didn't die, and the experience hardened her resolve to make that body so thin that the bone structure would be visible on stage, yet invincible. Eventually restored to her classes, she studied the clean line of the alien body-without-flesh, starved it, forced on it the ideal of the long neck, the exposed bones, the lithe and weightless torso. Thus, destined to perpetual hunger, she became obsessed with the joys of self-denial and an unrelenting fixation, waking and sleeping, on food.

After these early hardships in Leningrad came recognition for unusual talent and purity of form. By sixteen her clearly defined positions and precise classical steps won her a place in the *corps de ballet* at the Kirov. On the strength of athleticism, sculpted legs, and a beautiful line, she moved on to *coryphée* and solo roles. She was especially strong in the classical tutu: large extension; lovely poses in arabesque and attitude; straight, centered torso; expressive legs, arms, hands. She could travel across a stage effortlessly, leap and hang in the air in defiance of gravity, then land sinuous as a cat. In due course she learned the classical repertoire and began dancing the principal roles. Experience added lyrical line to technical proficiency, and she moved from allegro to the expressive adagio of the great romantic parts.

Seasons later, established as a prima ballerina, she traveled with the Kirov to the south of Europe where, one night in Monte Carlo after a performance of *Sleeping Beauty*, a young American lawyer brought flowers to her dressing room and invited her to dinner. He was shorter than she and stared at the world through slightly protruding eyes and little round glasses, an altogether unlikely suitor for a celebrated dancer, but she had her own reasons for accepting the invitation.

It was the middle of the Cold War, and the dancers were relatively free of intrusive surveillance by the company management or the KGB minders, so she was free to enjoy that night and the night after and the night after that. The result was that Tanya Marianenko and George Basson fell in love, though what exactly each fell in love *with* or what *falling* might mean for two such disciplined and self-absorbed people—those were unasked questions for which there would have been no satisfactory answers.

For weeks George followed the company—to Rome, Milan, Vienna, Paris, Stockholm, London. The whirlwind courtship through European capitals was itself the stuff of fairy tale. Obsessed by his fairy princess, George spared no effort amusing and indulging her, though he understood less than nothing about her life. Nothing about the fatigue of a company on tour, the cramped quarters and slow starvation, not even that the chocolates concealed in her clothes might signify something other than an innocent way, as she claimed, of keeping her energy up.

In fact, the time spent with him was an escape from a reality any-thing but glamorous and toward which she was secretly hostile. It was hard enough to maintain concentration and physical discipline on the road, but her perpetual struggle for mastery over the body made it torture. "George" meant relief! She could relax into the romantic image reflected in his bedazzled eyes and enjoy a whirlwind of excess. She ate and drank recklessly, lost sleep and stinted on exercise while he remained oblivious to the artistic price of indulgence.

As the tour wore on, the occasional sharp-eyed critic noticed her additional weight and the signs of fatigue that she, with characteristic inconsistency, blamed in turn on the body for sluggishness and her partners for caring more about their solos than the intricacies of partnering. But knowing very well the reasons and the consequences of being out of shape and earthbound, she suffered increasing distress. Then something quite different happened:

In London the night before the tour was to end and the company return to Leningrad, Tanya defected. She went with George first to Dublin, then Canada, and on to New York in a cloak-and-dagger climax to a theatrical fantasy of true love. But then, for her the world of chimeras was the only world worth inhabiting. An enchanted future in America was but an extension of the enchantment of the theater. For her, George embodied what she most admired and most hated: the principle of order and discipline by which she sought to subject the unruly body to her greed for mastery. In concealing her obsessions from herself, she concealed them from him as well, and that was more ominous than either could know.

Only much later, when George had pieced together the evidence of her inner warfare, did he suspect something pathological: a time bomb buried in that small, wiry frame, a nightmare of abstinence and excess, of transgression and retribution. As he respected the perfectionism of the artist, he accepted her self-absorption as an occupational hazard, though her intensity was so consuming that an evening spent in the same room could be exhausting.

Once when she was in a fit of temper he exclaimed, "Tanya Pavlivna, you're like a person who's broken in two. You spend all your energy trying to hold the pieces together."

If he was slow responding to all this, the cause may have been that, once married, the two resumed their careers and, like strangers, went their separate ways. Later she would tell a confidant, "Georgie loves Aurora and Juliet, not the skinny dancer the morning after." Rather than spoil the idol reflected in his eye, she retreated into herself, so that it only slowly emerged that *her* "George" and *his* "Tanya" had little to do with any actual Tanya or George. His tidy mind abhorred her inconsistency and retreated from her dark side into the equally illusive purity of public order and the law.

Private demons aside, her career went well in New York, though the occasional critic put his finger on something anomalous. After a performance of *Theme and Variations,* one described her as having turned in a strangely uneven performance that missed the pure liquidity of motion:

> This is not the first time we have seen a Russian dancer perform as though the point of the art were to strike a series of poses. In Marianenko there is a wall of calculation between her and the dance. Or maybe it's a private warfare that inhibits greatness. In this showpiece of classical precision, she danced against herself like a spirit trapped in a body, the ghost trying to force the machine to do its will. Then suddenly, unexpectedly, in the *pas de deux* she forgot herself. As though seduced by the muse, she launched gravity-defying suspensions in air and, in a thrilling finale, sailed across the stage in weightless orbit. At these moments, all too rare on Saturday night, she shows that when not weighed down by consciousness, she is equal to the best.

When Tanya moved to New Orleans, nothing essential changed in her artistic or her domestic life. She and George went on in the usual way, living different lives from the same address, he, trying to make the world come up to a higher mark; she, struggling to turn the drabness and sweat of the studio into an ideal that might save the same dreary world from tattered mediocrity.

—

Sunday morning at The Valmont, in early December. Two modern pagans lounging outdoors like extraterrestrials on a deck above a rectangular garden, oblivious of the old cloister below and the stone paths worn smooth in the service of an unremembered god. Unable to hear the old chant of the nuns passing through the cloister two by two, making their slow way to chapel for the service. Instead, Tanya and George sit lonely and apart among the pots that he calls her concentration camp for plants, immersed in discontent. He in chinos, tennis shoes, and a Hawaiian beach shirt intended to make work feel like leisure; she, behind sunglasses, lounging elegantly in slacks and a top that exposes the slim midriff. A turban on her head adds an exotic touch to late coffee on the sunny deck. The one engaged with his eternal briefs, the other eating a green apple and cottage cheese while amusing herself with a stack of new books.

Looking up from his work, he said, "Tanya Pavlivna, I never understand why you read cookbooks when you eat nothing and don't know how to cook." His tone is matter of fact, neither critical nor affectionate.

"These new! Recipes from whole world." The exuberance of her food-lust comes in a distinct tone he hates and fears: the devouring mother, for him inevitably the Jewish mother.

"This Creole and Acadian." She holds up a book with a large color picture: a Doric-columned Southern veranda commands a shaded alley of oak trees along the bank of a river. On an elegant linen tablecloth is a breakfast of Eggs Hussarde with tall pots of coffee and warm milk for *café au lait.*

In a wistful voice, "Take me out for big breakfast, Georgie."

He replies evasively, knowing such dark caprices too well. She may give the appearance of eating nothing but fruit and salads, but she dreams perpetually of food until she can no longer bear it. Then the binge begins. Driven to do the thing she least wants leads to a hell of recrimination. But most of the time, instead of eating, she collects recipe books and spends solitary hours slowly starving on the vicarious life of the imaginary epicure.

What George most dreads are the infrequent episodes when she loses control, though she never lets him see her until "the princess" is restored. But still, sharing the same house, he cannot *not* know about the diet pills and weight-reducing formulas, the laxatives and diuretics, the emetics and induced vomiting, the celery juice, enemas, and steam baths. Rather than consult a specialist as he advocates, she hides behind the mystique of Russian training, which has little to do with such extremities. Doctors, she says, would prescribe food, and food is the thing forbidden.

How is it that these two manage to get on together at all? George is an angry man. It's visible in the quick, impatient gestures of his hand as he turns the pages of his briefs and heard in the edginess of his voice when Tanya interrupts with random remarks. But it wasn't she who first made him angry. In that respect both are beneficiaries of his inheritance from Abraham, Moses, his father, or whichever patriarch it was that made him heir to legalism and despair.

If domestic discontent needs a particular point to condense around, food will serve. It occupies the center of Tanya's life and marks the crux of their life together. What is less clear to George is why something he regards as peripheral to the business of life should cause so much commotion.

Occasionally, when he leaves the office in time, he stops at the grocery, but he shops randomly because his efforts to plan ahead are always rebuffed. On the rare occasions when Tanya brings in food, he can't help seeing that there has been no thought of him. He keeps a shopping list in the kitchen, but she manages never to remember it or to see that the negligence matters. From every direction, food has become a power of negation, the thing that spoils the old appeal of her romantic exoticism, energy, and art.

> **א** Once, the sacrificial meal was shared with the god. The sacred offering consumed and incarnated in communal life. Start from living-together, and food means more than individual satisfaction. But start with brute appetite, and eating-together passes from ritual to neglect. The compulsion to do the thing she hates fractures the pronoun in "our daily bread."

George's resistance does not go unnoticed. It, too, feeds revenge, as when on Monday morning she goes early to the studio knowing it will be empty and puts on the costume of Nikia, the Hindu temple dancer in *Bayadère*. Then, to the music playing in her head, she faces the mirror and begins Nikia's command performance for the prince (her lover) and his fiancée. Tanya's sorrow is transferred to the character, who is about to be poisoned by the snake concealed in her basket of flowers. Then, as Nikia declines the antidote offered by the Hindu priest and dies, Tanya drops to the floor in tears, bereft by a loss all her own.

Recovering, she carefully dresses incognito in an Indian sari made of aqua-colored silk with a golden border. It's part of her art to expose herself to the gaze of others without being seen *as* herself. She darkens exposed skin and adds a costume choker and bangles for her wrists. Thus prepared to be seen without being visible, she sets out on a day-long ceremony of indulgence.

First into the Quarter for *beignets* and *café au lait* at the Morning Call. The chewy doughnut batter, deep-fried and sprinkled with powdered sugar, is paradise enow. Then she wanders through the Royal Street antique shops, passing the time until lunch. Across one shop is a Valmont neighbor named Gwendolyn Perdue examining linens, and Tanya has the satisfaction of being noticed without being recognized.

Toward noon she walks to the Acme Oyster House and stands at the bar, where the shuckers supply oysters on the half shell. The brackish taste of the Gulf is a unique indulgence, and she relishes one by one until she has devoured two dozen. These episodes of indulgence have a long history and have come on her in other great food cities like New York and Paris and London, but New Orleans is different. Here, temptation is the very spirit of the place.

Next, she leaves Iberville Street, returns to Canal, and takes the streetcar back uptown with other gastronomic fantasies in view. Getting off at Napoleon, she walks to Casamento's on Magazine Street. The cool Spanish tiles and bright interior refresh her as she waits for a table. Then, seated alone, she lingers in quiet anticipation of the mouth-filling tanginess of soft-shelled crab from the marshes.

The Valmont is not far away, but the glory of the day is too sweet for slacking off. She can keep up the eating only by punctuating it with long walks, and so she saunters through the Garden District back to the Avenue before returning to town. After a rest in the park by the river, she wanders along the riverboat docks and back again into the Quarter.

By midafternoon, her restlessness borders on the frenetic as though she were famished and could hardly find the patience to get from one restaurant to the next. George is in court and will not be home until late, so she makes a reservation for an early dinner at the Rib Room of the Royal Orleans.

At this stage, her spirits are sinking noticeably in warning of darker things to come. To forestall depression, she again sets herself in motion, crisscrossing the Quarter from Canal to Esplanade and from North Rampart and Congo Park back to the river. Along the way she casually buys a bag of pralines at the French Market and conceals it in the sari. Returning at last to the Royal Orleans, she chooses a solitary corner, orders a three-course dinner, and lingers over it for two hours in the company of a good bottle of Pinot Noir. The other patrons cannot fail to observe the elegant Eastern woman in aqua and gold, dining alone. Though they cannot read the signs of exhaustion or see how close she is to collapse, the waiter can, and he gently persuades her to let him call a cab.

Thus, at nine o'clock, staggering from exhaustion and barely conscious, she reaches The Valmont. Once inside the gate, she stumbles to a garden seat and collapses. No one is around, but the all-seeing Mr. B spots a body on a bench and calls Mary. "Someone is sick in the garden, or dead. You better go look."

—

Mary finds Tanya slumped across the arm of the garden seat, comatose. For all her gentle kindliness, Mary is a solid, round woman, experienced in handling the sick. She could easily pick Tanya up and haul her up the stairs but for the deference owed to celebrity. By patting her gently on the cheeks, she rouses her sufficiently to get her home.

Since George is not there, she takes Tanya in, unwraps the sari, removes her skirt and shoes, and tries to put her in bed. At that point, corpse-pale through smeared makeup, Tanya waves her aside with some unintelligible remark in slurred Russian, then lurches up and wobbles to the bathroom. Behind the locked door, Mary listens for a long while to the retching.

Eventually when all sound has ceased, Mary knocks. "Tanya? Tanya?"

No answer.

"Tanya, open the door!"

Frightened now, she settles on forcing the door and finds the body slumped on the floor, unconscious or asleep. She drags her to a sitting position against the wall and cleans her face with a washcloth that removes more patches of makeup. The long, mournful Russian face has become the face of a madwoman who has to be pulled to her feet and coaxed back to the bed, where she rallies just enough to sit up on the edge for a while, dazed and uncomprehending.

Mary keeps an arm around her for support until Tanya asks for water then, from a bedside drawer, retrieves various medicine vials and fumbles until she has poured a handful of pills into her lap. One by one she swallows them then falls back into the bed asleep. Mary, the practical nurse, covers her then reads the labels. Looking down at the sleeping figure that mumbles and writhes as though possessed by demons, Mary whispers, "Dear God! This is too much for me."

Near midnight—and still no George!—she calls the one person to whom she turns on the rare occasion when she's at a loss. Fr. Mark will know what to do.

And so he does. He alerts a doctor in the parish, who arrives within the hour. After consulting the medicine bottles, he pumps Tanya's stomach and gives her a sedative to let her sleep.

"You can safely leave her now," he says. "She'll be alright until morning. But her husband must be told."

Then, as on cue, the front door opens, and George enters grey and drawn with fatigue. At the sight of Mary and the doctor, and of Tanya on the bed in a feverish sleep, his face registers several responses in quick succession: astonishment, alarm, then grasp of the full situation. His shoulders slump as Mary introduces the doctor, who briefly describes circumstances that George absorbs without surprise.

"I should have seen it coming," he confesses, not adding that he has always seen it coming without taking precautions because it makes him so angry.

"She's so cursedly strong-willed that you can do little until she's helpless," he says with a shrug. "It's not the first time or the tenth. What can one do?"

Mary walks to a window and sees Papa in the cloister watching for her. As she makes a move to leave, George takes her by the hand, thanks her warmly, and escorts her from the bedroom. "She won't remember that you were here," he says at the front door. "Better not to mention it, or she'll blame you for seeing her like this."

As he returns, the doctor says, "She needs regular care. If there aren't physical causes, then she should consult a psychiatrist."

George nods. "I know, but I can do nothing. She is the strongest woman in the world and the weakest. You may know she's a dancer. A great one . . . or has been."

"Yes." The doctor checks Tanya's pulse then leads the way into the living room as George shuts the bedroom door behind them.

ℵ The "thinking-thing" living in the fog of first-person pronouns. The piece of inner equipment that does the thinking tries to bend the outer machine to its own purposes. Then consciousness discovers it does not own the body after all.

—

Finding these uninvited remarks scrawled across the unfinished pages of my account of gluttony, I decided to pose an equally cryptic question of my own as if there really were someone else here in my monastic cell. I can see that in some dark way the glutton suffers imprisonment in a recalcitrant body, trying and failing to control it, so I addressed a question to the empty room: "How does gluttony think?" Magically the following lines appeared in the white space of my text:

✗ Gluttony may think too much, "over-thinking" its own lack.

But it's her body! Surely she can do with it as she likes.

✗ She can try, and we can weigh the consequences. But beware, Scribe: Flesh has history and wisdom that thinking does not know.

Does Tanya love herself so little?

✗ She loves! But *what* she loves is stasis and her little vice. Protects it to the point of self-destruction! Preferring "I want" over "I can."

—

The morning after her binge, George can't leave Tanya alone. So he makes some calls and sits down with his anger to wait. Having covered up her responsibility for the trauma of the night before, it would not cross her mind that her vice might have consequences on him! Not even at the moment when his criminal investigations have reached a critical stage.

Rather than brood, he looks around and for a passing moment sees the living room as an emanation of the people who occupy it. No instinct here for dwelling. Just a waiting room where two professional nomads come to bunk and pass the time until the next appointment.

The furniture is all metal and canvas, expensive, impersonal, institutional. So portable that chairs and tables and racks migrate around the room looking in vain for a place to belong. No trace of a room inhabited like a second skin. Just design without aptitude for dwelling! Not even the dining room where no one dines. Just a glass table on a chrome base flanked by chrome and canvas chairs. On top, a scattering of newspapers and magazines. In the corners dust lies undisturbed awaiting monthly purgation by the cleaning ladies. The only evidence of human presence is a series of ballet posters on the wall, memorabilia of Tanya's European glory years and a woman whose image he had once loved.

His attention turns again to the hackneyed topic of Tanya's compulsions; he strains like a blind man trying to read a book written in invisible ink. Blind to the forces that drive his own life, he can ask without blinking how she can destroy herself when she's perfectly clear about her own interest, knowing that her career, her marriage, even her life depend on moderation, and yet . . .

Sometime in midmorning Tanya enters from her bedroom trying to hide behind the image of the princess who can bring an empty stage to life. But the performance fails. Instead, she sneaks in, a frail and naughty child who, occupying no space at all, curls up on a chair like a cat awakened from a hundred-year sleep. No Princess Aurora discovering a world of new possibilities *this* morning. It's the sorceress in *La Sylphide* with tangled hair and dark circles around bloodshot eyes.

Another person might apologize, but she never apologizes. Yet she does want to talk. "Georgie. I had a dream. A bad dream."

"Fighting the mirror again?" His tone is sardonic.

"Not the mirror. Old body in the mirror. You know what it means to be fortysomething, Georgie? This is what life comes to!"

She sits wringing her hands as he watches with as much detached curiosity as his anger will allow. Not saying the obvious, that she has been the ungrateful darling of two continents.

"Dancing is short life. If not a dancer, I have five children now."

"You chose the life you wanted, and you've enjoyed the rewards. A bit late now for regrets." He speaks firmly but not unkindly.

"I want to have baby, Georgie."

"You what?"

Dropping back into the broken English, "I vant to have baby please."

He stares. "Tanya Pavlivna, do you remember when I proposed to you? You had one stipulation. You made it an express precondition to marriage: no children. I wanted children. You didn't."

"*Then* I not vant children. Only dance. *Now* too old to dance. I vant children."

He holds his hands up as to an uncomprehending sky in a gesture as expressive as the well-controlled prosecutor can allow himself. "You made a contract with life and have enjoyed the benefits. Now you want to change the terms!"

He turns in his chair to face her directly. "You're a glutton, Tanya. You want to have it all. To possess everything. Consume the universe and remake it to your own image. When you can no longer punish your body in the dance, you want to punish it with children and probably punish them in turn. Well, now *I* don't want a child because of *my* career. I don't have time for children! You will please excuse me. I have work to do." And he leaves.

✗ God may be dead, but His throne is not vacant. It has been usurped by a pronoun: "I want, I want, I want."

—

An Arcadian scene on a sun-lit stage. A peasant cottage on the left, farm buildings on the right, mountains in the center distance. Rhineland girls, grape gatherers in colorful country dresses, accompany the ballerina in a wide crescent across the stage. One leads a waltz for the admiration of their male friends while these other children of the earth dance *terre-à-terre* with a lightness that lifts earth itself to the realm of spirit.

The whole scene breathes free in the first motion of a new world. Tanya as Giselle trips along in small leaps, joyously extending one leg then the other, followed by rocking steps back and forth like a boat on water. Giselle, the main character, smitten by a young count disguised as a peasant, is a creature of earth made weightless and innocent of care by the joy of first love. As she draws the young stranger into the dance and they glide, arm in arm, in unison, her body, forgetful of *outer* restraints, is restrained if at all only from *within*. Neither vertical and airborne nor dancing with abandon. Carefree, each unselfconscious step executed in elegant slow motion.

When the royal hunting party enters, she, unaware that her love is a nobleman, dances joyfully alone. Pliant footwork catches the high points and holds, never rushing, swimming melodiously across the stage. Yet something is out of joint in this Arcadia on the Rhine. Appearances notwithstanding, the captivated Giselle and Albrecht meet in body but not in soul, for deception casts long shadows of star-crossed love. On his side, it's his identity as a royal; on hers, a "heart condition" revealed by her mother via mime.

When her peasant suitor finds Albrecht's sword and discloses the deceit, Giselle is thrown into a torrent of disappointment. The dancing body loses its buoyancy, and gravity is restored to the whole stage, bodies and spirits all pulled downward. She stares absently as, with mad feet, weight on the heels, more acting than dancing, she tears her hair down around her face in a fit of madness.

The sword, meanwhile, lies abandoned on the stage, a neglected agent of unforeseeable consequence. Giselle stumbles on it, seizes it by the blade and, in a figure of the disobedient body enacting the distracted spirit, traces the image of a serpent in the garden across the earthen floor. In despair, she lifts the sword to stab herself. Whether she succeeds remains an open question. In either case the illusion is nearly broken when Giselle collapses on the stage, and the ballerina bends over in dry heaves as the curtain falls . . . early.

—

My editorial question, entr'acte, so to speak, is this: How are we to think of this perplexing performance? What, if anything, does Giselle's malady of body and mind reveal of the dancer who so splendidly enacts her? Why is Tanya, who runs the company, even dancing *Giselle* when she might be joyful dancing *Sleeping Beauty*? Is there a kinship between Giselle's inconsolable descent from joy through madness to death and a performer who cripples her art and her life by a rage for mastery?

In the practice-room mirror Tanya may search for herself in unacknowledged despair, but she only ever finds images of a tool driven by a tyrannical will to perform steps and strike poses as though she didn't know that the *art* of the dance requires something beyond exquisite physical control, some surplus or artistic remnant that belongs to neither. We can see as much when she *becomes* Giselle. Somehow, she must know that neither mind nor body can dance.

In Act I she incarnates Giselle! At such moments both Tanya-as-person and Tanya-as-dancer go missing. They pass into another being in another realm. It's the difference between ballet and athletics, Cézanne and a house painter, Paganini and an organ grinder. Does art, just at that point, suggest a paradigm of new life?

In any case, in this moment between the acts, Giselle is dead and there's one act to come.

—

Backstage, the ballerina lies unconscious on the floor, and someone folds towels for her head.

A voice cries, "Get a doctor!"

Another, "No! Call an ambulance!"

"Wait!" says the stage director kneeling beside her, holding her head and blotting her face and neck and arms. "She's coming to."

The director leans down. "How do you feel, dear?" Though the eyes are as mad as Giselle's in Act I, the director returns a maternal smile, concerned more for Tanya's well-being than the performance. "You were terrific! You've never danced better!"

The eyes slowly return to focus, and the director waves the cast members off to give her time. "Can you go on? You know there's no understudy. What do you think?"

Tanya pushes herself to a sitting position and bends over, holding her stomach with one hand and her head on her knees with the other. The gnawed lips look like an open wound as she raises her head and stares absently across the stage in a suppliant plea for help from someone who isn't there.

She murmurs, "Last act. Get me through last act. No more."

And so, the music resumes, and the curtain opens on a moonlit night in a forest. It's a kind of underworld with Giselle's grave on stage left, then, right and center, a space where the shades of jilted brides—the Wilis—convene nightly between midnight and dawn. During those hours any male who appears in the charmed space is condemned to dance until he dies of exhaustion.

The Queen of the Wilis enters with tiny steps on pointe that mark the clearing as theirs. The corps appears in diaphanous white skirts and bridal veils until they throw off the veils and hop in rows of elongated arabesque befitting the somber mood and the common destiny of undead lovers. In due course Albrecht enters, receives his sentence, and begins the fatal dance.

In the wings, still at the point of entering the scene, Tanya's eyes remain fixed on empty space. Then her gaze withdraws, the eyes glaze over, and only the figure of the suffering woman remains. Once in motion, she is transfigured. The director, still holding her by the arm, wipes her face and pushes her forward.

Enter stage left, the lost Giselle as phantom. Neither character nor dancer. Just the dancing body on the outer edge of materiality. The feet come together in a series of arabesques, spirit dancing on air invisible to the mourning Albrecht, who has brought white lilies for her grave.

Then the magical *pas de deux*. The two perform together and apart, he on earth in her aura, she encircling him with sustained floating motion in air, hovering, weightless, and insubstantial. Rather than touch, they seem to move past each other in quick parallel arcs, she passing through him, he responding to the bare breeze of her presence.

The invisible figure in white, refined to spirit, ascends in buoyant extension, holds, then descends with equal slowness, allowing each moment of airborne motion to disclose its own slow idea. Giselle, unconstrained by mortality, obeys only love across that inviolable separation.

Though Myrtha, Queen of the Wilis, has condemned Albrecht to die, Giselle repeatedly comes to his aid, intervening sometimes by distracting the Queen, sometimes by taking Albrecht's place to give him respite. Yet, eventually, he collapses. Myrtha commands him to continue, and so he does until the village bells herald the dawn and the visible fading of the Wilis' power. They drift away in the morning light, and he is saved.

Giselle's forgiveness saves him and enables her to return to a quiet grave, absolved of the vengeful half existence of jilted lovers. At their final parting, an ethereal hand offers him a single rose as she slips back into the earth forever. He collapses in grief. And the curtain falls.

When it opens again, to a deafening ovation, this once and only Giselle takes her bows as spirit still. Then Tanya, restored to herself, descends from the rapture of the dance into the subjection of ordinary existence.

—

On the day when Gwendolyn threw her savings in Lester's face, Tanya had been in court—the first time ever—for the climax of George's New Orleans assignment, unless it was for distraction from her own private hell.

When the trial ended and court was adjourned, she went to an office celebration and then came home alone. Now she sits in the living room submerged in a place beyond either feeling or thought, staring into the emptiness of the balcony doors and a rectangle of fading daylight, not thinking of George's triumph.

She untangles the long legs beneath her, hoists the body to its feet, and goes to the kitchen. Returning with a dish of ice cream, she slumps again into a chair and mutters, "Georgie not understand. Georgie just beginning. Tanya Pavlivna finished." No more applause, no more career, no more celebrity masquerading as love.

In her eye at this moment the patch of light on the deck outside becomes the warm glow of a hearth in a Ukrainian cottage, where "Mother" would understand. The eyes move to a line of crown molding above the doors like the long yellow crack in the plaster of a Leningrad garret where, as a student, she had been left alone to die. The only sound in this tropical swamp is the endless silence of imaginary snow between her and the homestead where the family gathers around the hearth after supper, stomachs full and faces red in the congenial warmth of the fire. The logs snap comfortably in the fireplace attended by the smell of fresh bread, the touch of her father's arms around her, and the puppy in her lap. Safe. Happy.

Then the telephone rings, and all vanishes into the pain of life as one long death.

—

About nine o'clock Mary and Papa are watching TV in his room, when a woman's scream cuts like shards of glass through the silent Quad. Mary rushes into the cloister and disappears into the stairwell opposite just as a second cry pierces the night with a long, guttural wail.

Later Mr. B watches the eleven o'clock news. "Welcome to the Wonderful World of Weather!" Papa never misses a chance to sneer at the neighbor weatherman, "that lazy toad" Claude Plauché, but tonight his irony is muted by the alarming cries two hours earlier.

A breaking story interrupts the weather report: "U.S. Attorney George Basson has been found dead on the east bank of the river under mysterious circumstances. Details to follow."

"Guess the Mob got him at last," he mutters, though there's no one there to hear. Having turned the TV off, he rolls himself back to the cloister door and waits. Every fiber of his being—the moist eyes in the bony face, the untrimmed hairs growing randomly from neck and nose and ears, the mouth sagging sadly on one side, even the shadow of his own mortality—all are suspended in concern for George Basson and poor Tanya.

No one's in the garden, where a light mist falls steadily across the gas lanterns, closing the night in on itself. The windows above are all dark except for Tanya's, and the eternal glow of the corner unit on the third floor. Mary doesn't call, and normally Mr. B would be in a panic, but there is no panic.

As the mist turns into a quiet patter of rain, audible through the open door, he addresses the room which, except for him, looks empty without feeling empty. The only light is the table lamp by the bed, which throws long shadows across the open terrazzo floor.

"I like your company," he says to nobody. "Whoever you are, I thank you. I don't know how it is, but when you're with me I forget about pain and this damn chair, sitting here day and night, watching the inmates." He chuckles dryly.

The voice that replies may be his own mind speaking, but that detail doesn't interest him: "The others crossing the garden want coherence, but you take the unexpected to heart. It takes courage to live a full life through a rear window."

Mr. B turns his chair half around, surprised by words too strange to be his. "Humph! I don't understand what you say, but I like hearing you say it."

He turns on the TV, and together they watch an old movie until the wee hours when Mary comes in.

"You've been with her?" he asks.

She nods sadly. "She got the call at nine, just after they found the body. You've been alright?"

He nods and adds a remark that doesn't surprise her. "I wasn't alone. It was on the news. And just when he had won! How strange." He blinks with incomprehension. "How is she?"

"When I got there, she wouldn't answer the door, so I used the passkey. She barely noticed. She was pacing the floor, raving against George, if you can believe it. Mostly in Russian, but I could tell she was cursing him as if the world and all were his fault."

She stopped, and both remained silent as they viewed and reviewed the situation.

"Did she ever talk?"

"Eventually she calmed down and seemed to take it in. Started speaking English, but not to me. Just talking about him, nonstop. At one moment as though he died years ago, the next moment falling into a rage again as though it was only about her and how she had been cheated."

Mary shakes her head, not comprehending, and goes to the kitchen to make cocoa. Promptly she returns and stands in the door, where she continues talking, trying to make it clear to herself.

"It's a terrible thing to say, but I don't think she's thinking of George at all. When I got there, she looked like a madwoman. Didn't say anything. Then what do you suppose she did? She went to the kitchen and cooked a huge breakfast. Nine thirty at night, if you can believe it! Eggs and ham and tomatoes and enough vodka to float a boat. I can't tell whether she's delirious from shock or happy."

Mary goes back into the kitchen for the cups and misses whatever answer Papa makes. Within two minutes she's standing in the door again, cups in hand as though she has forgotten them.

"I told you how nimble she was when she danced—like a cat. And how, right by herself on the stage, she could make the audience catch their breath with a single gesture. Now she's over there lunging and banging around that apartment like a tiger in a cage. Then suddenly she shrivels up on the sofa and just sits in that empty room that's so big she's lost in it. Staring with those sad eyes, she goes on eating and drinking vodka. Destroying herself. But you don't have the heart to interfere."

"Wouldn't do any good," Papa adds. "To her George is guilty, for having changed her place in the world."

After father and daughter drink their comforting middle-of-the-night cocoa, she goes to bed, and Mr. B speaks again to his inexistent companion. "Miss Mary's an angel in this infirmary of sick souls. But don't tell her. If she stops what she's doing to think about it, it'll interfere with the doing."

Then his tone takes a darker turn. "There's nothing *but* death at The Valmont. We live in a charnel house."

The Entrepreneur
Greed

As nudity is made visible in the un-dressing, so the
well-operating human being is made visible in its failures.

Next in the parade of vices, after lust and gluttony, comes greed.
Sins of the flesh, as they were once called. For a long while and for
compelling reasons, I avoided writing this story, because speaking of
Fabien Bergeron felt like betrayal. In truth it was written last because
I was incapable of writing it earlier. We had once been too close.
As fellow New Orleanians, growing up like brothers in the same
neighborhood, we lived in the economic and class divide that has
always afflicted the city.

He and I began school together and, in our early teens, were closer
than brothers until each of us was awarded a scholarship to a local
prep school, his Jewish, mine Catholic. Being Louisiana Creole of
Haitian descent (an "Ayisyen"), Fabien had no relation to the Jewish
confession, though as Creole of African descent and from southern
Louisiana, I was at least nominally Catholic.

These details allude to a fact about New Orleans that deserves
to be remembered. In class relations, as in everything else, this city
of which we remain proud was always unique. For better *and* for
worse, shades of color and hierarchies of class were always recognized,
measured, and finely exploited down to the smallest detectable frac-
tions of kinship. In part, perhaps because, like the Egyptians along
the Nile, people in this fluid world had to defy malicious definition
and cooperate sufficiently to survive. Not forgetting, however, the

long, slow emergence from a slave market at the end of the River into other, less conspicuous forms of servitude.

As neighborhoods grew, the masters lived on the front side of the block and the slaves—later servants—on the back side, but however wide the divisions, people at least knew one another. In our youth, Fabien's and mine, the Jewish and Catholic establishments were vigorous advocates for social justice long before the challenges to segregation became intense. That fact has everything to do with the advantages we enjoyed.

However different our backgrounds, I, who lived with my widowed mother, was always welcome in his family. Both his parents were teachers, except that teaching wasn't something they chose. *They* were *chosen*! Teachers by vocation. It was their mode of being. They were rooted in the ancient understanding of people as historical creatures, open to unforeseeable possibilities, nourished by love and wonder of everything available within the range of experience. Their way of life—the way they lived their world—required the same attentive care for the soul in thinking and speaking as care for the body in eating and breathing.

In their house, the dinner table was a place to nourish the body and feed the soul in discussions that held everything up for examination till long after the table was cleared. There was a certain nobility in their bearing and an evident joy in a materially modest life lived in the perpetual exploration of ideas. I had never known people who passed through the day "considering the lilies," giving thought to everything around them. At the time I admired the Bergerons more than anyone I had known in my constricted childhood. Much later, in hindsight, I discovered it wasn't just admiration; it was love of a kind it took me years to recognize.

Another dimension of the Bergeron way of living that had especially dramatic effects on both Fabien and me was that, for them, summer vacations from learning amounted to so much life lost. So during our high school years they arranged for the four of us—parents and boys—to meet formally at their house several mornings each week during those four summers to read the classics together, especially the great American Black writers. The consequences were huge.

Our meetings were formal, because the purpose was too important and the aims too high for informality. At the time, I took the pomp and circumstance as eccentric, even pretentious, but how wrong I was! Seen in retrospect, those summer mornings were life-shaping, even life-saving, rituals. All about becoming responsive to language as the realm where happiness requires far more than physical and material security. They didn't blush to call it "the satisfaction of a life well lived." But that, they said, requires courage to love a fickle and freckled world.

At each meeting the four of us took turns reading—aloud, if you can believe it—to get the music of the language in our ears and the spirit of the words in our hearts. I still hear the lyric voice of Mrs. Bergeron saying that one must learn to read a new book the way a musician learns a new score: by listening attentively and learning to perform the music of the sentences. "We read first with our ears," she said. As for the meaning of that music, she took delight in quoting an ancient adage, "Let me write a nation's songs and I care not who writes her laws." Every time she repeated that line—and she did it often, as one teaches a child its first language—you would have thought from the sound of her voice it was a Hallelujah Chorus. Some days we would read a single page together, then stop and spend the rest of the morning in conversation, letting the book soak into us, flesh and bone.

Fabien's father was the more socially conscious of our two teachers. Closest to his heart were questions of opportunity and justice, rooted in ethical development. He often described how when a collective goes decadent—he meant when social acts no longer add up to a vital consistency—renewal typically comes for the excluded underclasses. This argument, as I may call it, was to be especially influential on Fabien. But it was Mrs. Bergeron who was the artist and dreamer. She could open the adventure of everything from the minute details of everyday life to the ancient mythologies. To her we were heirs to it all, and her intention was to graft it permanently into the conscious texture of our lives.

Along the way, these two gave us our histories in stories as new as yesterday and as old as Africa and Phoenicia. Several enduring modern influences began here: for Fabien, especially Du Bois' *Souls of Black Folks*; for me, Ellison's *Invisible Man*; and for both, Wright's *Native Son*. Across those four summers we navigated these and many other seas together, venturing far beyond single themes, as one always does in developing an ear for the great books.

The summer ritual kindled in us the ambition to translate these vacation adventures into practical action, and yet we were destined to take different roads. Fabien—rather like his father—took the road forward toward opportunity for all, while I, more like his mother, took the way back, deeper into the perplexities of human nature. That difference alone makes his life too important to neglect, and it's the heart of his place in my portrait gallery. Not because he exemplifies greed—though I mustn't compromise just because he's my friend—rather, as it turned out, because of what he was to suffer in the struggle against a greedy world.

Our paths began to diverge when his passion for science and practicality won him a scholarship to MIT, where he excelled in physics and, odd as it was for a son of the Louisiana swamps, eventually took a graduate degree in metallurgy. I, meanwhile, took the "road less traveled" and remained at home with my ailing mother while studying the humanities, also on scholarship, at Tulane. My path felt like I was a guest at the banquet of the gods within a mile of the backside of the block where I was born, and there the task of my life became the still odder one of finding words to set things in the open that otherwise remain concealed.

Fabien's story proper begins while he was working toward the undergraduate degree in physics. During those years he became friends with another undergrad at Boston University named Reagan Achebe, whose father was a distinguished research professor in metallurgy at MIT. As friendship turned to love, the lover and the father got better acquainted, and that resulted in the professor's hiring Fabien in his senior year as research assistant in his laboratory. So it happened that while Reagan finished her degree in English at BU, Fabien earned a master's in metallurgy.

The most thrilling experience of my life to that point was being invited to Boston for the wedding as his best man. It was the only place I'd ever been, but the greatest benefit, as it turned out, was being welcomed into the Achebe family—mother, father, sister, and bride—all of whom I saw with bedazzled eyes. Reagan I especially liked. She was as well read as young people can easily be, and we had books in common. Until that moment—the Bergerons aside—I had never realized the gift of seeing the world through the eyes of others and developing an understanding and a taste for their world. The wedding directly followed the two graduations, after which Fabien brought Reagan back to New Orleans, where he had accepted a position in an engineering firm.

For several years he thrived, until the business got entangled in corruption schemes and went broke. But he soon picked up the pieces and invested his experience with metals and marine construction in a firm of his own that became a successful part of the offshore oil industry. In time his company's horizons expanded to the busy port along both banks of the Mississippi that extends well south of the city and beyond for 100 miles.

We met rarely during those years, just enough for me to follow the narrative of the family and, mainly through accounts in the press, the events of his career. Not that we callously neglected the old friendship, but our paths, when they occasionally crossed, did so at oblique angles. He was not proud nor was I disposed to intimidation, though I lived very simply. In fact, if either of us had been asked to name the most important people in his life, I'm reasonably sure each would have set the other high on his list. The relevant fact is that while he busily burned his candle at both ends to the point of neglecting his family, a mile away I led as different a life as can be imagined, like a monk in a cave on a three-story mountain.

How much greater the surprise then, when one day some twenty years later, he turned up unannounced at The Valmont. Alerted by the buzzer at the gate, I watched as he climbed the narrow metal staircase that led from the cloister to my corner apartment. I was startled by the man I saw. He had always been large, with broad shoulders and an athletic build, usually dressed in a business suit as though he had just come from the office. On this day the face was still round and sensitive and the deep-set eyes still left an impression of detachment from the world outside, but a deeply furrowed brow and a pensive disposition suggested a troubled mind.

As he stepped into my room, the old convent library, the space seemed to shrink. At any time, the writing table in front of the window, the two chairs, and the bookshelves on four walls left barely enough room for a second person, but it was clearly too small for him and left no room at all for whatever he had come to say. Thus before I could offer him a chair, he proposed that we go to lunch at a nearby restaurant.

So it happened that I had no chance to study the changes in him until we were seated and had ordered our food. As a teenager Fabien's manner had been thoughtful and gentle. He seemed to live outward into the world from some remote inner reserve. This day his gaze was still direct and personable, but I saw pain across the table no longer disguised behind his characteristic stoicism. The forthrightness and resolution were still there but not the tranquility. Even the diminished energy of his speech hinted at some magnitude of distress I was about to share.

Without reservation or pretense, he began quite solemnly. "I have asked to see you for a particular reason. You may hardly believe it, but there have been few days in my life that I have not thought of you and our happy years together. Now I find that I have something to say that, after the loss of my parents, can only be said to you. There are things that must be spoken, but only to a friend of uncompromising honesty and judgment—the way other people without religion or the benefit of such a friend may speak in solitude to the open sea, to the mountains, or to a hole in a tree."

By this time we were eating po boys with glasses of beer, and he took a drink before continuing. "I need to tell you—or say to myself in your presence—that my wife has filed for divorce and that I both don't care *and* am devastated by the failure."

In the face of those words, I could do nothing but sit still and try not to blink.

"You know all about what people call my success story, but my private life, to the extent any remains, is another thing entirely. The fact is, my children grew up without a father, while I lived a separate life in the city. It's not that they or Reagan suffered materially. In the early years she loved the comfortable, affluent life with the children. She loved the money especially. I never cared much about the money, but I let it corrupt them. Her social life at the country club—playing the loving mom who lived for her children and spoiled them while primarily pleasing herself—I was glad to escape all that. The alternative was a domestic battle I couldn't, or wouldn't, fight. I blithely used the cliché of a reasonable division of labors to bow out. In doing what I most wanted to do, I declined responsibility for the family as though bags of gold could substitute for authority in the ethical decisions of modern life."

He stopped, and I sat like a witness staring at a stark reality for which I had no words. Not that he had come to ask questions or seek my advice. That would have been ludicrous. But he had already said something I wouldn't understand until later: that the role of witness is not to supply words, but to hold open the horizon where we can confront ourselves and our task clearly. It's a kind of triangulation between two persons and the world and testifies to the idea that things exist only in being communicable. But all that comes hereafter. Little did I imagine at lunch that he was telling me only half—and the simpler half—of the story.

After we had finished eating he showed no inclination to say more, but we sat on in that discreet back corner of the room and ordered another beer. Eventually he resumed: "You may hardly believe this, but what I most need from you is not commentary on my tangled life. I will do what I have to do."

Hesitantly, I asked, "And what is that?"

"I won't protest the divorce and, fortunately, there's enough money to make everyone as happy as they're capable of being. What I need is a perspective outside my own soap opera. You have lived very differently, and you haven't lost the fire. I need to hear how you have lived since we were young together."

Lacking the courage either to take umbrage or to refuse, I replied, "You might say nothing much has happened. I can put my simple life in a few sentences. It's what I learned from a Sufi wise man of the twelfth century named Ibn 'Arabi. He calls them the Four Pillars of Wisdom: silence, solitude, hunger, and vigilance."

He frowned. "Which means what?"

"Whatever he intended, here's what I've worked out over the years. To be a seeker, we must be delivered from cravings and the internal prattle of idle minds. That deliverance requires silence. If we want to speak truly, we must learn to be quiet inside and out, to draw close to things—even the blade of grass or the hinge on a bread box—letting things show their own characters.

"For silence we need solitude. Where there's no one to talk to and we're as detached as possible from practical distractions, we're free to concentrate and let the mystery of all things flow through us."

He stopped me with a raised hand, puzzled over that for a moment, then waved me on.

"The hunger. It doesn't mean bread and water. It means attention and moderation. If happiness results from contemplation, we need to be liberated from the distractions of the world, and that's the role of vigilance. Vigilance awakens us from the careless purposes of everyday life to the point even of sleeplessness. If we can rid ourselves of the idea that the purpose of life is a good night's sleep, we may discover that wakefulness from identity and security opens new potentialities. These four stages along the way of happiness are what I have tried to live by."

There I stopped. What one might have expected to be the beginning of a long conversation, like our interminable debates of old, ended in silence, though I could see that my summary had struck a nerve or a memory somewhere behind Fabien's sad eyes. Yet, instead of replying, he stood up, extended his hand across the table and, without more words, we parted.

For several months after that I heard nothing more from him, but I used the interim to try for a consistent view of his life based on what I could learn from my scant sources.

—

It's hard to imagine a marriage beginning with higher promise than Fabien's. Both he and Reagan were endowed with all the blessings that should have led to a coherent life. They were equals in energy and intelligence, imaginative, socially accomplished, and perpetually engaged in conversation together. In their company one could imagine—with a dash of philosophy added—that this might even be a remarriage of the arts and sciences. And their physical comportment toward each other, along with the birth of two children within two years, seemed to confirm an equally healthy intimate life. It was what might have been expected under the auspices of the families Bergeron and Achebe.

My perplexity over Fabien's story began with what he had called his "failure." Did that mean that the two lovers had lost faith in their ideal of life together? Had the world intervened, forcing conformity, until they had lost their way and wandered off in different directions? Perhaps by the time he was absorbed in his engineering firm, Reagan's life would have been transformed by motherhood and the die cast.

Because she was a good mother, the children would predictably have narrowed the scope of her life. Likewise, he, who had chosen—had already chosen before returning to New Orleans—the other half of a well-recognized division of married life, was absorbed in the construction business. It's an oft-told tale that over-investment of energy—erotic energy—in one activity can leave a deficit for the remainder of life. Little wonder that as even the best become mired in prosaic routine, marriage dwindles into dull conjugality.

At some point along the way, Reagan persuaded Fabien to move the family across the lake. The reasons were obvious, even clichéd: safety, better schools, social opportunities, along with the other conventional objects of desire that often work like the hand of fate in family matters.

But, after getting this far and realizing I was getting nowhere, I gave up. Until, in the middle of one night, my phone rang.

—

"**A**lex? This is Fabien. Would you meet me in the morning in my office? In the International Trade Center?"

I made some stammering noise of acceptance.

"At nine."

Though I promptly agreed, there were misgivings that this time it might be a confession, and I felt embarrassed. As it happened, my fears were justified, but whatever he wanted, at least it wasn't advice.

When I arrived on the top floor of the International Trade Center at the foot of Canal Street, a secretary ushered me into an elegant office. Fabien stood with his back turned, gazing down at the river traffic in the harbor far below. He didn't seem to notice me until the secretary left the room.

Then he turned slowly as though weighed down by burdens too heavy to bear. I was astonished at the difference two months had made in his face. That world-weary visage approaching from across the room had the texture of a relief map deeply etched by anxiety, disappointment, even despair, all barely held together by an ingrained stoicism he had still not lost.

He approached with what was meant to be a cordial smile, shook my hand, waved me to a seat, and began: "Please forgive the sudden call." Then, dismissing that and all other preliminaries, "You have been much in my thoughts since we last met."

He waved me to a seat in a leather chair and continued, "I have a question for you. Not at all what we spoke of last time. The question is this: Do you think a person can know all his life that he's living a lie without ever recognizing it? If so, how responsible is he? Even if he covers things over with the habits of ambition and cowardice?"

Without expecting an answer to these rhetorical questions, he began pouring out the anguish of his public life. The voice was nothing like the beaming optimism I had once known nor the commanding voice of a captain of industry. Not even the quieter, sadder voice of the family saga. Now it was halting, monotonal, disembodied:

"You may know that I have had two careers. The first has been what people call a great success. In fact, I learned early in business that the price of success is to join the legions of Mammon, but I covered it over with confidence in my own immunity to the disease. In the early days I didn't know that who we are, our habits and instincts, derive from *how* we use ourselves and the time allotted, how we spend every moment of our days and years. Mine have been spent where graft and greed corrode the spirit even of the best. I've brushed shoulders with the Mafia and lived in an atmosphere where business is often conducted by bribery and enforced by violence. I may not have participated directly, but I enabled evil, and I bear the taint.

"My greater guilt—my greater *greed*!—arose from my lauded humanitarian project. The dream never was to make money. I rarely thought of that. My ruling passion must have been the desire for respect, mainly my own. I needed to earn my own respect in ways that went unexamined. My ambition was for heroic deeds, for saving people like us who were born at the bottom of the heap, on the assumption that equality and what is called economic opportunity would result in a good life for all."

Listening to these words I remembered how he had been celebrated for an exemplary educational project that bore the identifying marks of our old summer reading. He had recruited and mentored young people of color, opening the way to education and successful careers for many who might have lost themselves and whose talents might otherwise have been lost to the world. But there had been bitter disappointments as well, and he went on to speak of them.

"Everyone on the Gulf Coast knows about Amos Williams, whom I proudly rescued from the streets and eventually raised to an executive in the corporation only to witness his arrest by the FBI for running theft and prostitution rings for the Dixie Mafia. That story is infamous, but it tells all. The details don't matter here, since they have been splashed all over the press for years. What does matter is that my thoughtless generosity was prodigality. I didn't know then that prodigality and greed are the same weakness: the greed for righteousness! That both use the ambition to intervene and destroy the relations that, for better or worse, make a coherent world."

There he stopped and turned about-face. Rather than wallow in this self-inflicted last judgment, he shifted in his chair, as though to recover a sense of direction.

"Do you remember how excited and filled with hope we were by our reading of Du Bois? Remember the passage about 'teaching workers to work, teachers to teach, thinkers to think, without ever pretending that fops are not fools?' I think my ambition began with that sentence, and I still admire it. But I had picked it up and made it a slogan without really listening to it. The sentence doesn't say that we have the skill to tell who a person may become. That only emerges slowly.

"Du Bois speaks of workers and teachers and thinkers, but he says nothing about employees whose consuming passions are greed and owning things. Nothing about the idolatry of success and pleasure, or wealth and the banality of creature comforts that distract us from responsible living. I turned Du Bois' sentence into a social gospel about picking up the young like a piece of clay to mold and manage into healthy, worthy citizens. That doctrine may not be wholly false, but it has turned my life to ashes.

"Of course the press will miss the part about turning the best into the worst and diagnose my fate as personal 'burnout.' That's the common disposition to ensure that nothing really changes! It's what people often say who lack names for the soul and its maladies. Something has burned out all right: I've decided to renounce it all. I'm selling the company!"

With that astounding announcement he terminated this sketchy confession, leaving me with no choice but to respond. The only thing my numbed mind could invent was repetitious and pragmatic: "Then what will you do?"

"I'll put most of the proceeds in trusts for my wife and children. I've already told you about being an absentee husband and father. It's what naturally happens when we're recreated in the form of employee and tool of economy, always itching to get back to *work*, our familiar form of slavery. Once the publicity dies down, the family will hardly notice the difference. I'll reserve a modest annuity for myself, so I'll try to learn how to live again."

He paused as before endless and still unresolved complexities. "That's as far as I'd gotten when I called you."

Again he stopped, but not for me to ask another lame question. "Not to fear," he added, as though to cover my embarrassment. "I don't care for melodramatic gestures like jumping out of windows or shooting the employees. The fact is, I needed to convey my renunciation to you first. Perhaps because you're the living person whom I have known longest, but it's also related to those summer books, to the last time I remember having a soul."

That was all. Without another word Fabien stood up, thanked me for my help, and I left. The next thing I heard came from Lester King, of all people. He and I happened to meet in the convent refectory one afternoon, where he stopped me and said with a grin of surprise, "I understand you are friends with the industrialist Fabien Bergeron."

Keeping the surprise out of my voice, I acknowledged that we had grown up together, and he added, "Did you know that he has just bought the vacant unit on the third floor? His agent gave your name as a reference. You know that he"—he meant Fabien—"has recently divorced his wife after thirty years."

For some reason the fact appeared to give Lester particular pleasure. But as he expected no answer to his question, I said nothing, and he scarcely noticed. The implication was that no reference was required, especially from a person like me, so I smiled and passed on.

Too many years had passed since Fabien's life and mine had meshed for either of us to try to renew the intimacy artificially. But our occasional meetings have been cordial enough, and I've kept up with his movements. Hence, the place of his life in my little gallery of vices.

Shortly after he moved to The Valmont, he took up photography with such a passion that most of his time was—and still is—spent traveling with his camera. I know his movements, because when he's out of town, I water the plants on his side of the mountain. That fact enables me to give you a sense of where his great renunciation led. But for that I must describe some photographs that he allows no one else to see.

—

In Fabien's unit, each wall of a dining-room, where no one comes to eat, displays six startling black and white pictures, all alike in size and minimally framed by thin slats of raw wood.

The briefest glance at these twelve works rouses wonder. All are outdoor settings with a human provenance, mostly urban and, in appearance, quite ordinary until we realize, by the effect on our mood, that no one's there. Everywhere, the works of human hands but otherwise deserted. Negative scenes bearing the weight of stasis and loss.

As you enter the well-furnished but somehow empty room, the first image to catch your eye is of a bench in a deserted riverside park, viewed at eye level from behind. The bench is set on the brow of a slight grassy hill that declines to a sidewalk with a horizontal railing along the bank: the Mississippi viewed from the French Quarter. To the right and slightly nearer the picture plane, a lone, leafless tree balances the composition without adding anything of life or motion.

The River, beyond the grass and the railing, is leaden-colored and still, under a sunless sky. A human world, everything in order, but human only by subtraction. Not that the people have walked out of the picture. The effect is much stronger than of no-one-in-sight. Along with the sense of the missing human, every detail supports an uncanny impression of no motion and no time.

Across the dead water of a river that comes from nowhere and will never reach the sea is a ferry landing and a stretch of the port. But it's a landing without a ferry and a port without workers. Boats, but no sailors; barges and tugs secured to piers pointlessly, where there is no current to resist. And not a breath of air in the dull light.

Yet as the eye passes over the static picture plane, a conviction grows that what's present isn't what matters, that the thing itself is missing, unavailable for inclusion. The negation is so heavy we think of little else. It extends even to what *is* given, as though without the people and a world of relations in motion, nothing composes. No composure anywhere, and—most startling—utter silence.

Passing to a second picture on that wall, we gaze into the distance along an elevated urban freeway without traffic. In the middle the ribbon of concrete curves gradually away to the left toward a vanishing point on a not-quite-visible horizon. Below to the right, city streets are dark and deserted except for intermittent lamp posts encircled by globes of dead light, without power to penetrate the shadows beyond.

No cars here either, and no pedestrians. Absent even the energy field that might hold the tall buildings in dynamic relation with one another. The missing forces weigh more strongly because the buildings match the inertia of the highway above. Material objects but no world. Again, it's not that the people have absconded or been purged without trace. Instead, "here" and "there," "now" and "then" have lost the power to relate.

Among the most uncanny qualities of this small collection of twelve pictures is their unrelatedness to each other. Scanning the set around three walls is like looking through just so many windows at atoms of reality randomly distributed across an expanse that doesn't add up to a place. Tombs in a boundless graveyard without memory or epitaph. Each isolated in the expanse of empty wall within slats of frame that ambiguously limit the visual field without enclosing it. The edges of the frames are less boundaries than points of entry from which there is no escape, like the rim of a black hole. We're drawn into those empty windows by nothing but the energy of our own gaze.

Across more chasms of wall, one picture might be Virgil's "unlovely swamp of dull dead water." An old rowboat has been marooned in a remote bayou—but remote from where? Nothing stirs, not even the base elements of earth, air, fire, water. Not so much as a leaf moves on the trees above, and the only hint of time is the boat itself, stranded so long ago that the boards have rotted and left only a skeleton of keel and gunnels and ribs. But what the eye can't escape is the water. The closer one looks the more one feels that it's not *this* water alone, but that all the tides of the world have died in a general abdication of nature.

I have pored over these pictures for months, yet they still puzzle me. I struggle to see the implications beyond visual composition and historical references. The photographer gives us a context in which all the bonds are missing that might compose a living world. As given, the world is atomized into dead objects juxtaposed. Even we are detached as observers, isolated on the outside where we feel only the loss.

That skeleton of a boat, its decay aside, seems to exist divorced from an integral world of boats. A ghostly, even nostalgic shadow from which the meaning's gone. Imagine, if you will, aliens from space happening across this—or any boat—for the first time! Lacking access to the bonds that make an integrated world, wouldn't they see it as a bare and meaningless object? Nor would collecting it as an artifact help. Even for that they would have to belong to a boat-world. Perhaps the question posed by the pictures is this: Do relations among things belong to the things themselves or does their "thingliness" belong first to an incorporeal network?

If world comes first, then isn't the disposition to regard any world as a collection of discrete objects—collectible and exploitable as possessions—the product of greed? Reality anatomized in the interest of holding a living world and all its people in a safely manageable stasis where nothing dies because nothing is alive? But that still doesn't say what difference Fabien's pictures make. In the context of so much unrelatedness there is a tone of renunciation. As if he knew, without knowing that he knew, that his dining-room gallery, like the tomb of the nuns in the garden below, might also be a place of "resurrection."

Two other scenes, disconnected by anonymous space, face each other across the dining-room. In some other time and place—except that history too has gone missing!—they may once have been related to each other. The site is upriver from the city, along the River Road, where elegant plantation houses of another era survive alongside industrial enterprises that have for a century marred the banks of this once noble stream.

In the first of the two scenes a decayed mansion house lies like a cliché at the end of a perfectly symmetrical oak alley. The geometry of the two-story country house of gracious columns and deep galleries might be elegant still but for a long, diagonal crack from eaves to ground across the front entrance. Another absence, felt if unseen, is a double row of slave cabins that would have been concealed behind the repressed backside of the building. Despite the vertical trees, the horizontal porches, the earthen road between the trees, and the diagonal scar across the front, the picture is geometry without motion. Another missing field of relations, the bare residue of objects without world. In the absence, photographic realism becomes hyperreal and contradicts nature itself.

The scene directly across the room captures in one image countless industrial sites that gradually intrude on the still-older agrarian order of the river. The background, in parody of nature, is a jungle of rusty oil storage tanks squatting in a tangle of pipelines that look like nothing so much as dead roots. In the foreground, a slender line of decaying piers extends left to right along a slant of riverbank where ships once gorged and disgorged their cargo. Farther left in this slovenly wilderness, a dry ditch with the texture of corroded metal marks the place where chemical waste once overflowed into the river.

What I wonder is whether the photographer is witness to something unavailable for presentation? Something even about himself? I have often studied these unique works searching for the artist, not finding him. Yet since they hang in his room as works of his eye and his camera, they must in some sense *be* him. Like the portrait of Dorian Gray in the attic, they must reveal an aspect of his sensibility and his capacity too remote for me to describe and too private for public exposure. I say "must reveal," because works that refuse kinship with each other have the potential to show the artist and the fate of a fundamentally good man in a greedy world. And more!

As usual, when I'm puzzled and summon the phantom Nuntius, he doesn't respond. Either he has abandoned me or thinks I'm not ready to hear until I've poked around in the void on my own, searching for the unnameable unknown. Yet even in lodging this complaint against him, I feel an intimation—less than an idea—that in contemplating the last picture I'm facing a judgment where the ruin of the world is on trial and I'm a collaborator.

Is it possible that imagining the worst opens space for what's not-the-worst? Desire roused? Even obligation imposed? Does the desire for something more provoke intimations of still formless possibilities?

The fact that the photographs are vaguely attributable to different historical eras strengthens the weight of such last-day accounting and calls us to testify to the desolation of the world—and more. No evidence is cited against anyone. Certainly, no judge points a finger. Yet transgression, accusation, judgment, punishment—all are present. Even if, having once seen, we shut our eyes and walk away, we carry a burden that demands "more," for a Last Judgment is also, is it not, a cry for redemption?

The Talking Head
Sloth

"**W**elcome to the Wonderful World of Weather. I'm Claude Plauché." The hypnotic, perfectly pitched baritone voice offers consolation and cheer without the exertion of having to listen.

"Well folks, we have a hurricane!" News of the thing most dreaded and the thing most awaited. News useful for swapping opinions in a world without thought.

"Who said there's no adventure living in New Orleans? Tropical storm Hendrik has pumped itself up into a Category 1. My present prediction is that it will pass over Hispaniola and Cuba then get stronger. And in the warm open waters of the Gulf? Who knows? So keep those TVs tuned to Channel 3. Whatever happens we'll br-r-r-ave it together!"

Measured in advertising dollars, the natural buoyancy of such un-thinking is invaluable. Chatter without cease disguises uncertainty and assures that the world is stable and the heavens benign.

"Tomorrow? Variable clouds with scattered showers and thunderstorms, mainly during the afternoon hours." He reads off names and numbers on a giant map that an audience less indolent might perfectly well read for themselves.

Claude is the man for the job. A modern talent deft at producing and consuming images. Listening or speaking, he can neutralize language into clichés with a semblance of imagination and conviction that never wanders into meaning. His breezy magnetism spreads comfort indiscriminately. A smile and a voice so caressing might suggest Narcissus or a camera fetish, but his "public" loves it. He's the young man next door, so familiar that strangers greet him in the street. And yet, stepping from behind the camera, all vanishes. Where the audience is missing, as in coming home alone and crossing the garden, he is a surprisingly short man with dyed but well-trimmed brown hair, stocky in build, tending toward round where one might expect angles, cheeks pudgy like a baby's behind, and a face drained of energy without a trace of interest in life.

And yet he's a local celebrity, popular, even "charming," in demand on the party circuit, pleased with everyone and everything. No danger of offending complacency or of naming the despair behind the symptoms of boredom.

—

"**I** can't believe that Claude Plauché."

Mr. Bourdieu moves his chair across the foyer to the kitchen door the better to talk while Mary cooks supper. "When he isn't 'working' or 'mingling,' he sits up there on that deck in his rocker listening to animal music through headphones. Or he's indoors watching TV day and night like there's nothing in the world worth getting up and doing."

"He holds down a good job," Mary protests as she brings the food to the table.

"Oh yes. Once a day he drags himself out of his chair to go downtown, but what he calls work is just another way of standing still."

"I don't see why you dislike him . . ."

Mr. B. interrupts, "I don't dislike him. There's nobody there to dislike."

Mary assumes her patient look. "Well, I don't think he's as bad as all that. He dresses nice and has good manners. People like watching him on TV. Even you do. And he's very sociable. I always think what the song says: 'People who need people are the luckiest people in the world.'"

"And I think you're a goose!"

She pays no attention to his ill humor. "It's nice that Claude is always surrounded by friends. They like his company."

Mr. B's mottled face reddens as he interrupts again with all the energy he can muster. "All but him! I don't think he likes himself much. Shows *some* sense. Prancing around on TV like God Almighty reading the temperatures. Then comes home to his private Dead Sea."

The old man adds extra Tabasco to his bowl. At their proletarian supper hour these two oddly paired creatures, father and daughter, sit across the little table in the kitchen and "have a gossip."

As they eat his favorite gumbo, he remarks, "This morning . . . Now this is really something. You won't believe this."

The wizened face grins, and he searches with a gnarly hand for his napkin. "Meg Daeger was sitting in the garden buried in a book, and Lester went over to her. You know she never comes down if anyone's around. Well, they passed the time of day, Lester like the Lord of the Manor and Meg wishing him at the devil.

"Then who do you think turned up? You're right! Claude! You know how the sparks fly when those two get together. She pointed at him and said to Lester, 'Why don't you take that wart in hand and make something of him? Apprentice him to your legions of Mammon.'

"Lester squared his shoulders and chuckled. 'I might corrupt him.'

"'Slugs are incorruptible,' she said. 'There's nothing lower.' She wasn't joking either."

"Tsk, tsk," Mary clicks her tongue in disapproval. "And what did Claude say to all that?"

"Just stood there grinning, schmoozing, pleased with himself. Not that he didn't understand. He's a damned juvenile delinquent. Takes any kind of attention as proof he exists." Mr. B stops as though that's the end of his tale. Then suddenly makes an aside under his breath, addressed more to himself than to her. "Can't believe they're kin!"

Mary stops, startled, her spoon in midair. "Who's kin?"

"They are. Meg and Claude. She's his aunt!" Mr. B enjoys telling her things she doesn't already know about the "inmates" she's so proud of.

Her round face glows with astonishment. Then brushing back the wandering lock of hair that's always getting in her eyes, "Are you sure you've got it right, Papa? How do you know that?"

He purses his lips and squints as though it helps when he has a new idea to ponder. "You have to admit, they hate each other enough to be kin." Then he breaks off as though there's nothing more to be said. He likes holding her in suspense as she sits, one hand pulling anxiously on her round chin, waiting.

"So, go on! Tell me the rest."

"Well, after Claude left, Meg and Lester went on talking. It seems that when she was retiring, Lester called her about the unit that was for sale at the time. And what do you think? Claude put him up to it! And she knew nothing about it until today! That bit of news shut her up for a while, I can tell you. She sat there like the cat had got her tongue. Didn't like it, either. Then she told him that Claude is her sister's boy."

Mr. B's eyes modulate from sardonic to thoughtful. "But he must have meant it kindly—Claude, I mean. He didn't have to have her on his doorstep."

Mary gets up and begins collecting the dishes from the table and putting them in the sink. "Did she say anything about the sister and brother-in-law? You know how proud Claude is of his family history." Mary comes back and leans two chubby hands on the table, patiently waiting.

"Apparently, she—I mean the sister—married a rich foreigner, a count of something or other, but the marriage didn't last. As a child Claude lived with his mother in hotels all over Europe. Meg was sarcastic about it. Said he grew up in elegant halls and gardens surrounded by beautiful people.

"Downhill ever since, I should think. Always finding an excuse to mention the fashionable world. It all fits. Accounts for his poses. That ring on his pinky like he's some kind of aristocrat! Degenerate enough for an aristocrat, I say. Always cutting a figure. Imagining he was born to glamour."

Mr. B throws down his napkin and pushes himself back from the table, ready to return to his "observation post."

Mary maneuvers the wheelchair across the foyer and places it facing the cloister door that he calls his "window on the damned."

As she stands behind, towering over the old man, he seems diminutive by comparison, though mass to volume, more substantial by half. She goes over to the TV. "Now I've got to go down to the refectory, Papa. Do you want the TV on?"

"Hell no. It's all crap this time of night. I'll go outside later." He maneuvers his chair closer to the door but doesn't open the curtain.

At the hall door she pauses to relieve herself of a burden. "I don't care what you say. I think Claude's one of the sweetest people at The Valmont. I've never had any trouble from him, and he always remembers me at Christmas."

When she's gone, Mr. B opens the curtains and continues talking, knowing there is more than one person in the room, but fewer than two. Through the slurring of his speech he pushes vigorously on. "No reason to try to explain to Miss Mary. She's half in love with all these people, women *and* men."

He sniggers then continues with his story, spoken to some presence in the room, if no more than a breeze moving the curtain. "When Claude was about twelve, the mother sent him home to boarding school in the East. Then down here for college. Didn't even know where his aunt was until he found her by accident. First time they'd ever met, if you can believe that. She made it pretty clear that she didn't like him, so after he graduated, they didn't meet again until years later after he started his TV career. Then he looked her up, probably to show off. But she wasn't impressed."

Mr. B is enjoying himself too much to desist. "Oh, yes. One other thing." He giggles as though the other thing is *too* delicious. "Along the way Claude spent a year in Paris as the special friend of some fine lady. Probably her gigolo. I know people say he's gay, but I doubt it." His brow remains flushed. For some reason Claude is an affront to him. "To be gay you have to be alive!"

Then he adds, quite seriously, "He's a pretender. His two favorite things when he's not on camera are his mirror and his echo." But a frown betrays concern, and he squints as though trying to see more clearly. "I don't understand him."

He may speak cynically about the residents, but Mr. B frets about them too. His grizzled head shakes sadly. "He's young and healthy and intelligent. Has a good job. But wastes his life. It's not that he can't do anything."

Under his breath he concludes, "A lazy man is such a coward. What I want to know is: What's he afraid of?"

——

Trying to sketch the character of Claude Plauché is like reaching for a soap bubble. Touch it and it vanishes. For months I've made no headway whatever. Direct observation helps little where even the face is not *his* face. The features keep changing. And between what he says and what he does there's only negative consistency. Even from one moment to the next he doesn't coincide with himself. His indifference to the flat plane of his existence leaves him featureless. Even the dead nuns in the garden are more distinct. They don't show themselves, but they leave traces in the world. Perhaps because they're only dead, while he's dead otherwise.

Sometimes I think I'll give it up and cut him out altogether. Then I decide I must go on, because the blight on his existence clarifies something about the human condition, if I could only tell what! Even in his lack of imagination and unacknowledged despair, he must have been at least touched by experience. Time surely leaves sufficient traces of habit and character for him to operate minimally in his present environment. As for the future, he can hardly *not* look ahead at least as far as his dinner, and yet his indifference to possibilities leaves him unacquainted with himself. Deaf to meaning and blind to hope.

So, I'm reduced to describing the TV personality indirectly by his effects on other people. Leaving aside his virtual audience on the tube for whom he is only an image, there are just four people who, taken together, must know whatever of him is knowable. The first is Marty Berenson, the station manager of Channel 3 who judges him with contempt. Then there's kindhearted Mary Bourdieu, who lives in a cloud of sentiment; Mr. B, the keen satirist with more insight than charity; and last, his aunt, the professor, who gives satire a bad name. And yet it's true that Claude's sorry condition, his preference not to-be at all, makes him a comic figure and fodder for satire.

All see Claude in sharp relief either as a type or as an individual with better or worse traits of character, but none see with the disinterest it takes to catch the singularity of a person. To all but Mary he's a cluster of weaknesses, and even she sees him only as a member of the class of humanity toward which she is benevolently disposed even when they don't take the trouble to exist. So, I'm caught again: How, pray, does one love Claude Plauché enough to understand him? To catch the singular Claude, I really need the inspiration of my phantom muse, but he usually speaks up only after I've taken a leap and landed in befuddlement. So, I'll begin his portrait with a story from the TV station.

It seems that one morning on the streetcar, Claude overheard a conversation between two men about the hurricane that was threatening to dump the lake on New Orleans and drown it. One man mentioned a news article he had read on the subject, and the other responded with an account of how the Dutch, who had faced the same danger for 1,000 years, had finally "tamed the North Sea" by a system of dikes and high-tech sluices.

When Claude got to the station that morning, he went straight to Berenson's office and proposed that the manager send him to Amsterdam to file a series of reports on flood control. Of course Berenson dismissed the idea, but Claude responded, "It's public opinion, Marty. I'm your biggest asset. I have the highest viewer ratings in town for news programming. My popularity can stir up the public and get things done. It's all about public opinion."

Berenson, knowing his "meteorologist" better than he knew himself, laughed him off, and that would have been the end of it had station gossip not picked up the story and spread it as far as a senior executive who knew less about Plauché than about the menace to the city. When even the network became interested in this project in which nothing whatever had been projected, Berenson had to produce a plan with a budget. The short version of a long story is that Berenson charged

Claude with the task and set a deadline. Predictably, Claude temporized and evaded until his job was in danger. The point for me is that this managerial episode might shed some light on the weatherman's particular form of madness. But that's entangled with another of my four witnesses.

—

The most accessible and transparent of Plauché's relations is his aunt. And that comes with a history of its own.

Years earlier, when he first came to New Orleans for college, she was nothing to him but a name that turned up occasionally in his mother's letters. Once he was established in the same neighborhood, he chanced to hear of a Professor Margaret Daeger in the Department of Romance Languages at Tulane. Here's what followed:

Chancing to pass the language building one afternoon, Claude turned in to look for her office. The door with her name was open, and he saw a family resemblance in the woman standing at a bookcase, casually smoking. Despite the wrinkled and leathery face, the frizzled dry hair, and the pinched look of one whose youth has been eaten away by some obscure vice, he recognized the astute eyes.

"Auntie Meg?"

A message from another planet would not have been more startling or more unwelcome to the professor. The familial diminutive in the voice of a half-forgotten sister seemed to claim possession and cut her down to its size. Her lips tightened at the aggression as she returned to a time-worn desk and sat down a bit belligerently. In silence she stared casually at the nephew she had never seen before.

"I came here for school in the fall. I've been meaning to look you up." The social voice was confident if unconvincing.

She continued to sit and left him standing in the light of the single window in the room. A half turn of her chair would have put them face to face, but she didn't turn. She sat examining the rough skin of her hand instead. For a few moments she scratched at a scaly spot as though she might have forgotten his existence. Then with a quick side glance, just enough to take the measure of the pudgy face, "So you're a freshman."

The remark was pronounced with the degree of interest one takes in an unpleasant duty. "Isn't New Orleans an odd choice? After the European childhood and the Eastern boarding school?"

He missed the point. "Well, I *am* half-French. That's something, isn't it?"

"Something. Depending on which half and what you do with the other half." This, neither sarcastic nor friendly. Pleasant, for her, but then, he didn't know her.

They chatted for a few minutes about his mother, her sister, the one topic they had in common, though Meg's news was only as recent as last year's unanswered Christmas card, and his was mainly about himself.

Suddenly the chair swiveled enough to make her square body and forbidding gaze unavoidable in his line of vision. She inspected him with conspicuous care, searching for the language of character in a body that knew no such language. She found what of him there was to find physically attractive but not at home with himself.

By looking away he bore her scrutiny well enough and made his own survey of the office, the walls of books and the jumbled desk, searching perhaps for a trace of kinship and finding none.

At long last she gave him a Meg Daeger half smile. "I saw your father once when you were still a child. We met by accident during a research trip to Paris. I'm not sure where you and your mother were then, but your father and I recognized each other in the lobby of the Paris Opera."

She paused to call up a forgotten image. "I remember it clearly. At the Palais Garnier during intermission. They were divorced by then and he was with friends, so we spoke briefly and only of you. He took great pride in . . . what did he call it? Your 'destiny?' Yes, that was his word, '*your destiny.*'" She watched with a practiced eye for some response.

Claude cowered a bit under the gaze, then replied, "I'd be interested to hear more about him if you have the time. My mother's view is not . . . well, unbiased."

"Nor is mine, I think you'd find." Then instead of satisfying his curiosity, she got up abruptly and collected her books. "I'm off to class now. You may walk with me if you like."

And so he did. They set off across campus, the heels of the matronly lace-up shoes digging into the sidewalk as though she were at enmity with the earth; he, passing over the ground with the light swagger of self-consciousness and a touch of defiance. Instead of speaking to his interest, she asked what he had come to study.

"I haven't decided. I need to be sure before I decide. First year, you know. I'll just get my feet wet before deciding." He didn't try to make all this deciding sound true.

That was what the first meeting amounted to, and there was no second. Meg might have sought him out, invited him to her house for dinner, done whatever aunts can do for nephews, but her interest in family extended no further than the occasional whiff of curiosity. So she forgot about him.

From time to time, he formed a vague intention of seeing her again then didn't. Was it his fault if the word "destiny"—his father's word, now hers—checked his enthusiasm, such as it was? And so he procrastinated with the more-than-procrastination that usually accompanies the phenomenon. Hadn't he received a message and a summons in that single word and, the better to evade it, transferred responsibility for the message to the messenger who could be more easily evaded? Meg's physical presence, sitting in that office gazing at him face-on with the sternness of a judge—her demeanor more than her words hinted at something he was to do, which registered as a rebuke.

Thus time passed without their meeting again. Meanwhile, he spent a year in France, then returned and showed up once more unannounced at her door. He acted on no idea. A habit of evasion had closed the imaginative space between acts and intentions. Maybe he secretly hoped not to find her in on a Friday afternoon. But she was in. When she opened the door and recognized him, he saw the creases in her square face tighten with surprise and a slight trace of interest.

Since they last met, his posture had improved and the boyish flesh of the cheeks had tightened, but his gaze was looser and more ambiguous. He had acquired a stylish wardrobe but not the character to wear it. Instead of maturity and self-possession, there were traces of compromise. Three years apparently came down to just so much ground lost.

As he was in no hurry to come to the point, he mentioned Paris.

"And what did you do in Paris? Were you studying? How did you spend your time?"

He mentioned time spent with his mother then spoke in a livelier voice of a woman friend with whom he had found room and board. She had introduced him to the *beau monde*, as he put it, had, he hoped, added a little polish, certainly had taught him a bit about the world.

From his enthusiasm for these details, Meg surmised that he had played the passive lover to some minor aristocrat with social pretentions. As for the polish, it was the veneer of a poseur. He had grown up bilingual and could justly pride himself on fluency in the language, but there was no evidence of his having used it for anything more significant than to amuse a bored mistress and order his dinner.

"So now the fun's over and you're back at the grind. Are you learning a lot? What courses are you taking?"

He hesitated before replying, more than a little defiantly. "I've decided on communications. Yes, I think I'll go into television."

She stared at the slight flush that made his fat cheeks pink. "You'll what?"

"TV." As if the plan were being fixed even as he spoke, "I'm going into TV. I don't have to, you know. There's always the annuity from my father, so I don't need to work. Free to do what I like, you might say." And he grinned with very white, very straight American teeth.

She barely heard the remark about the annuity. There were a great many things Meg Daeger loathed, but she loathed nothing more than "the media" and the childish prattle that passed in them for thinking. Refused even to own a television. If the clatter of public opinion eroded the capacity for thinking, how much worse the substitution of a picture for a thousand words? In her view bored generations had fallen under the spell of mindless spectacle. Now here was a young man, presumably of some promise, proposing to squander his life in that morass of simulation and self-indulgence. And for what? Money? Celebrity? Alms for oblivion.

In all this Meg was half-wrong, because she was incapable of imagining a rational being who lived without any desire whatever, and when she spoke again, she made no effort to conceal the contempt. "Since you're back, all polished up with your new knowledge of the world, why not get an education? One might have thought that to be alive was to grow without ceasing."

He chuckled apologetically, paying unintentional homage to some obscure ideal that his version of Paris had not quite eradicated. Lacking the finesse to circle about a topic at a safe distance, he let her remark drop and veered in another direction. "You said something when I was here before that I have wondered about. Having to do with my father."

"You mean, I suppose, what he said about you that cold night in Paris." She took time to conjure up the scene again. "We spoke for only a couple of minutes."

He frowned, then insisted, "And yet he said something you never forgot."

"It was the only time I ever saw him except at their wedding." She calculated how to put it, what tone to adopt. "He said that you were a precocious child, capable of anything and destined for something grand."

Claude stared at a formulation too general for flattery and too specific for comfort. "What did he mean?"

"Oh, he didn't mean you'd become important and make a great stir. You weren't to become emperor of Louisiana. Your father would never have been so vulgar as to want you in the guild of movers and shakers. It would have been some distinction worthy of remarkable talent, talent inherited from him, of course. God knows from your mother you could have inherited only sloth."

She watched Claude's face cloud over like a pond after a fresh stirring of the mud. Not quite knowing that her rough hand had touched a forgotten wound or roused an enemy within. Of all this she recognized little.

Only a sorceress could have known the effect of her words, and Professor Margaret Daeger was no sorceress. Yet if a single word from her had roused some indistinct idea from which he might defect but never escape, then his Aunt Meg had become the one person who knew! Those bloodshot eyes, present or absent, might accuse him forever after.

She went on, meanwhile, with her blunt truth-telling, a puppet master blindly twitching his strings. "So has the thing your father foresaw come to be? The thing that was to happen?"

The question put him momentarily in danger of recognizing himself as a person to whom something ought, but nothing had, so far, happened. For evoking that "nothing" and making him a haunted man—for that too, if he could rouse himself sufficiently, he might learn to hate her.

In time, Claude took his degree and stayed on in New Orleans. The slackness of the city suited him. Less the hedonism than the autonomy of people who wanted to live free of costs and responsibilities. He liked the torpor of a place where one could enjoy life without having to improve or be useful. The slow movement of a feverish climate and a humid atmosphere that made industry absurd were about right for him. His neighbors might be possessed by the demons of commerce and progress, but he was blessedly free of their vices. He knew how to enjoy life. It was his special talent.

After that second meeting with his aunt, they lived for several years in the same neighborhood without meeting. Meanwhile he became as conspicuous as a person can well be in a modern city. Meg even heard his name occasionally, without curiosity, while he managed likewise not to think of her lest it irritate a sore spot.

Occasionally, when the sore smarted, he resolved to find some worthy aim to relieve the flatness of his life, but the impulse faded, and such thoughts thinned with the thinning of his hair. He had contempt for success, which didn't quite come to the same thing as his indifference to failure. It belonged to the aristocratic side of his heritage not to regard scandal or insolvency as failure, or to blush at being turned out of his house or caught in a crime. Yet in a different sense, failure haunted him as what his life thus far added up to. As he grew a little rounder and a little balder, he lived more and more in the shadow of a European childhood and a magical year when he had "seen the world."

✗ Beware Scribe. A talking head and a scribbling hand may share the same world! Isn't there some lucidity in Claude's regarding all things as vanity? Isn't his empty world the same the artist-thinker contemplates in joy and perplexity? You may be his closest kin at The Valmont! Your tone reveals proximity. The words may come from the professor, but you're writing them down—all of them.

—

In proposing the flood control project to Marty Berenson, Claude had felt a slight quickening of the pulse. Then the interest flowed out again and left him marooned in lethargy. For him TV was a distraction; another was the repetitive rhythms of pop music. The one formed the bland, the other the garish wallpaper of his life. Something like an artificial bio-support system for maintaining the pulse of the organism by numbing the mind.

One Friday morning in the middle of such a brutal therapy session the telephone rang. Berenson calling.

"Clauché!" He says, taking satisfaction in melding Claude's names. "I've got to talk to you about that Dutch water-management thing you got me tangled up in. I'm downtown now and I'm coming by your place in a few minutes."

Claude cleared his throat and stammered, "I . . . I . . . I've got too much on my plate today, Marty. It's almost the weekend. Work can wait for Dismal Monday. How about early next week?" Suffering the weight of inertia, he stretched his sandaled feet out in front of his chair the better to feel free.

Berenson shouted into the phone, "You get your act together, Clauché! I want to see some paper—what you plan to do and what it's going to cost me. I'll be there in twenty minutes."

Not to waste that twenty minutes as Claude wasted it, we might *use* it to examine more closely Claude's state of mind. Rather than facing the fact that he has done nothing and has nothing to show, he settles back into his chair and spends the twenty minutes pondering his own misfortune. In fact, that non-response casts a peculiar light on sloth.

Just at noon, Berenson finds him on his deck lounging in a rocker, in shorts, shirt, and Panama hat. Claude looks at him as though for the first time and says, "You don't look good, Marty. You're working too hard."

"Just tired," he answers in a voice pitched about three steps too high. "The thing is, Plauché, the company president is interested in this thing of yours and wants to see what you have in mind. To him it means money."

At that moment Berenson spots someone waving from the garden below. He raises a tentative hand in response. "Isn't that Lester King, the real estate tycoon?" He waves again more vigorously. "His office is across the street from the station."

"Yeah, that's him. He's running around town on this lovely day piling up more money."

Marty, impressed that a person like King should live at The Valmont, cranes his neck to have a better look around. "Expensive!" He looks askance at Claude, wondering how he manages it. "Successful people, eh?"

"Ambitious, restless types. Forever on the move. Lester's not as bad as the rest. It was an old dump of a nunnery until he bought it and renovated it. The people here are like you, busy grinding themselves up trying to make money they don't know how to enjoy or to improve the world that doesn't improve. Why do you people live like that? Why bother? In the long run we're all dead."

Claude sniggers modestly as though to stress the profundity of the remark. "At least Lester makes his money between times. Mainly he collects women."

Then, pointing across to the Quad, "Over there is where the federal prosecutor—your fellow New Yorker George Basson—and his wife live. He busies himself trying to clean up the town, while Tanya, the dancer, is completely miserable in New Orleans, if you ask me."

He modulates the tone. "But if you really want to be impressed, there's a couple who pass their time with their heads in books. One's a priest, researching something about the river delta. Always looking backward, these bookish types, avoiding life on the front lines."

Marty puts aside his own impatience and sits still during this astonishing speech. Its length and its passion—not to mention the heresy of it—leaves him staring with open mouth. Eventually he answers the question why. "Maybe it's that we aren't all fools. Maybe some of us know what side the butter's on."

In recording this singular speech by Claude, what strikes me is its coherence. It's arresting. Astonishing, even, to hear cogent criticism from one who never lets thinking disturb his idle mind. But motives aside, I keep asking myself how a person with no ideas can occasionally see so far. Can vision result from willful blindness?

✘ Where character, measure, and purpose are the same, doesn't Plauché's sloth touch on an ethical measure? The same life in the same world but lived differently? Adrift in limbo, relating to nothing, giving nothing, measuring himself by vanity.

Meanwhile, sitting on the deck still and sensing that his Friday-morning speech on the vanity of life has done nothing to improve Berenson's mood, Claude goes inside and returns with copies of several articles on how the flood control systems work in The Netherlands.

Marty shuffles through, then flings them down on the glass table between the chairs. Leaning forward, he cries, "Damn it, Plauché. You haven't done a thing!" And he pounds the glass table with his fist so hard it cracks.

Claude nearly leaps from his chair and stands gaping in horror at the ruined tabletop, then at Marty, and back again. "What's wrong?"

As though sensing some indistinct danger for himself in the situation, Claude sits down again and leans forward. "I never promised a deadline for this thing, Marty. It's true I'm a bit behind, but it's not my fault. I've been distracted by other things." He isn't lying or trying consciously to mislead. It wouldn't occur to him that misleading is possible.

For a moment Berenson looks like a man defeated: shoulders stooped, head dropped on his chest. He turns around and says quite earnestly, "Plauché, you don't give a damn about anyone but yourself and not yourself enough to do what's good for you."

Then, pointing a finger, "You bring me a proposal by tomorrow afternoon or you're finished." And he stamps back through the condo and slams the door behind him.

Claude remains in place, still whimpering, "It's not my fault."

—

By Saturday morning all this has washed away and Claude sits in the leather lounger in front of the TV, catching up on the news until it's time to check the mail. Still a bit stung by the scene with Berenson, he looks around for his "project folder" and takes the pages to the kitchen. Perched on a bar stool, he begins reading. After a paragraph he breaks off to find a yellow note pad, but by then it's time for the mail.

Downstairs further procrastination is carefully covered over. The mail carrier has just opened the bank of boxes, but when the waiting's over, Claude sits down on a bench in the garden—a thing he never does—and passes half an hour paging through *TV Broadcaster* and *TV Guide*.

On the way back upstairs, chancing to notice Meg Daeger hunched over a book in the cloister opposite, he crosses the garden. "Auntie Meg!" He enjoys seeing her wince at the words, but this time his motives are different.

Facing her at close range across her table, he's astonished. Has it been so long since he really looked at her? She has become a disheveled old woman: faded sweatshirt and shapeless slacks; stringy hair, grey and unbrushed; with eyes and mouth permanently stamped by discontent.

"I'm having a party tonight." He watches the words make no impression on her. "Why don't you come? It helps to be around people."

The tone is by no means insistent or imploring, yet a trace of pleading in his voice is not quite neutral.

Meg closes her book and forces her eyes up to him. The effort seems to gather the disassembled parts of her face. "Go to your party? Why would I do that?" The questions sound almost innocent. Then, with the finality of completing a syllogism, "Being at a cocktail party is like being in a coma!"

He gives her the condescending TV grin and the voice of fake optimism. "That's your opinion, but I don't agree. You need to get out. Meet people."

The round face reddens with indignation. "Opinion!" She pauses and glares. "Is everything to you a fluttering of opinions? Is there nothing real or true in your world?" The abruptness and the critical eyes leave the impression of his having been turned inside out and found hollow in both directions.

The indignation continues. "Whose pleasure are you consulting? You think I want to listen to the nattering of your friends? Or that they want to listen to one who would make them feel brain dead? If neither of these, what?"

He chooses to appear scandalized by her contempt and stares in disbelief.

As she grows more thoughtful, he physically shrinks. "Family sentiment, is it?"

That leaves Claude completely adrift, though he understands enough of the music without the words . . . until she changes keys.

"But you know all that! Whatever else you aren't, you aren't stupid. That's where we're kin. Your bet is that I won't upset the punch bowl because I know it would make no difference. So what's the point?"

"That's not true, Aunt!" He may not intend to give the impression that she matters to him, but now he *is* pleading.

She waves the subject aside. "Well, we'll see." Abruptly she climbs to her feet and walks away.

As Mr. B says, Claude may be a man adrift in a small boat on a private dead sea, but it's not quite true that he does nothing whatever.

One thing he does to avoid solitude and his acquaintance with himself is go to parties.

That evening people fill his living and dining rooms, continuously arriving and departing. Some from the TV station, some whom he hangs out with after hours, some from The Valmont, and a number to whom social obligations can be thus repaid without inconvenience.

Usually the residents don't mix, but one way inconspicuously not to mix is to drop by Claude's place for a drink on the odd Saturday night, invitations unnecessary.

The room is filled with the noise of voices. Amid the babel, Claude, wearing the face of prophylactic sociability, is astonished to see Fr. Joseph Barthes across the room, drink in hand. Then he shakes hands with George Basson—no sign of Tanya—but when Lester arrives with Gwendolyn Perdue (of all people), he conducts Lester through the bodies to the bar then draws Gwenda to one side.

Because neither threatens the other, these two get on in good party style. He's the only one to whom she can safely prattle, and she's the only one to whom he can talk without the danger of being trapped by words. Neither really intends to say anything, and each intends not to do so by constant talking without listening:

"Have you seen the new furnishings shop on Chartres Street?"

"Don't you just love to shop? Found anything good lately?"

"I hate everything new. I was born old." Then he checks the clock.

Eventually Meg arrives. The sweatshirt has been exchanged for a wrinkled, shapeless blouse, but otherwise she looks much as she did earlier in the garden. Without anyone's noticing, the sea of bodies parts for her to pass, while the voices measured in decibels remain safely undiminished.

Without preamble Meg directs a question to Fr. Joe. "What is all this talk about that's trying so hard to be about nothing?"

He stares back without replying as she passes on to the bar, gets a drink, and parks on the deck alone where she sits looking across at her own place barely thirty yards away, wondering why she has come.

"You came!" Claude is beside her chair, looking down. "I'm glad." The words ring truer than he may intend.

Without looking up, she replies in a toneless voice. "I was just wondering why."

"That's absurd, Auntie Meg. What do you want from life?"

"I want to die."

Before he can reply, the doorbell causes a stir in the living room, followed by an ominous silence. He leaves Meg and returns to the crowd, where he spots an uninvited guest just entering.

Marty Berenson—who hasn't come for a party. In his anger he scowls at the crowd and plows across the room toward the deck. Along the way he catches Claude's arm and drags him along.

"Didn't I tell you to bring that proposal of yours in this afternoon?"

The angle of Meg's chair makes her invisible from the door, and in his surprise, Claude has forgotten about her. Thus she becomes an unseen witness to Berenson ranting and Claude almost pleading.

The Weatherman eases Marty farther from the door until they are standing just behind his aunt as he announces that he has decided to withdraw the proposal.

Berenson throws a cigarette butt over the balcony into the garden like a grenade. Then, "You're fired!" and turns on his heel to leave.

Claude reaches for his elbow and pulls him back. "Marty, you don't mean that. Where would your advertising budget be without me?"

"Just you watch! I'll have you replaced tomorrow before lunch. You know nothing about TV, Clauché!" Then continuing in a tone of calm contempt, "People will watch anything so long as they don't have to be alone with themselves or talk to their wives. We'll say you're on assignment. By the end of the week, they'll have forgotten all about you."

"Don't get excited, Marty. Cool down."

"I'm *very* cool! You can pick up your severance pay on Monday, minus the hundred."

"What hundred?"

"The bet, goofy! You bet me that something would come of this thing. That should leave about two dollars."

Berenson begins walking away, and Claude again catches his arm. But just as the manager swings, Meg stands up in their faces. His right hook lands squarely on her left jaw, and she collapses at their feet.

It broke the jaw, and chaos followed. Claude dropped into his chair from where he took no notice as the paramedics hauled Meg away, nor when Berenson left, not even when the party dissolved. He sat on into the night repeating, "It's not my fault."

The morning after, he turns up at the hospital with a bouquet of roses, though the flowers only add to the awkwardness. Meg can't speak, and he can think of nothing to say. All he manages is, "How are you Auntie?" and offers the roses. She stares as though neither he nor his flowers make sense. He lays them beside her on the bed then pulls up a chair. Finding that awkward, he gets up to fiddle with the window blinds and sits down again.

Eventually he shrugs and rises to leave. Meg gestures for a pad and pencil that lie on the table by the bed. She scribbles one line, folds the page twice, and hands it to him. He stares at it for a moment, then deliberately opens it and stares again, first at it, then at her and, stuffing it into a pocket, leaves the room.

Later, discovering a random scrap of paper in his jacket, he opens it before dropping it in the trash. It contains only one line, and the line makes no sense whatever: "How long must a row of zeroes be to add up to more than zero?"

The Man of Law
Wrath

Precisely at seven ten each morning, going out to his office, George Basson takes the long way through the cloister rather than the short way across the Quad. So regular, says Mr. B, that you can set your clock by it. Basson is a brooding, straitlaced little man, impeccably dressed in conservative suit, white shirt, and bow tie. He walks with military discipline, briefcase in the left hand and umbrella tucked under, then passed across the right forearm. Not handsome, but notable in a crowd for self-possession and the bearing of authority. Less about the small eyes behind wire-framed glasses or the bald head than about the thin, firm face and sensitive mouth. Somehow it's easy to guess that the man of authority might also be a lover of books and the arts.

Four years ago, when he and Tanya Marianenko moved into unit 206, he made a first-day tour of The Valmont and surprised Mr. B in the act of retreating into his room. The old man turned his head at the sound of footsteps, recognized the new resident, and spun his chair around to face him. Holding up a finger on his weathered right hand, he burbled slightly as stroke victims sometimes do, "You're George Basson, the U.S. attorney."

George paused and nodded.

"I'd like to ask you something." The tone was sardonic, more goad than question. "What makes you think you can stop corruption in this city? It's been lawless for three hundred years. Since it was a fur-trading post. You'll wear yourself out, and the city will be the same."

George lifted a friendly hand, smiled, and passed on without replying. Thereafter they did not meet, though Mr. Bourdieu kept an eye on the prosecutor's gradual decline from cheerful resolve into sallow-faced disillusion and anger. By the morning we are about to speak of, George appears to have arrived at whatever truth those words foretold as he hammers the ground with his heels and scowls at the slate walkway.

As Basson exits onto the Avenue, Papa says in one of his usual addresses to the universe, "That man's control frightens me. Behind that calm surface he's ready to erupt. He carries that umbrella like a hunter carries his gun. Used to have a friendly smile, but now there's only that fixed grin. Why is he always grinning when there's no one there to see? He smiles and smiles as though if he stopped smiling, he'd snarl."

The old man shakes his head and grimaces. "Sacrifices himself as though he hated himself. I wonder if a rigid conscience belongs to self-destruction."

George lets the gate slam shut behind him and crosses impatiently to the streetcar stop in the median. Taking the morning paper from his briefcase, he folds it like a New York commuter on the train and reads the front page:

THE PITBULL'S LAST SNARL?

U.S. Attorney George Basson returns to Judge Philip Lerner's court this week, seeking a conviction in his last corruption trial. The defendant, state Judge James Chappell, is under indictment for bribery, obstruction of justice, and mail fraud.

The contentious issue in this trial has been the use of wiretaps and hidden cameras by the federal government. What one side calls evidence of criminal intent, the other calls entrapment. So far the case has rested almost entirely on an FBI sting operation.

The proceedings are expected to move rapidly toward closing arguments by prosecutor Basson and defender Gerhardt Schwartz.

Judge Chappell is the last of eighteen government officials and employees to be indicted by the grand jury. So far, the federal probe has led to the conviction of the district attorney, the assistant DA, three city commissioners, five attorneys, and six employees at City Hall. Only police Chief Henry Renfro escaped conviction, thanks to a hung jury.

The year-long drama has been amusing to a city with a sporting taste for wheeling and dealing, mistresses and payoffs. Observers expect the case to go to the jury before the day is out. The question on everybody's lips is, "Will this be George Basson's last snarl?"

As the streetcar makes its slow progress into town, George notices other passengers craning their necks to get a look at the man who is regularly vilified in the press. Even going to work in this city where he is an alien, he carries a burden of a personal history that's never far from his mind. In his family the word "law" was spoken often, and always with reverence. It's the culturally rather than confessionally Jewish family living above his father's storefront law office in Brooklyn, heir to an ancient, if diminished, ideal of law. Law based on a sovereign covenant performed face to face, so to speak, between Yahweh and Abraham that eventually descended, as human affairs will, into legalism and stasis. No longer a promise made, but law as sovereign command.

George learned his political axioms at his father's knee: "Through your seed the nations of the earth shall be blest" and "We hold these truths to be self-evident." The father's proudest achievement was producing a son who became a Rhodes Scholar and took a law degree at NYU. Schooled in these traditions, he entered the noble service of political justice never suspecting that it might be a path to despair.

After law school, working as a public defender upstate, George eventually got frustrated with "making the worse appear the better cause," as though human waywardness might be corrected by social management. He had listened to his clients' voices and his own in court until he had come to believe that it was law rather than criminals that needed defending. So, blind to the collusion between law and transgression, he took up arms against barbarism and become the defender of order against chaos.

From the streetcar stop at Carondelet, George walks a block to Lafayette Square and crosses to a coffee shop where he waits in line for "coffee black," then scowls at the taste of chicory that gives an unpleasant surprise each morning. Passing on to Poydras Street, he navigates the crush of pedestrians with a New York gait like an alien from a different dimension of being. It's the difference between Lester King strolling through the Quarter with proud slackness and a man concentrated on rectitude.

At age forty-eight and at the top of his profession, he brought the same quietly uncompromising spirit that had made him successful in Upstate New York to his appointment as U.S. attorney for the Eastern District of Louisiana. What inspired him, though he would not have expressed it so ostentatiously, was a vision of turning a notoriously corrupt city into a just, which meant an orderly, city.

Before moving to New Orleans, he had been here for conventions and for Mardi Gras, but in preparation for the new post he read more deeply into its long and untidy history. He knew it as one of the crossroads of the world during its evolution from lawless frontier to governance—if any—first by France then Spain, then France, the U.S., the Confederacy, and the U.S. again. Knew its Mediterranean hedonism, its Sicilian opportunism, and the Mafioso wars down to the reign of Carlos Marcello. Knew the tradition of prostitution so extensive that Storyville qualified as a reform movement and knew the long history of sleaze that made City Hall a college for felons. And he knew that people survived it all by forgetting care, as in the annual orgasm of carnival.

But there were things an outsider could not know. For example, that Mardi Gras was not just a holiday escape. To understand its erotic power, he had to live *into* the city. But the idea that Eros might be the reverse side of law itself was a dimension in which he permitted himself to be well deceived.

✘ Violations of law, erotic suspensions of rule—the energy of desire behind the law. Perhaps the city's "letting," in excess of law, may hint at means *without* ends?

Soon enough George came to see how the city worked: bribes to public officials from the oil industry, sales of posts in government agencies, preferential treatment for companies dealing with state institutions, influence peddling in insurance contracts, vote buying. These, while not unique to New Orleans, were commonplace. And it got worse. Police-court hustlers making a living by passing money to fix anything—parking tickets, hit-and-runs, petty theft, drug dealing, possession—anything could be fixed, for a price. Even in criminal cases, when judges handed down sentences containing errors so that they could be reversed on appeal—all for money.

Where there was no standard of measure, corruption wasn't corrupt. Just the business of business-as-usual, and a condition of employment. Elected officials, office workers, attorneys, the police, janitors—all had mortgages to pay, families to feed, children to clothe. It wasn't about being honest or crooked. It was a system, and everybody knew how it worked. The language of justice simply shifted accordingly, and to defect was to be blackballed: no work in the city and no references. A lawyer would never practice again. A judge's political support would evaporate. An office worker would wind up a day laborer or leave town without recommendations. All prisoners of the machine. If they toed the line, they and their families were fixed for life. So the question: If you arrested all the guilty, who would be left to serve on the jury and what jury would dare convict?

George could hardly remember what it felt like not to be angry, angry at the hostile glances in restaurants, at the theater, on the streetcar. Angry at the public for following the court proceedings like a soap opera staged for their amusement. Angry at the daily efforts of the press to discredit him and the FBI as outside troublemakers. Angry that a depraved public took a cynical view of law as a mask for raw power. The job he thought he had accepted was to bring to justice crooks in high places, but the job as he found it was far more difficult. It was pedagogical: to establish respect for law in a topsy-turvy city.

As reward for defending citizens against dysfunctional government, he faced accusations of demagoguery and of interfering with the New Orleans way of life. Thus every case he won left him more defeated.

In the last block of his march to the office, the man who is forever debating one side or the other of some argument silently examines himself. "Why bother enforcing rules in the face of this desire for anarchy?" Not just complacency, but lawlessness as good-in-itself. Hate toward the very impulse to harmonize human behavior, passion to tear the fences down. Then, who is the real enemy here? Eventually you begin to suspect yourself of moral fanaticism.

—

One evening George sits at home alone reviewing another day in court, Tanya being either still at the studio or at a performance. When he finds nothing to eat, he reaches for the phone book. He races through, looking for a number, and calls out for pizza. Not that he especially likes pizza, but the gesture gives satisfaction because Tanya thinks it too low for words. On the surface he remains calm with the calmness of pure will to control. He takes a beer from the fridge and instead of pouring it into a glass, as he prefers, drinks from the bottle, because Tanya hates that too. Beer in hand, he goes out to the deck.

It's a spring evening, dark except for the city lights glowing against an overhang of clouds. All day the clouds have lain there barely moving, without rain. Left alone against his will, he pulls up one of the canvas chairs that's piled with food magazines and jerks the chair so that they scatter over the floor. Instead of picking them up like a defender of order, he kicks them aside and settles down to review the day in court.

A few minutes later the door buzzer sounds, and he goes through to get the food. Returning with it and another beer, he pulls up a table, picks a piece of sausage off the pizza—slovenly town; he had not ordered sausage!—and throws it into one of Tanya's pots for dead plants.

Shortly thereafter she comes in from a rehearsal and drops down in her chair without noticing the scattered magazines or his forbidden food. "I've had such a day, Georgie!"

The remark finally provides a target for his anger. *"I've* had such a day!" And he begins doing a thing he never does but resents not being free to do: He defiantly recounts his day in court against the current of her waning attention.

—

A cloud of lethargy hangs thick in the air of Judge Philip Lerner's courtroom. The morning session of the second day has been taken up with complaints by the defense about one of the jurors who violated the judge's order not to talk about the case. The offender, a postman, had already petitioned the judge to replace him on the grounds that his wife was ill, but the request was denied. Now he is reprimanded and dismissed, making it appear that he leaked to a reporter with this result in mind. As usual there are disputes between the attorneys about his replacement, and by the time all is settled, it's eleven thirty. So Judge Lerner declares a break for lunch.

In the afternoon, the courtroom reeks of human smells: tobacco breath and sweat, trapped in the closed space for weeks, but disguised in the morning session by aftershave and cologne. Now the scent of Creole spices is added as the audience and press wander back to their seats and settle into the semi-somnolence of after-lunch.

The series of trials has dragged on for months, faithfully attended by jaded reporters and regular spectators for fear of missing the one moment that might matter. But today is different. Though experienced observers continue to express doubts that the prosecution has the goods to pull off another conviction, a measure of curiosity has returned to the tired proceedings.

George Basson and assistant Tony Bouchette sit together at the prosecution table on one side of the room, while the defendant, Judge James Chappell, and counsel, Gerhardt (Gerry) Schwartz, sit on the opposite side, all waiting for court to reconvene.

Chappell is a burly man who, in another life, might have been an LSU linebacker. He and his counsel share a grinning, back-slapping demeanor at odds with the dignity of the law. On the scale of impressiveness, George's short stature, balding head, and glasses are no match for the commanding presence of such men, but *he* plays the game differently. In his quiet way—immaculately dressed in dark grey suit and bow tie, self-possessed, and intensely intelligent—he takes it for granted that the proceedings of the court are not about him and the figure he cuts in the room.

If misgivings simmer behind this air of rationality and quiet humanity, they don't show. As everyone waits for the judge, the prosecutor sits straight in his chair, feet flat on the floor, hands folded on the table in front. The studious eyes are slightly out of focus as he considers the obstacles ahead and his strategy for dealing with them. Can this jury be persuaded by evidence collected from traps set by federal agents? Will twelve not-very-intelligent men take the word of the diminutive but courageous woman who is soon to be called as star witness for the prosecution and asked to betray her employer? Whatever the evidence, can such a jury rise to the challenge and find a respected judge and pillar of the community guilty as charged? It's a lot to ask of any jury, but it's what he must ask.

The jurors file in, and a hush of respect passes over the room. Everyone stands for Judge Lerner's entrance. The old Southern aristocrat, white-haired and black-robed, at once Olympian and folksy, resumes his place of quiet authority above the fray, and one of George's assistants begins tying up the loose ends of the case for the prosecution before giving it to the defense . . . or so it seems.

When the assistant finishes, George stands, and in a droning voice befitting a lazy afternoon in a river town on the Mississippi, speaks as though he is about to rest the case. Then he wheels around as by sudden inspiration and says, "Your honor, the prosecution calls Ms. Christy Dalbert."

He puts no particular emphasis on the words, but the whole room snaps to attention.

Christy Dalbert had appeared earlier as a witness in a case against the district attorney and testified to having seen money pass to her friend Terri Gattuso from a man later identified as an agent. Ostensibly the money was for delivery to the DA's office. So now, calling Ms. Dalbert to the stand so late in the trial prompts observers to leap to the conclusion that she may have been a mole in Judge Chappell's office, where she is well known to have been employed.

The heavy wooden doors at the back of the room swing open and a petite blond enters. A middle-aged, fading beauty, but striking in a modest dark suit, light blouse, and black pumps. She walks to the witness stand and speaks in a clear voice as she is sworn in. Basson asks her to identify herself, and in response to the question about employment she answers that she was until recently secretary to Judge James Chappell.

Then beginning quietly, "Ms. Dalbert, how long did you work for Judge Chappell?"

The answer comes in a calm monotone. "Since his election six years ago."

"And when did your employment end?"

"On September the third last year."

"Had you known him before you worked as his secretary?"

"I'd worked in his law firm for five years before he was elected."

"And what was your personal relation with him?" He gives her a reassuring smile.

But she needs no reassurance. "I was his secretary. We were friends, I think. There are a lot of confidential affairs in an office like that. I was responsible for most of them."

George turns to the matter at hand. "Will you please tell the court what happened on the night of October 27th, 1976?"

"I went out to dinner with a friend. To Galatoire's."

"And who was this friend?"

"Terri Gattuso." The name makes a stir in the audience, and the judge raps the gavel for order.

"Please tell the court what happened that night."

"Nothing unusual until a man stopped at our table. He knew Terri and there was a minute or two of small talk, then he walked away."

"What happened next?"

"We paid our check and left. When we got to my car in the parking ramp—I was driving Terri home—the same man came up to her side of the car and handed her two thick brown envelopes. I noticed there was nothing on the outside like an address or anything."

"Were you surprised? Was she?"

"I sure was. But Terri didn't seem to be. She just took them and put one in her shopping bag and laid the other on the seat between us. Then the man left without a word."

The self-possessed witness speaks in an even voice without emotion, as one might expect of a person who has spent years in the halls of justice. And yet a closely attuned observer might sense a touch of the theatrical, as though ground were being prepared for an unexpected moment.

Meanwhile she continues. "Nothing else was said. We drove uptown and, when Terri got out of the car, she left the second envelope on the seat. So I handed it to her."

"Then what happened?"

"Terri held up a hand and said, 'That one's for you.'"

Basson, "The envelope was for you?"

"Yes."

"And then?"

"I looked at her sort of puzzled, I guess, and picked up the envelope next to me as though to open it. She said, 'I wouldn't do that now. Just put it in your bag.' She was already out of the car, but the door was open, and she waited while I put the envelope away. Then she gestured toward my purse on the seat. 'Take care of that. There's a lot inside. There'll be a piece of paper telling you what to do with it.'"

"When did you open the envelope?" Basson asks.

"Not until I got home."

"And what did you find inside?"

"Money."

"Did you count the money?"

"Why, yes." A self-conscious smile touched her mouth at the corners. "Who could resist counting it?"

"How much was in it?"

"Ten thousand dollars." George allows himself to appear surprised at a figure that causes another stir in the audience. The judge raps his gavel. The noise subsides. Without prompting, the witness adds detail. "In hundred-dollar bills neatly divided into little stacks held together with rubber bands."

Basson pushes ahead, cool, detached, with barely a hint that he might be enjoying the moment. "And were there instructions for what you were to do with all this money?"

"There was a piece of paper that said, 'For the Judge.' That's all."

Another stir, longer and louder than before. The journalists who have been sifting the dry sand of this trial for days leap in unison on the new bit of information and begin furiously scribbling.

Another call for order, and George resumes. "So what did you do with this envelope with the ten thousand dollars inside?"

"The next morning, I took it into Judge Chappell's office and handed it to him."

"And what did he say?"

"He took it and said, 'Thank you.'"

"Did he open it or ask any questions?"

"No."

Again, murmuring from the audience.

"Did you get the impression that he knew what it was?"

"All I know is he wasn't surprised. Just took it and put it in a drawer of his desk."

"Did you know his office was bugged?"

"Yes."

"How did you know?"

"Several months earlier I had let a man into the office after hours. I was there while he put a listening device in the bookcase." The witness quite enjoys dropping this bombshell, though Basson seems less sanguine about the consequences.

"Who was this man?"

"I don't know his name. He was from the FBI."

"How did you know that?"

"I had been contacted by them and had agreed to cooperate."

"And why did you agree to cooperate?"

"I knew what went on. About the bribes, I mean. It was just the way business was done."

Basson turns to the judge. "Your honor, I request permission to play these tapes to the court."

An hour passes in vigorous contention, especially when it comes to light that there are videotapes as well and that the witness had used a concealed camera on a number of occasions. Defense attorney Gerry Schwartz goes into high dudgeon. He dives and surfaces, leaps and blows like a great fish hooked on a sportsman's line. As he rants at the idea of anyone committing such a "*hy-ē-nus* outrage," George does nothing but keep the line taut, quietly, patiently, citing legal precedents.

Eventually Judge Lerner admits the tapes into evidence with the result that Judge Chappell is tied to the same web of bribes and payoffs that had been established in earlier cases. But the old question remains: Will this jury convict on the basis of secret federal surveillance?

Then comes the cross-examination. Gerry Schwartz stands up, lays aside his usual urbane bearing and coaxing voice. This time, the bully. However vulnerable Christy Dalbert might appear, he swaggers up to the witness box and glares at her with all his six feet plus of height and addresses her in a hostile, authoritarian voice that implies, "I'll break you, little lady!" Presumably to rattle her into saying more than she has rehearsed.

"*Miss* Dalbert," he begins, continuing to glare, using the "Miss" as a term of contempt. "You *are* unmarried, aren't you?"

"Yes." She looks him steadily in the eye, indifferent to his efforts to intimidate. The impression is that she knows exactly where the power lies between them, and he doesn't have it.

"*Miss* Dalbert," he repeats. "When you were working for Judge Chappell, were you privy to *all* his affairs?"

"I suppose so. Most of them anyway."

"What about affairs in bed?"

"I don't know what you mean."

"Come *Miss* Dalbert," he growls. "Weren't you his mistress at the time of his election? And hadn't you been his mistress while he was still in private practice? And didn't your confidential affair continue after he became judge?"

"Objection, your Honor," George calls out. "Ms. Dalbert's private life is not on trial here. And counsel is not letting the witness answer."

Judge Lerner: "What are you trying to establish, Mr. Schwartz?"

"Your honor, I'm trying to test the credibility of the testimony the witness has given this court."

"Proceed, Mr. Schwartz, but allow the witness to answer."

This revelation from a person George has somehow needed to believe in comes as a personal blow at a critical moment. Wanting to believe, he has too casually taken her as a symbol of the innocents who make the struggle worthwhile. Now he is shaken by the proof that, like all the rest, she too is guilty.

Without quite dropping his head into his hands, he stares at the implication. The culprits are not only the ones who violate the law. They are also the employees who depend on them. And not just the ones who profit indirectly but the cowardly bureaucrats who know but won't tell. Not just the friends and friends of friends more loyal to friends than to the law, but those who don't understand the causes (or no longer understand them) and those who don't want to understand.

Meanwhile, Schwartz continues to snarl at the witness. "How did your intimate relation with Judge Chappell end, Miss Dalbert?"

She remains unflappable as though to say, "Go ahead. Do your worst. I have nothing to lose."

"By mutual consent, I'd say."

He sneers. "Let's try again. Didn't Judge Chappell tell you on July the 10th, 1975, that his wife had found out about your affair and that he was ending it?"

"Maybe. I don't quite remember."

"Don't remember what? What happened? Or when?"

She answers in an even voice. "I don't remember the exact time."

And from that point Schwartz went on in the same vein, setting traps that had little to do with the case, intended only to discredit the witness in the eyes of the jurors. Dalbert coolly evaded or readily admitted her faults as anyone with her legal experience might, as he portrayed her and her friend as cast mistresses motivated by revenge, and all in the following substance and tone:

"Isn't it true that you, Miss Dalbert, and your friend—both mistresses who had been discarded by their lovers—tried to blackmail them and, when that failed, you invented this cock-and-bull story about a courier service for bribes—bribes which were on offer from the federal government, by the way—all as a way to besmirch the reputation of our good local officials?"

Not for the first time George cries, "Objection!"

"Sustained."

But Schwartz hardly notices. He might be a hellfire-and-brimstone preacher crying out against a sinful world. "Are you telling this court, Miss Dalbert, that you are here today trying to bring down a distinguished judge, elected by a grateful community, and that you're doing that out of concern for civic morality?" He doesn't wait for an answer or an objection. "No more questions, your Honor!"

Christy Dalbert is excused. As she makes the long walk back down the center aisle of the crowded courtroom, looking to neither side, she betrays no more self-consciousness than if she were walking down a Canal Street sidewalk.

—

Court having adjourned early, George has dinner with an official from the Department of Justice in Washington, in town to witness the end of the trial. Afterward he takes the trolley uptown and arrives at The Valmont early in the evening. Tanya is at a fundraiser for the ballet and will be out till all hours, so he'll have quiet time to collect his thoughts and review tomorrow's summation. But the best-laid plans, like the best-crafted laws, rarely go as intended.

At the gate of The Valmont, he searches in vain for his keys, buzzes Mary, and gets no response. Until a moment later when Mr. B appears in his chair on the inside and opens the gate.

"Sorry, Mr. Basson. Mary's in the infectory with Lester." Then giggles at his own mistake as he opens the gate. "I mean the re-fectory."

That rouses a smile in the weary face of the prosecutor. "Thank you. How are you, Mr. Bourdieu? Nice evening."

The old man is sensitive about being seen in public and half apologizes. "No one's around, so I'm out early for the fresh air and the smell of the earth."

They pass through to the cloister and the opening into the garden then, instead of walking on, George pauses. It's a thing he's never done before, and Mr. B adds, "Mary won't be long."

George sighs deeply. "Don't trouble yourself. I'm in no hurry." And he sits down close by on one of the benches in the inner wall of the cloister. Casting a summary glance over the garden, he adds as though it's a new idea, "It's a pleasant place to come home to."

His eye rests for a moment on the tombs in the far corner, and he continues in an agreeable conversational tone. "I've always wondered what real estate law preserved that old tomb. Any idea?"

"Mary says the Dominicans stipulated that no owner could ever destroy the garden or remove the tombs or the cloister. That's one reason why the building was derelict for years. Lowered its value on the market. Before you came, Lester proposed replacing the garden with a swimming pool. But even the residents balked at that idea."

"So the law would have stopped him, in any event. But it's odd that people who might not especially want to live with dead nuns on their doorstep should also not want it changed. In the abstract the tombs are rather ghoulish. Not to mention all the religious superstition." Then with a companionable smile, "But it's pleasantly spooky."

Mr. B looks up at him curiously. "You like it then?"

"The odd thing is I rather *do* like it, though I don't know why."

"The Hermit over there"—Mr. B points toward the corner beyond the tombs and above the old chapel—"you know he lived up there for several years before Lester bought the place. He says at night he used to see the ghosts of the nuns among the ruins of the garden. In those days there was no electricity. It was just an overgrown piece of wilderness."

"Ghosts, huh?" Basson chuckles at the old man's sense of humor. "A bit morbid, isn't it?"

"Ghosts aside, I'd say it's a companionable place, especially at night. That's when I'm often out on my balcony." He points across the garden. "The tombs have a sort of historical, sentimental value, I suppose. Not very useful though, are they?"

Mr. B. answers in a ponderous tone new to George: "I once asked Fr. Mark why these fossils from the dead past are important. He's Mark Maloney, Mary's parish priest. He and Mary knew this place long before the nuns got too old and the convent had to be closed. Her mother sent Mary to school here as a child, and for years Fr. Mark was the nuns' confessor."

George tries inconspicuously to keep the old man on the subject. "And what did he say about the tombs?"

"First, he said that a place of death is also a place of resurrection. Then, seeing that wasn't especially useful to me, he quoted something from poetry. Shakespeare, of all people. I only remember one line. Something like, if we only had what we need, we'd be no better than the beasts of the field. I remember it began, 'Reason not the need.' But it was all over my head."

"I know the passage!" Basson says with an enthusiasm that seems to displace his gloomy mood. "It's old mad Lear after he gives his kingdom to his daughters. The daughters immediately take away everything else he has on the grounds that he no longer *needs* anything. Then in anguish Lear protests: 'Oh, reason not the need! . . . Allow not nature more than nature needs. Man's life's as cheap as beast's.'"

"That's it, though Mary says it better. I mean in a way a person can understand. She says the garden's a place for gratitude for more than we can know. Even for death, since it's an investment in life. It's what the nuns passed on to their pupils. Fr. Mark says if we listen carefully, we can still hear their silent prayers that anchor life like we anchor boats in the river."

Basson looks askance. "That sounds poetic and nice, but I wonder what it all means."

Mr. B snickers. "So do I."

At that point in a conversation as far off George Basson's beaten path as a conversation could be, Mary arrives and ends it. But it ends with a cordiality between the attorney and the riverfront philosopher that must have astonished her.

Upstairs, Basson makes himself a New York toddy with Old Overholt Rye Whiskey and goes out to the deck. For a while he contemplates the garden from a new angle, then he sets all that aside and turns toward tomorrow and the business of the law.

From the beginning George had sensed in Christy Dalbert a reserve of cold revenge against Judge Chappell, but she had entered the scene late in his preparation for the trial, and her testimony was needed only to get the recordings into the record. He had known about the Gattuso affair with District Attorney Alan Bowles in advance but hadn't needed to trust her, since she was only to provide a missing link, identifying sources and confirming evidence. Last-minute rush or not, his missing the possible revenge motive for Dalbert's suit against Chappell was serious professional negligence on his own part. His judgment had been impaired by the tenor of his own private life. The unexpected revelation that Christy is no better than the rest leaves him alone and bitter, again questioning who he is defending.

He continues, speaking aloud as though there were still someone there to hear: "For these people law is the enemy. Lawfulness bores them. They're proud of being run like the Mafia. From the beginning this city was less opposed to reform than indifferent—which is worse."

Such conversations with himself are not unusual, however much they may resemble mentally impaired street people. He speaks quietly, deliberately, in a rumbling voice, face to face with an imaginary audience, emphasizing points with flourishes of face and hands. For years he has been honing the rhetorical skills for swaying others with words. By long habit he thinks in dialogue, speaking for both sides, constructing and refuting arguments, testing lines of questions on imaginary witnesses.

And so, if he hears himself being answered by a spectral voice or feels another mind pushing against his thought like a gentle breath against a candle flame, he barely notices. Only the words count. Except for one thing: a voice emanating with authority from no recognizable point of origin—whether demon, angel, or chimera—since it can't exist, cannot *not* be listened to:

> ℵ "Haven't you heard, Jew? The law kills! What is your ideal law-abiding city *for*? To preserve citizens from unfair practices? For economic housekeeping? Saving them *from* . . . but *for* what? What is the good of your evil?"

The prosecutor does not miss the point, and at that moment his search for the one just man opens another direction: "What *is* the city *for*?"

It's a difficult question for which he has no ready answer. But preferring the tree of knowledge to the tree of life, and with a sense of being heard by someone, he goes on arguing the negative case:

"When the city doesn't work, people suffer. You must find causes and stop the suffering."

In his preoccupation with the guilty, he lets the remarks about law slip away. He gets out of his chair, walks to the railing, and looks down blindly into the garden. Then, restless still, he returns and continues the line he had begun, speaking aloud, musingly:

"The corruption in government is routine. A secret only in that people decline to think about the way things are, how they got that way, and where they may lead. In this town the only unpardonable sin is repetition. Boredom. But law *is* repetition. That's what it does. Its system."

The question about the law continues to hang in the air as, in a further gesture of self-blinding, he takes off his glasses, and his indignation toward the world descends into wrath. But imagination has not quite died, and he lets the unaccountable words continue to resonate.

✗ "Is your ideal city a laboratory of political invention or a harmonious ant heap? Affirmation or prohibition? Pedagogy or the police? Can your law be kept without poisoning the springs of life?"

—

When the court is called to order on the morning presumed to be the last day, there is standing room only. The press is squeezed into a few rows on the left behind the table for the prosecution and the VIPs—wives and friends of the judge and the attorneys, alongside state and city officials. Out-of-town press quickly overflow the designated rows into every available space.

Tanya Pavlivna has not been in court before, so when she enters in all her conscious, elegant celebrity, an extra wave of interest spreads in whispers across the room. The jury—twelve men, eight white and four black and no women—enter looking tired and bored, but even they are roused by the excitement in the room.

The prosecution having opened the trial, closing arguments begin with the defense, so Gerhardt Schwartz strolls over to the jury box and leans on the rail without a trace of the bullying demeanor he used against "*Miss* Dalbert." The twelve men might be golfing buddies at the country club or his Sunday school class at the First Methodist Church.

"My good friends, first I want to thank you for being so patient and attentive during this trial. I know how inconvenient it has been to be sequestered so long, for you and for your families. But I want to remind you that what you're doing is protecting the Democratic Way of Life. I thank you for that, because in this trial we have witnessed an unprecedented arrogance of power in agencies of the federal government. These moralistic Washington bureaucrats think they know how to run our state and our parish and our city"—he pauses for effect—"even to run *our lives*, better than we do. So they've sent their secret police and their fancy Northern lawyers down here to sniff around and try to persuade you that our democratically elected officials are dishonest and corrupt.

"Well, if that was true . . . I say 'if,' because I don't believe it is true anymore than you do . . . but if it *was* true, we have ways of correcting it without these outsiders laying traps. The United States of America was founded on the principle of local government, and we the people are the basis of the law. If it's broken—and I'm not saying it is—then we can fix it in our own way and in our own time." His voice rises with patriotic indignation. "We don't need federal investigators and U.S. attorneys down here trying to undermine your confidence and mine in our God-given right to govern ourselves."

Meanwhile, George Basson sits at the prosecutors' table listening impassively, hands folded in front of him, face still but concentrated, though the cheeks are sucked in, making a dimple on the left side of his mouth, and the lines are more defined in his forehead than usual.

His thoughts run along these lines: "He, Schwartz, has no case and he knows it. What can he say about guilt and innocence? He must invent the best arguments he can, but an honorable man would make the best case and stop. And those dunces! They're going to acquit! God! Why did I ever get into this cesspool? Why try to save animal contentment from itself? Let them all be damned!"

Meanwhile Mr. Schwartz continues to the jury: "So, you see, what's on trial here is Orleans Parish and our dear city herself up against the Eastern Establishment! Enough, I say—and I think you'll agree with me—I say, enough of spending our tax dollars to trap our officials into doing something they can then turn around and indict them for."

Schwartz passes on to the details of the case. "Now, let's consider the witnesses for the prosecution, because at the end of the day it always comes down to the witnesses, doesn't it?"

He paces up and down thoughtfully in front of the jury box like a lone actor on a stage, filling the theater with his presence. "What I ask you to consider is this: Can you trust them? This snooping Big-Brother government has had the *ti*-merity to rest its case on the last-minute testimony of *Miss* Christy Dalbert. And who is this Christy Dalbert? She's a woman who we've heard admit—under oath—that she prostituted herself, and when she got rejected, she turned state's witness. For revenge! And not just for revenge, but to avoid being prosecuted herself. So, you see, if there was a conspiracy—and I sure as heck don't say there was—then she was part of it.

"The prosecution is asking you to find our honorable Judge James Chappell, this proud and humble civil servant, guilty of *hy-ē-nus* crimes on the word of a fallen woman who wants nothing but revenge on her ex-lover and to escape prosecution."

Suddenly he stops, raps the knuckles of both hands on the railing, and leans there a few seconds as though studying what might be added to an airtight case.

"Well now! Under the rules of this great state the prosecution gets to have the last word in this trial, but don't think that makes what they say true. No. They will harp on the letter of the law and how their secret police have made it appear that our client has crossed some invisible line and . . . "

For another ten minutes he goes on doing what he can to weaken the prosecution's closing argument, finally concluding, "Gentlemen of the jury, I'm asking you to defend the unique culture of our great city, to see the difference between the letter of the law that kills and the spirit of mercy that gives life. I'm asking you to stand up for justice and find our client innocent of all charges."

Schwartz straightens his tall figure and strides confidently back to the defense table as though it's a victory march. Before resuming his seat, a slow survey of the courtroom might be a bow to an enthusiastic audience.

—

George allows a moment for the air to clear after Schwartz's summation. Then he rises as inconspicuously as possible and makes his way across the room to the jury box. It's a moment and a figure that a cartoonist might catch and circulate as evidence of who knows what: the little man in dapper suit and bow tie, bald head slightly bowed, hands clasped pensively behind his back. He gives the jury a long, friendly look, shuffles through some notes, then lays the notes aside as though they're unnecessary. In a clear, calm voice laced with consideration for the patience of twelve good men and true, he begins to review the path they have traveled together to this moment. Looking into the eye of one after another, person to person, taking his time, avoiding rhetorical flourishes as though he and they understand that his case needs no embellishing. And so it goes, all friendly, all rational, all business, until he gets to the case for the defense.

He begins this point almost lightheartedly. "I was listening while the defense predicted what we would say in this summation. Well"—he directs a slight ironic bow toward the defense table—"I want to thank Mr. Schwartz for his help. That's the one thing he's gotten right in this trial.

"Now, how do you suppose he knew what we would say?" His voice grows firmer. "I'll tell you how. He knew because the truth of this case is as plain as the back of your hand. Still, the burden of proof is on the state, and that's as it should be. The state must show proof beyond a reasonable doubt that the accused did what you have seen him do, that he said what you have heard him say, that he has deliberately and persistently violated the law and the trust of his high office. And please don't overlook the strenuous efforts the defense has made to prevent your seeing and hearing those telltale audio and video tapes. Ask yourself why they wanted to guarantee that your judgment would be blind and deaf to the facts.

"The defense promised to show Judge Chappell as the innocent victim of a government conspiracy. That promise"—he looks down at the floor and makes a sweeping motion with his arm—"that promise lies in shards before you on this floor. A shattered promise! In desperation they have tried to put the federal government on trial."

He shrugs. "What else could they do? They're as overwhelmed as the rest of us by"—he turns and glares at the defendant, pointing an accusing finger—"by the blatant contempt for the law in that man's office."

He backs away from the jury box and assumes the indignation and the conviction of an Old Testament prophet, only modulated so it isn't *his*, but the indignation of all reasonable people. "Don't think for a minute that this is all about money."

He takes a few steps this way and that, looking at the floor, searching for what, if not money, it might be. "No, it's much worse than money. Taking bribes is one thing. Peddling influence is one thing. Selling your honor and your soul for filthy lucre is one thing. But it's quite a different thing for an official who has sworn to uphold the law to act as though the law doesn't apply to him. This trial is about one thing and one thing only."

He holds up a finger and passes it slowly back and fro before the jurors' eyes. "That man"—the finger moves around with a boldness that causes a stir in the visitors' gallery until it points directly at Judge Chappell—"that man, sworn to hold the law above reproach, has proved a liar and a cheat. You know! You've heard! You've seen him violating the public trust. You've seen why your national government has to spend money to investigate and bring crooks to judgment in New York, in Chicago, and now in New Orleans—to assure law and order for you, for me, and for our fellow citizens."

Again, he takes the time to search each face with a gaze that is unavoidable. He knows exactly how to elicit an involuntary reply from each man in turn. The glasses don't hide the eyes. They direct and concentrate the gaze. It takes greater boldness to evade those eyes than to meet them straight on. It may be judgment day for James Chappell, but for each juror it's like standing before their own bar of judgment.

"James Chappell lied on his sacred oath. He cheated every citizen who voted him into office and everyone who didn't vote for him. In accepting payoff money, he stole from every person in New Orleans. He took the bread from your table, the shoes off your children's feet. I don't have to repeat it all. With your own eyes and ears, you've witnessed a man unworthy of our trust."

There's a shuffling in the audience and George knows he has touched, if not the conscience of the city, at least an uncomfortable truth. Several jurymen exchange glances, which, however, does nothing to reassure him that his gambit will pay off.

If the darker side of his mood at that moment could be measured out in a sequence of ideas, it would go something like this: "I'm going to lose this case, and the rest won't have mattered. The whole of my life comes down to this moment! Not because the city believes the Chappells of the world are innocent. Everyone assumes their guilt. But they hate the law and admire the man who flaunts it. May God damn them! They deserve the desolation they're asking for! Without the will to an ordered life, nothing can be done. Destiny blinks and the moment of civilization passes us by once again."

Forcing the mountain of resentment back into some dark void of his being, he continues. "Finally, Mr. Schwartz has struggled to obscure the real issue by discrediting the state's witnesses. Now I'm not going to stand here and claim they're all angels."

He stops, smiles mischievously at the jurors, and asks in an intimate voice, "Wouldn't it be nice if all witnesses were saints or nuns?"

Then the solemn public voice again: "But this is the real world. This is New Orleans." A subdued snigger from the audience. "They"—pointing to the defense table—"they have tried to persuade you that the state's witnesses are in a conspiracy to frame honest officials. They say that Ms. Dalbert's testimony is tainted by revenge."

He exhales audibly. "Well now, what are we to think about that charge? I know Mr. Schwartz is a smart man, but can even so smart a man as Mr. Schwartz look into the human heart and see its motives? How can I know Ms. Dalbert's motives? How can you? Does she even know all her own motives? Don't your motives and mine change from one day to the next? The law doesn't ask you to play God and decide the secrets of the witness' heart. The heart isn't on trial here."

He walks up close to the jury box, lays both hands on the rail, and leans forward in an earnest man-to-man posture. His voice lowers to a tone of intimacy that can still be heard on the back rows of the courtroom. "But what if her motive *were* revenge?

"Let's consider that charge for a moment. What if she *had* conspired to take revenge on Judge Chappell for betraying her? Wouldn't her only hope for success be that her testimony is true? And would her true evidence be any less convincing if she were acting from revenge? Wouldn't it be still more convincing? Whatever the witness may have done, whatever her complicity, she has stared down her own reservations and come forward to perform her civic duty of exposing the cancer of corruption that has afflicted this city for decades."

He ceases and stands in quiet thought. Then takes a few paces up and down in front of the box, hands behind his back, eyes on the floor, reviewing and digesting the situation along with the jurors.

"My friends, the law doesn't require you to trust the witness! All the law requires of you is to call the words you have heard and the acts you have seen by their proper name and acknowledge the culprit's guilt."

He pauses to let the force of the argument leave an impression on the jurors' minds. "I'm not going to keep you here all afternoon repeating the obvious. I'll just leave you with the words of that great president and patriot Teddy Roosevelt."

He holds up a book that looks very much like a Bible, and in ringing tones that fill the room, he quotes: "Teddy Roosevelt said, 'Unless a man is honest, we have no right to keep him in public life, it matters not how brilliant his capacity, it hardly matters how great his power of doing good service … No man who is corrupt, no man who condones corruption in others, can possibly do his duty by the community.' That, my friends, is what Teddy Roosevelt said. Now I ask you to uphold that standard of honor in public service and return the only possible verdict in this case: guilty as charged."

He lowers his head and returns to his table as the audience audibly relaxes, shuffles in their seats, and coughs. Then Judge Lerner promptly reads his charge to the jury, sends them out to consider their verdict, and calls a recess.

The bets have suddenly shifted, and everyone now expects a long deliberation. There are sticky issues of entrapment, of questionable witnesses, especially the exalted respect ordinary people have for judges—and this jury is nothing if not ordinary. Yet in less than an hour, a buzz spreads through the halls of the building.

"The jury is coming! The jury is coming!" And a surge toward the courtroom creates a crush at the doors.

Once order is restored, all stand for Judge Lerner to enter. He takes his seat and calmly asks, "Gentlemen of the jury, have you reached a verdict?"

The foreman stands. "We have, your honor." He passes a paper to the bench.

The judge glances at it and asks, "What is your verdict?

"Guilty on all charges."

The audience erupts in cries of wonder and peals of laughter. People fill the aisles shouting with joy. Not joy in justice perhaps, but the release of the joy that comes when the theater curtain comes down on the suspenseful fifth act of a comedy.

Judge Lerner raps his gavel and calls, "Order! Order in the court! Order! This court will come to order!" He continues banging the gavel until the room is silent. Then the jurors are polled, and the judge ends the trial of the decade with a last firm rap of the gavel, and the jury files out.

Outside, the street is filled with a sea of people and an army of press. Lights flash, reporters yell questions, TV cameras roll. As the prosecutor emerges, a reporter in front of the crush asks a question. George recognizes him as Richard Perdue, who had left that pretty little wife Gwendolyn at The Valmont. As he answers, a female photographer at Richard's side asks Tanya to close in beside her husband for a picture. Thus the play concludes, all questions answered, all passion spent. God's justice and the rule of law restored. Unless it's Mardi Gras.

—

"**T**hat was an awesome summation, boss!" Tony Bouchette cries as he, George, and Tanya walk away from the courthouse together. "At first I thought it might be too subtle, but you really knew what you were doing. Really great!"

George returns an artificial smile as though he isn't much enjoying his triumph. "Thanks Tony. At least it didn't hurt us."

Tony is happy enough for both. "This is a day to celebrate. Let's go up to the office and collect the others and go to the Carousel. We'll start there and make a night of it."

"You go ahead. I need to clear my head a bit." Then to Tanya, who always likes a party, he adds, "You go with Tony. I'll catch up."

It's a sunny afternoon in April with unusually low humidity. After weeks of confinement in a stuffy courtroom, the open air is invigorating. Turning up Camp Street away from the office, he should feel free and happy after winning the most important case of his career—a series of most important cases. Instead, he moves as though the present is insufficient, as though his thoughts are somewhere out in front of him, and he must hurry to catch up. Walking at a rapid clip toward no destination whatever, prepared for action with nothing left to act upon, he continues for blocks in the general direction of Lee Circle, asking himself in multiple versions, "So what? Where everything remains as it was, what has been won?"

He calls it being honest with himself, looking his evil in the eye, not knowing that one can no more survive the facelessness of Evil than the bare face of Good. He may have learned his political axioms at his father's knee, but his father is dead, and his axioms have dwindled to random social ideals and fleeting norms. Where the measure is gone, there is no "measuring up." So even his own efforts come down at last to nothing more than opinion driven by a disposition for revenge.

✗ What then of the man who can only love a perfected world? Who bears the greater guilt, the one who bends the rules or the one who acts against the world as it's given? Punish all the guilty and destroy possibility. With nowhere else to live, resent lawlessness and endure a lifelong suicide!

The man in the suit with the umbrella over his arm reaches the elevated expressway. Oblivious of the traffic and the absence of a pedestrian walk, he climbs the ramp onto the high bridge over the River. If there is any idea in mind, it certainly isn't crossing to the West Bank. The impulse, more instinct than idea, is to escape the city and breathe free in the bright air between the cumulus clouds and the muddy Mississippi rushing seaward. The traffic is not yet heavy as he walks alongside, paying no attention when horns blare at the mad pedestrian or when cars swerve to miss him.

As the bridge leaves the bank and reaches out across the grey water, he begins the climb into the sky, stopping occasionally to look back on the city and its neighborhoods along the great crescent below. The ancient Greeks may have felt a bit as George feels, leaving the city, carrying the burdens of everyday life up to the theater for the tragedy, to become for a time one with the god and be renewed. Except that the lone modern man, at once inside and outside the city, is a homeless speck between a desolate earth and an empty sky where no god offers purgation.

In the middle of the span, he stops, leans on the rail, and stares for a while at the water below. The river is deceptively placid, except where the concrete pylons of the bridge emerge and provide stiff resistance to the current. The opacity and the invisible forces match his state of mind. On this of all days, the bridge might have been his triumphal arch, but it's only a fragile suspension over a churning void, leading nowhere.

He hates this city, hates it for its profligacy, hates it for its unruliness, hates it for its ridicule. Now, in the moment of vindication, the city will have conveniently forgotten that a week earlier it vilified him and now lauds him for his achievement.

Here, in solitude, he almost acknowledges something else as the source of his anger, something not about the press and the public and the crooks. It's the persistent voice of a tempter trying to expose his illusions. To this opponent, too, he addresses his best arguments, knowing he will lose on appeal to one who judges disinterestedly.

It must be a curious sight for the passersby to see a man, well-dressed and alone, standing at the railing of the high bridge, ranting to empty air and to water on its final hundred-mile surge to an indifferent sea.

"I cannot remember not being angry." The voice, below the noise of the traffic, is little more than a sigh of defeat. The arms fling out impatiently, then the hands, closed into fists, pass the anger on impotently to the steel railing in front of him.

Then, willing himself to be calm, he stops and switches sides of the case. "If the others are guilty, does that make me innocent?"

✗ Which limit of the law do you serve, Counselor, its penal end or its instructive beginning?

He stands a long while sending words out over the River toward the sea, face to face with an ideal that would, if it could, prosecute the whole world.

A gull lands unnoticed and remains perched on the rail not five feet away. It angles its head one way then the other, a double scrutiny with each eye in turn on the face of the man of law glowing red in the afternoon light. The bird hops down the rail to an empty point beside him as though to decipher the fixed smile now twisted into a scowl.

George leans on the rail, hands clasped, looking outward, longingly, at the distant bend where the River opens into the great S curve south. Yet the mind holds its focus: "Without order, what's the point?"

He removes his glasses and carefully deposits them in a convenient pocket. Climbing onto the railing, he steadies himself with his hands and, thoughtless as the gull, sits, legs dangling over the water far, far below. His head inclines as though listening again to the voice, then lifting his hands, he slowly leans toward the River.

✗ It is time to reflect again on rivers and gardens. Not just the Ojibwe's Misi-ziibi and the monastery garden, but all such cyphers for immanent possibilities. We, who were here before the rivers ran into the seas and before people cultivated the earth, observed for millennia as the beings called "human"—named for the *humus*—learned to cooperate in "humility"—also named for the *humus*—with the earth, doing no harm to either. Eventually, growing blind to the inherent connections of all things, they became the masters and possessors and lost themselves.

Seeing this much but baffled by the secret communication between vice and virtue, the Scribe now seeks cures for these careless souls, to prevent the evil and encourage the good. Yet isn't he as puzzled about life and law as George Basson? Why won't Lester and Tanya and Claude make better use of their lives? But would his neighbors benefit from being told that it's possible to stride resolutely, joyfully through the gate of The Valmont without knowing where the road might lead or who one might be at the end of that road? That one can read a book *from within* the book-being-read or be in time and out of time at the same time? That they *are* the transactions *between*?

Real questions, but who would understand? Words so remote, requiring minds willing to be disrupted and realigned, would pass them by without a trace.

So let us speak instead of time and the River, of disjointed lives trying to navigate the currents of changing worlds. Rivers like gardens—the Mississippi and all rivers even to the Indus, the Donau, and the Nile—offer parables of human being and its changes.

When Joseph Barthes and Mark Maloney first met in the garden, they spoke of the precarious history of the Mississippi, of its geological system that came to ruin under the calculations of the managers and the planners. What the two priests did not speak of is the poetry of the River, of its full character and pulse such as one encounters in *Huckleberry Finn*.

It's the difference between engineering the River into a planned economy and discovering, along its unpredictable course from boundary waters to the ocean-sea, an ethics and a poetry of being human.

Here's the question: How does the use and abuse of the River relate to a prosecutor who wants the city to stand at moral attention? And isn't that more or less what the Scribe also wants from his neighbors? No vices, just virtues: an empty, invisible good without reference to evil. Has he yet discovered that the point of his book is not to prove good principles and make people believe them but to lure the Valmontese into loving the shifting sandbars, the unstable channels of their desires and harmonizing them? Could even a god, deprived of hate, know love?

The artist who gathers scraps from the town dump and constructs a collage accomplishes more than he can know. In loving the unlovable enough to see differently, he finds a way where there is no way. The sacred and the profane may not be strangers after all. Even in this scribe's bitterest lamentations, one can hear the resonances of love for a freckled world.

A messenger from elsewhere sees this enigma of the yes and the no on every face. He hears in every voice the rivalry between loving all and settling for transient indulgences that end in emptiness:

In the tipsy prostitute among the midnight shadows of the cathedral, threadbare scarf draggling along the gutter. Giving words to a distant trumpet: "Lord, I want to be in that number, when the saints go marchin' in."

In the aging beauty with the facelift and dyed hair, on a bench in Jackson Square holding a poodle by a rhinestone leash: "So Sister Martha is dead at last, and I don't care. Why should I care? She never loved me."

In the old man with the ashen face and broken voice: "Five years since I saw him. Wonder what he's doing now. Why doesn't he come to see his mother before she dies? Or write at least?"

In the waitress on tired feet hauling herself up the stairs to a bare room at the top of the house: "I'm dead beat. Always hitting on me. Maybe I'll go back to Houston. No one there either."

Not one of these without a glimmer of infinity. Disappointed and out of phase with themselves. Defending the mirage of self, demanding all, risking nothing, loving nothing, dying of lack.

Yet from Chartres Street behind the Square, the asthmatic groan of a tenor sax: "It's that old black magic called love."

The Professor
Envy

Mary has brought a package to Meg Daeger's third-floor apartment because Meg is not home. She puts the package inside, then pauses, looks around, sensing a familiar presence like the inexistent visitor who keeps Papa company late at night. The charged spot in the room is in the vicinity of Meg's favorite chair.

"I know you're here. You may as well show yourself."

She's never heard the voice, but she has overheard Mr. B conversing with an emptiness that cannot be nothing, since Papa is the most reasonable person she knows. The truth is she and I share a disposition to honor names as bonds between language and things known *and* unknown. Especially names for things unseen like hope and love and truth.

Thus, she proceeds without embarrassment to address the indiscernible other in the room "This is where Meg spends her time, you know. Smoking endless cigarettes and drinking whiskey with a bit of reading from the French poets." For the first time, because she's not alone, Mary gives attention to the books lying all around and looks amused.

"Meg may not be a good housekeeper, but there's only her after all. I guess she has better things to do than straighten up. She's a very intelligent woman, a professor, you know. Was until she retired and moved here."

Getting no reply, Mary walks through the rooms as though to see that everything is in order in a place that hasn't seen order in years. The peculiar presence of another opens her eyes to details she overlooks when she's here alone so, as usual, she feels called on to defend her tenant.

The living room is a cluttered lair. Freestanding bookcases in dark wood fill the walls, killing the spaciousness of the room. Books overflow onto the floor north, south, east, and west, coming to rest in crooked piles in the corners under ubiquities of dust. Journals and old papers yellowed with age bury all the furniture but for the overstuffed chair, molded to the imprint of Meg's ample body.

Her chair is flanked on one side by its own stack of books, each with a marker as though six or eight volumes are underway at once. On the opposite side, a small table in front of a reading lamp supports a large bowl piled with ash and cigarette butts, adding to the stench of smoke in the not-fresh-air of the room. In the kitchen dirty dishes fill the sink and counter. On the dining room table, the dregs of breakfast sit dried and crusty on a plate. Likewise unkempt, the bedroom consists of a single bed unmade, another stack of books on the floor within reach, a second overflowing ash tray on a night table where the lamp has been left burning for who knows how long.

Mary mutters to herself, "Still, she shouldn't let herself go!"

Of course, I, as commentator on the scene, can't be sure what she heard, but as all understanding is translation, I can report what I heard her hearing and what I saw her not seeing as in the old Italian pun, *traduttore, traditore*, the writer and translator as traitor.

Returning to the living room, Meg feels "the presence" before the mantel, the only uncluttered spot in the room, and it lends an aura of a sacred space like an altar to some past glory. On the shelf stands an old photograph of Meg as a young woman.

"That's Meg in her late twenties," she says. "Not a handsome face; no sex appeal, snub nose, blunt features. But you see all that only for a moment. It's the gaze that's arresting."

✗ The same eyes. Beautiful in their prime but already smoldering with unforgiving heat. Impatience behind the social mask, avoiding truth, trying to be everyone else. Neither happy with happiness nor complacent in complacency. Disappointment already, feeding envy.

Mary studies the face. "What a lovely girl Meg was. Have you noticed how she has started talking to herself lately? In the garden last week I saw her on a bench having a conversation with the air. Couldn't have been you, because I'd have felt it, wouldn't I?"

Mary breaks away with a chuckle and, having performed her duty, goes to the front door and opens it. "You coming?"

She shrugs and shuts the door.

Sometime later Meg enters, slacks covering short stout legs, the old sweatshirt over the square torso, short hair greasy and grey, probably chopped off with scissors at the bathroom mirror. The unkempt look of one who doesn't think of appearances. She goes to the kitchen, pours whiskey into a dirty glass, and takes it to the dark living room. Turns on a lamp, sits down heavily in the chair, and sips from the glass.

The face in the lamplight from the garden is marked by more than age. Not so old but molded by the deep frown of some inner warfare survived but lost. The face might be called happy in one respect only: happy in not suffering the half erasure of experience by paint or surgery. A vestigial instinct for truth?

Looking around for something, she finds the reading glasses on one of the towers of books, puts them on, then jerks impatiently on the sweatshirt that's gotten twisted. She picks up a book at random and, instead of opening it, stares, pensive, over the top of the glasses across the dark room. Lays the book down, discouraged, and lights a cigarette.

Looking about suspiciously as though something is out of order, she says, "I can feel something's going to happen." Looking again, searching, hostile this time. "I won't let it happen! I won't!"

The other, imperceptible still at the mantel, also waits, then moves to the bookcase and surveys row upon row of books that, taken as a whole, look less like the tools of intellectual life than the protective wall of a ruined fortress. But protection from what? At the same moment Meg looks around the room again, suspicious, as though someone else might be there, then ignores it, or forgets.

When she speaks next, her voice, in soliloquy, is enervated and limp yet retains the clarity of an address to an imaginary auditor listening in judicious silence to words that rustle like a stale wind through dry leaves.

"I shan't go to bed tonight." She sighs then takes a long draft of the whiskey and continues smoking.

"Why not sleep?" he asks, if you can call it asking when an idea without a source reaches another mind.

Meg hisses as though in reply yet saying what she would never say to another person: "Envy never sleeps!" Thinking it because something in the air inspires it, yet accustomed to monologue, not thinking it as exchange.

"If I sleep, I dream. A swarm of guilty dreams pickled in the brine of the long disease of my life. Timeless, those few months forty years ago. More vivid than yesterday."

She exhales in a smoky sigh. "So old. But the pain endures forever." The face closes like a shutter, leaving a trace of violence on a countenance long settled into futility.

"Let it go," he says, voicelessly.

"Some things go on and on, unchanged. Memory is a curse. If only one could forget."

"Memory plays tricks, like remembering the beginning of the sentence at the end but never quite the same beginning or the same end."

Then more energetic, defensive: "No change. Memory is a prehistoric beast, grinning at you from beneath an ice floe. The primordial yelp of the undead, arrested in mid-growl, ready to spring again. Always with the same fresh passion."

"Unless the trap is forgetting that memory forgets itself, and in forgetting, forgives. Without facing-up and forgiving, it only pushes one thing into the shadows to make room for another."

She coughs the smoker's cough, takes another drink, and stares straight ahead for some minutes before going on. Eventually, "There's the one real thing. The rest is shadows and shadows of shadows." She deliberates over the one real thing.

"I'll show you. Where have I put those notebooks?" Meg thinks for a minute. Then gets up, reels across the room to a coat closet by the front door, drags some old boxes off a shelf, and begins taking out stacks of ancient softbound books of the kind used for class notes. She sits on the floor and reads the covers, then drops them one by one: "Fall 1941." "Winter '40." "Spring '39." "Winter '37." And so on until "Fall '35." Opens this one and searches inside briefly.

"Found her!" Laboriously she gets up from the floor and takes several of the notebooks back to the chair.

"Let's see." Then addressing the silent, attentive witness . . . or no one: "Listen to this":

> *Lisa was in the office today when Sam Stallings came swaggering in, shaking flecks of light from his mop of curly blond hair as if he were the Pythian Apollo. He began flirting with her in that bragging, condescending way. Instead of cutting him as he deserved, she was friendly, as she is with everybody. He took it as encouragement, of course, perched on top of her desk, leering down at her. Insufferable man! I put him in his place, though: 'Sam Stallings, you're a moral paralytic. An abscess on the universe!' Of course, Lisa thinks I'm too hard on him, but God, how I hate that man's arrogance!*

"No, that's not what I want." She turns back several pages and reads again:

> *Lisa said tonight that Maria Baumgarten got the highest teaching scores last term. She's so happy for her. The simpleton! Of course she did! I could have gotten higher scores too if I'd looked over my students' shoulders while they marked the evaluation sheets.*

Another stop as she finds another page:

> *Taking the required course in structural linguistics this term from that ass Martin Basil. So distinguished. He also admires Stallings! Pays no attention to the rest of us. Can't stand him.*

An impatient pause. "Hell! Where is it?" She turns back several pages more, then brightens. "Here. Listen."

24 August 1935

*This morning one of the new teaching assistants arrived in
our office. A young woman, a conscientious creature. Clever
but clueless. She took the desk next to mine and we introduced
ourselves. Name's Lisa Walters, accepted into the Comp Lit
program from some school in the Southwest. Scared to death.
She'll be teaching first-year German, not French. Seems her
mother is German and she's bilingual. We didn't say much until
later when she caught me staring at her, absentminded.*

"Why are you staring at me?"

*"Sorry. I wasn't thinking." Then really looking at her,
"You're too pretty to be here." I was thinking that men—and
women too—must always be falling in love with her, so soft
and vulnerable in a naïve, unselfconscious way. Drawn in by
those intelligent green eyes that know nothing of their power.*

*My remark made her self-conscious, but directness doesn't
scare her. "Thanks for the compliment! I guess you mean that
attractive women are all dull." She bubbles when she speaks.*

*"Not quite. Still, women as handsome as you don't usually
become intellectuals. They have easier ways of getting what they
want."*

*She said nothing to that, and that was all until this afternoon
at the general staff meeting. She came in and sat down beside me,
I suppose because she knows no one else. For some reason I felt
responsible and invited her afterward to Mattie's, where the grad
students hang out. Several others came in, so she met them and had
a good time, I think. Stallings couldn't keep his eyes off her, kept
showing off like the arrogant slug he is. We all drank too much as
usual, told stories about our summer travels, and renewed last year's
critical debates. It was midnight when we left, so I walked Lisa
back to her rooming house, though it was out of my way. When we
reached the house, instead of saying goodnight, she turned around
and said in a mournful voice, "I think I've made a mistake."*

"What mistake?"

"I'm just a country girl from a backwater school who's in
way over her head." Then the pitiful impressions of the evening
came pouring out. "These people. They've gone to good schools
and traveled all over, while I've been nowhere and know
nothing. This isn't going to work."

"Give yourself time," I said. "I've been in the program
for two years and just began to feel comfortable last spring.
We're knowledge junkies, so we all overrate anyone who knows
something we don't know."

"Yes, but they've read all those philosophers I've barely heard
of. It's all gibberish to me."

"None of this matters, Lisa. Shit, some of them aren't half
as good as you think. Some are bright but undisciplined; others
make up for being ordinary assholes by working hard. Me, I'm
probably a mix of the two. How you fare will depend more on
character and discipline than what you bring with you."

She probably paid no attention to my little sermon, but
the polite girl from the West thanked me and said goodnight.
I came home feeling quite good, charmed even. I like having
someone dependent on me, especially someone as pretty as Lisa.

The other, listening to the words from the yellowed journal,
watches Meg sitting in the old chair living two lives at once, haunted
by a remote past that's restored to presence in those pages, immersed
in cigarettes and whiskey and a wave of despair that engulfs her
whenever she stops reading.

"Did you fall in love with her the first night?"

"Was I in love with her? I wonder. It certainly didn't turn out
like that in the end. I always needed to be admired; it was my ruling
passion, my preferred poison. It's why I worked so hard to distinguish
myself. From her I got admiration. More than admiration. A bit of
worship, even. She was vulnerable and needy, and that was flattering;
so I became a mentor—protector, friend, eventually her roommate

and finally The Enemy." She stares outward into the room, seeing only detached images that don't congeal into a world.

"What crap!" Meg throws the old notebook aside on the stack by the chair and goes to the kitchen to replenish the whiskey. Returns, lights another cigarette, and stands before the window looking with an atavistic gaze into the garden and beyond into the sky where Venus is prominent but unloved. From the east, a heavy cloud intervening between earth and sky gradually extinguishes the stars a handful at a time. Then rain, first pattering then pounding against the windows.

She turns around and says aloud, "I haven't really thought about all this in years, but it's always there at the back of the mind, contaminating everything." Then, more wistful than despairing, "The heart dies, but it dies oh so slowly."

Taking a long drag on the cigarette, she inhales deeply. "Burns down slowly like a candle in the window of a ruined house, then flickers and goes out, leaving a dark and empty shell. Even remorse eventually fails and the heart goes cold as blue ice, reflecting light but giving none. Ambition survives, of course, and you run on like an automaton, giving your classes, writing your articles, attending your mindless meetings, receiving your petty honors.

"All alike: the Slocum Family Award for Excellence in Teaching, distinction for the Best Book on Baudelaire in '59, best critical article on French feminism in '65, emeritus professor of French. Success is the worst part. Distractions from the catastrophe of life, punished by commendations you don't deserve and by memory of lovers who never last. Each day caring less. All added up, it comes to less than a gold watch at retirement. At least the watch is a gift of the time remaining. Reminder that it's later than you think.

"An early lover said, 'Making love to you is like being devoured by a fire-breathing dragon.' The last one said, 'You're a cold, dead thing. Being with you is like screwing a corpse.' True. Yet we crave that last judgment because we want to be seen truly, just once!"

She returns to her chair defeated. And the uninvited guest, passing over the fierce energy and the loving invention of lamentation, brings her back to Lisa. "Did Lisa succeed? Was she bright enough?"

"Oh, she was bright enough alright." She pauses for an instant before subsiding into despondency. "The little bitch! Sometimes I can't decide whether I loved her or hated her for it. Within two years she became one of the most promising students in the program, with an illustrious career before her. So it appeared then. That, too, has haunted me all my life. She poisoned my life by letting me poison hers. Poisoned first by loving her, then by destroying what I loved." She sighs again. "But that's running on too fast."

✗ So, not quite dead. Tell it slowly and tell it all. Relish the bitterness and the remorse. Desire survives even the wasteland.

She picks up the notebook again and looks for another passage. "Here."

5 January 1936:

> *Lisa, back after the holidays, moved her things in today. I'm delighted to have the company and someone to share the expenses. She's much more orderly than I am, so that will be a good influence. Good for her too. Maternal instinct, I suppose. Thanks to our late-night discussions, she had a good first term and got a strong teaching review. On top of everything else, she's never spent a winter in the North. Doesn't even have clothes heavy enough. Yesterday morning when she left for her German 2 class, the wind chill was zero. I had to wrap her in an extra sweater and spare scarf to keep her from freezing. But she's learning. I'm proud of her. I think I envy her a bit.*
>
> *Tonight as we were reading in our little parlor, she looked up and said, "I'd like to be like you."*
>
> *"Whatever can you mean?"*
>
> *"You have everything: intelligence, an amazing education, you're a good teacher, self-possessed, and you're a lovely person."*

Meg stops reading and sits staring again, not blankly this time, living in recollection. A trace of smile around the mouth does not reach the eyes before she gives herself a melancholy shake, returns to the notebook, and repeats greedily: "You have everything: intelligence, an amazing education, you're a good teacher, self-possessed, and you're a lovely person."

"No, Lisa, I'm quite plain. Remember what I said to you the day we met? You're the one who's too pretty to be in grad school."

"Oh, yes." She replied, mocking, effervescent. "Then you went on to explain that pretty women are not all stupid." She got serious again. "I'm sure you must see how men admire you even if you won't give them the time of day. You don't know your power over other people."

I was so grateful I went over and put my arms around her and held her close for a moment. Her shift slipped off her shoulder, and I was more aware than I should have been of the fine thinness of that warm shoulder against my cheek. The whole room echoed my pounding heart, but Lisa didn't hear. Sometimes I think I may end up falling in love with her.

"After that, whenever I happened to touch her"—Meg's eyes glow, living it all again—"her hand in passing a cup, a plate, a book; brushing an arm; even occasionally her cheek—I would tremble so violently I'd have to leave the room not to be discovered. Roommates are always touching one another without noticing, but I noticed. And not only touching. I've never forgotten one of those discreet caresses."

The joy on Meg's face quickly fades into impassivity. Suddenly she looks up like one who has decided something important and pushes her voice across the room toward the inexistent confidant. "No, I wasn't in love with her. Not at first!"

Her voice is a smoky rattle in the dark room. "Not until after she moved in, and not immediately then. But there was anxiety and irritation. Irritation expanded into an exquisite jewel of misery. When we weren't together, I was driven to distraction by images of what she might be doing, tortured by thoughts of her enjoying what I couldn't enjoy, persecuted by fantasies of deceit, of her plotting against me, ignoring me. I wanted all her attention. What went to others was my loss, and she loved everyone indiscriminately. I hated that, and I became testy."

Another pause before adding in summary, "If I had been in love with her, wouldn't I have wanted her good, to make her happy and strong? No. What happened, the only thing that has ever happened, wasn't love. It was something else."

The other wasn't listening to the words in the room but to the music, which tells more. Listening away from the words, beyond the judgments of herself, remembered as objects of reflection. "Why did you write these things down?"

Meg: "To piece it all together. To keep it. To understand, I suppose."

"To preserve the fantasy or to celebrate it?" The question hung in the air without response. "And all the rest, those stacks of notebooks, what were they for?"

"To hold the experience close, enjoy it, preserve it. If you don't write down what happens as it happens, it gets muddled in memory. A way of holding on."

"Of not letting go, the way memory does?"

"Not letting yourself slip away."

"Not breaking the chains and marching forward freely into an open future?"

By now Meg was somewhere else, thumbing through another notebook as she spoke. "Here. This shows how it was. I had forgotten this."

15 February 1936

I don't want to write about this, because I'm jealous and I don't know why. It's humiliating. Lisa, of course, but is it Lisa herself or the way people court her? Is she what I want or is it the love she inspires?

It happened this afternoon during office hours when one of her teachers showed up at the bullpen.

We called the teaching assistants' office the bullpen in ridicule of the sexist term.

He came in to ask Lisa out for a drink. A good-looking man, new on the faculty and married. But he's hot for Lisa, and she likes him. Ordinarily it wouldn't win her any friends among the other female students since they're all half in love with him, but then they're in love with her too. When the two walked out together, my blood was on fire.

A few minutes after they left, I followed. I knew it was crazy. More than crazy. It was hell! But I had to see what was going on. They went to Maggie's, and through the window I saw the two deep in conversation, having a great time. To me wormwood! Lisa was in a coquettish mood, unmistakably attracted to that dishonest oaf. Leaning across the table, her blouse open by one button more than was necessary. I was so distraught I could hardly stand. I turned away and leaned against the wall until I had recovered enough to walk home and go straight to bed, physically ill. When Lisa . . . Lisa—God, how I love writing that name!—when Lisa came in later a little tipsy, she thought I was sick and tried to take care of me.

I didn't handle it well. We had a terrible fight. I screamed and cried and accused her of behaving like a whore, knowing the whole time that she isn't a whore, but that I'm a fury, driving her away. Finally, I yelled at her to shut the door and leave me alone. At that moment I hated her for my pain and hated myself for being jealous. I sank back into bed with the most horrible emptiness, as though my existence had been negated. I couldn't help myself. I wanted to die.

It's several hours later now, and I see I've gotten way out of my depth. I am falling in love with her! I can't let that happen, because she would have to leave. What choice would she have? That tender heart would recoil from the black void of my love. So I have to get over it. I must conquer this thing.

Meg stops reading and relapses into misery, hunched over in her chair, slowly wringing her hands and muttering as the world about her breaks up into spectral images. Eventually the eyes go flat, and the face at rest has the ravaged look of a person forsaken. There would be tears, if the tears—and hence her vision—had not dried up years ago and the parched heart become a desert. So whence this tsunami of passion?

The head gradually rises, and she stares vacuously at the floor in front of her as if having forgotten the notebook in her lap. One hand contracts like a claw over the page just read so that it pulls slowly away from the binding and ends as a ball in a clenched fist. Then, collecting herself, consciousness returns to the face, alive again to the sense of not being alone. Without seeming to notice, she drops the crumpled paper on the floor at her feet.

After a long stare across the empty room, she confesses, "You see, I knew. But I still don't know whether it was love or envy. Or love struggling against envy."

"Or cruel, idolatrous love?"

She scans the room as though looking for a source for that question, then shrugs and continues. "In the few months before that night, I was as close to paradise as I would ever get, happy to live in the green light of her eyes, happy to live on the crumbs and dream the rest. I wasn't fully aware at the time, of course. Vision needs distance and the courage to understand. I couldn't, or wouldn't, know until it was over. But I have known through forty rotten years.

"In that miserable night and others that would follow, I thought I would die of hopelessness and loss. Only later did I see that I was suffering an excruciating joy and squandering it. At the time I just held on by tooth and claw."

"That picture on the mantel, is it part of the holding on?"

Meg gets up, goes over to the hearth, and stands in front of the lone photograph. She picks it up and stares at it. "From grad school. Lisa took it on our first vacation together. If only I could be the girl in that picture again. Look at her! The heart is already afflicted, but she doesn't know it. The world lies before her still. Not yet sick with hatred for the whole race of mortals. She hasn't yet discovered that she's living a transitive, paranoid existence, desiring what others desire only because they desire it. Look at the ambition in those eyes. My God, a single moment of honesty would destroy her. She wants her share and means to have it. Especially to be thought well of. Look at the care she takes for the admiration even of a camera!"

"Then it was envy and not love?"

"Lisa was such a loving person! I continued to enjoy her affection for a time, but it was a daily rebuke. I think I thought it was love, but it wasn't. It wasn't Lisa's welfare I wanted when I helped her. I was living on her like a parasite. From the day she disappeared—oh yes, she just vanished, but I'm coming to that—ever since Lisa disappeared, I have envied that girl in the photograph who still had a chance of getting it right but could not or would not."

"'Does 'can't' mean 'won't?'"

She snorts, "Of course, idiot!"

Meg drops off again into silence and, preoccupied, wanders back to her chair and takes a drink from the glass. Then picks up another notebook, pages wearily through it, and resumes reading.

8 November 1937

Lisa makes great strides in her program. She didn't teach during the summer. Took a full load of courses and worked very hard. At least when she works, she doesn't have time for a lover, which is what I fear most. Sometimes I feel rivalry with her. Or is it that her desperate need of me is fading? At least there has been no recurrence of the jealous scenes. But I watch her, and she knows I watch. She pretends not to mind, but she does. I'm beginning to make her life miserable. She hasn't had time to think of a new place to live, and so, if I'm careful, I may have her for another year. I don't know why she stays on in the apartment, but if she left, I'd be devastated. Will be, I should say, because it's inevitable if I don't get myself under control.

*Tonight, she told me about her research on that Claus
Neumann person she's been secretive about for weeks. She's taking
her first research course and spending so much time in the library
that I've lost track of her work. It's an idea about a schizophrenic
German poet. When she first mentioned him, I read the poems
and didn't like them at all, but she's excited about them.*

*It appears that the Neumann manuscripts, which are in Special
Collections at the library, were all typed and later revised by hand.
She says that the typed copies are pedestrian and uninteresting,
almost prose arranged like poetry on the page, but the music is in the
revisions. They're inspired. Her discovery—theory is more like it—
is that Frau Neumann did the revisions and then the poems were
published under the name of Claus alone. If she can prove that, it'll
be a big thing. Lisa has found a sample of the wife's handwriting
that nobody else has noticed. It could launch her career, since there's
something of a Neumann critical industry just now.*

*Lisa had the good sense to have a handwriting specialist
compare the sample with the revisions of the manuscripts and with
Claus' own hand. That's detective work, not very intellectual, but
then Lisa's not really an intellectual, is she? She wants to show that
Herr Neumann had the mind and Frau Neumann had the lyre.
That might be more substantial, but I doubt it, since it's more
about the author than the poems. Anyway, she has only one week
left before her seminar presentation, so we'll see what happens.
Her professor is a well-known expert on the subject, so if she can
convince him, she'll have the research paper and a dissertation
topic in one package—and the beginning of a scholarly career!
Still, it's not a very weighty idea, is it? It'll be a shallow success.*

"A bloody lightweight!" Meg breaks off, unaccountably angry as the
malice of a lifetime surges into her face from the internal upheaval. The
mouth sharpens into a brutal line and emits a growl: "That's what she
was, a lightweight. Oh, it was clever of her to unearth that letter and
make the connections, but that sort of thing is only good for a historical

footnote. She didn't have the intellectual balls to do anything with it, and yet you would hardly believe how she was celebrated. For weeks no one could talk of anything else. It was enough to make you vomit."

Between her finger and thumb Meg unconsciously holds the corner of the page she has just read. Then with an angry gesture and shudder of revulsion rips the sheet from the book and drops it on the floor with the other.

At the gesture of violence against herself, Nuntius, still leaning against the bookshelves, moves behind her chair and lays an imperceptible hand on her shoulder. She jerks at her sweatshirt as though it's at fault for the kinks in her life then, remembering the book on her lap, turns several more pages as he watches from above.

"Here." She jabs the page with a stubby finger in refutation of something unsaid. "See! See!" she barks as though to silence an opposition that opposes still in its silence.

24 November 1937

The jury is in. Lisa has convinced Professor Müller. He's so enthusiastic that he has invited her to give a version of her paper in his session at the Modern Language Association in New York next month. It appears that someone has canceled, and he's putting her in the slot. He says that she can expand the project into a dissertation. Says that if she does a good job with the supporting research, he'll get her a book contract with his publisher. So, she's all set, isn't she? And I'm in hell! Damn the little bitch. After all I've done for her!

We had a terrible fight last night. It was her night to cook and she forgot, after I've done all the cooking for weeks and the cleaning, too, while she was busy with that damned paper.

"I can't go on like this," I said, trying to keep the tremors out of my voice. She asked what I was so upset about. So I told her.

"I'm sorry Meg. I see that I've been very inconsiderate. I'll make it up to you. You've been very good to me, and I appreciate it." Then she started crying.

> *I can't bear it when she cries. Turns me to vinegar Jell-O. I
> wanted to rush over and hold her in my arms like a baby. But
> I hardened myself. "I don't want you to make it up! And I don't
> want your gratitude!" I yelled. "I just want you out!"*
>
> *"Out? You mean . . . you want me to move?" She could
> hardly speak for sobbing.*
>
> *I gritted my teeth and answered, "When you come back
> from your celebrity performance at the MLA, you can find
> other digs. I've had it!" And I left her slobbering on the floor.*

Meg remains composed, though while she was reading, the other
had returned to the center of the room and settled unseen into a chair
opposite, like a gentleman guest in conversation with a friend. This
time not leaning, as one might imagine, against the furniture or for
hours together against a wall, and not sitting wherever, on a table or
a fence or the corner of a tomb like a gargoyle, to observe whatever
there is to observe.

Still possessed by the momentum of the narrative, Meg selects
another notebook and reads without commentary.

11 February 1938

> *I rarely see Lisa now. What a fool I was to let such a simpleton
> get to me. Today I was in the library all day doing research for a
> paper. At lunch I went over to the union for a sandwich and saw
> her across the room with Müller and several other students from
> his seminar. It so upset me that I left my sandwich half-eaten and
> took a walk to calm down. Back in my carrel at the library, it
> occurred to me to look up the Neumann manuscripts. They don't
> look like much. A homemade binding to preserve the poems and
> a kind of pocket in the back cover. Concealed inside were two
> pieces of old paper. Just a banal letter that looked and read like
> trash. No reason why anyone would have given it a second thought
> except for being written in the same hand as the marginalia of the
> poems! Like most discoveries, it's obvious once someone has had the*

*imagination to find it, and Lisa was just dumb enough to notice
and just imaginative enough to make the connection. A more
incisive mind would have dismissed it as worthless.*

*As I sat with the letter in my hand, I realized that it hadn't
been catalogued separately so there was no record of it. On an
impulse, with no particular idea in mind—I swear to that!—I
slipped the letter into my pocket and left. Now as I think about
it, I'm startled at what I've done. It's like having blood on my
hands. What is it Lady Macbeth says after she's stabbed the king
in his bed? "Will all great Neptune's flood wash this blood clean
from my hand?" So what will I do now? Take it back? Destroy
it? Or put it away and do nothing?*

As she reads, Meg's hand trembles so violently and the book
shakes so she can hardly see the words. Her face red with shame or
embarrassment or guilt, she slaps the book hard against the arm of
the chair and adds, "That's the moment my life stopped. From then
on, I lived under a curse."

She looks up as though steadily at a person in the chair opposite.
"Envy and love. It was always warfare of envy *and* love with that girl."
She points toward her own photograph on the mantel, "*Her* envy
destroyed her love." Then, spirits sagging again, she drops her head to
her chest and murmurs, "And here I sit a smoky wreck with a cracked
soul." Her lip curls as though she has drunk wormwood.

The calm, disinterested voice remarks: "But a soul still."

"With only enough life left to suffer."

"And desire to remember: Desire, the agent of possibility."

Meg looks up startled and explodes in a burst of derisive laughter that
quickly subsides and is forgotten. She scans a few pages more and stops.

1 March 1938

*There has been a great scandal. It's Lisa's thesis. It seems
Professor Müller checked the Neumann manuscript and didn't
find the letter that Lisa has been displaying copies of all over the*

Western world. Instead of trying by intelligent means to account for the problem, he has apparently decided to play the victim of a hoax that has compromised his scholarly reputation. What a vain man! What will all his MLA buddies think when he can't produce the letter? Who would have thought that Müller, the Ass, would jump to such an absurd conclusion? If he had done his job, he would have looked at the original months ago.

The upshot is that Lisa has quit the program and disappeared. Nobody knows where, just vanished. So it's too late to do anything about the manuscript, though of course I'll return it as I always intended to. Just haven't gotten around to it, because I've been so busy.

In a way it's all my fault, though who would have thought the little fool would run away? Didn't even drop her courses and take a leave of absence. Left a note for the secretary saying her German 2 sections would have to be assigned to someone else. In the middle of the term, no less! Well, serves her right if she's going to be that irresponsible. I didn't mean her any harm even after all the pain she gave me. I only intended to give her a scare. That asshole Müller is as responsible as I am.

Meg's face is a grinning, demonic mask as she stares down every hostile object in the room. "The last time I saw Lisa she was sitting alone at the bar at Maggie's. It was one early morning, and she was drinking what looked from a distance like whiskey. She never drank more than a little wine. I saw her first through the window on my way to class.

"That day I cut my class. The only time I ever did that. Just went in and sat in a dark corner and watched. I'm sure she had not been to bed. Her face was puffy, her eyes red, her hair disheveled, but I sat there watching without remorse, unfeeling, drinking in the effects of the evil I had perpetrated.

"That's the image that has never faded. Forty years and only that face, the only face. Forty years and one name, one thought, one betrayal. And why? Because I had to have it all."

The decades of accumulated revenge against herself gather visibly in Meg's face as she snatches the page she has just read from the book, crumples it, throws it to the floor and stomps it with her foot three times. "There! How do you like that?"

"What will you do now?" The voice, calm as though all that has been said doesn't have to matter.

"Do? What is there to do?" she snarls. "I'll keep on *doing* what I have always been *doing*—nothing!" But the question momentarily appeases her and makes her thoughtful. "I destroyed my life long ago when I entered the Lisa-darkness. Now there's nothing but to sit here smoking and drinking, waiting to die."

Nuntius murmurs something under his breath, just for the two of them as though the books mustn't hear, and her face contorts into a bestial scowl that makes it unrecognizable. He utters the word a second time.

"Forgiveness!" she shouts through a grimace of pain. "Balderdash! There is no forgiveness. What's done can't be undone." She stares startled, then looks all around as though there might be a ghost in the room after all. "I must be going soft in the head. I'm hearing voices babbling garbage about religion."

She shakes her head fiercely and makes the room echo with a fiendish laugh. "Why did I think that? I don't even know what that means." A raspy laugh like a death rattle. "It's absurd."

"Where is Lisa now?"

"I have no idea. At the devil I hope."

Then through the wide, brutal slit of mouth she hisses, "That wasn't the last word. Wait!" She goes back to the piles of notebooks on the floor by the closet and hunts for a while, looking into one after the other for dates. She finally settles on one, finds an old envelope in it and takes out a Christmas card that, remembering or forgetting, she has kept for years. "Here! Listen!"

10 December 1958

Dear Margaret,
    It has taken me twenty years to write this. I know what

*happened to the Neumann letter. I saw you watching me
that last morning at Maggie's, and I understood. It has taken
me this long to forgive you. I went back home after that and
married a man I'd grown up with. From the middle of a
successful career as a corporate director of personnel, I can, at
last, say from the heart that I hope the years have been as good
to you. You were once very kind to me, and for that I remain
grateful. Merry Christmas, Margaret.*

Lisa Sutherland, née Walters.

"She forgives me! How could anyone forgive all that damage? No one has that power."

Meg gets up and goes to the mantel again and stares at the youthful photograph. "This picture . . . did I mention that she took it? I've been looking at it for decades, thinking if that girl had only known how lucky she was. I have spent years wishing to be her. But doing what she did, she stole my life from me."

She seizes the frame and smashes it against the hearth then goes back to her chair, collects the notebooks on her lap, and coldly, methodically tears them page by page until nothing is left but the covers in her lap and wads of paper at her feet.

"There," she points to the crumpled paper, "that's what life comes to!"

"You think nothing can be done about the past?"

Cynically, mockingly, she asks someone, not herself, "What? What can be done?"

"Change the meaning. Use all that energy to reinvent life."

Meg stares straight ahead, attentive, as though a new idea has occurred to her. "Starting where?"

"Find Lisa. Find her and say you're sorry."

Meg stares at the absurdity. "She'd spit in my face."

"It doesn't matter what she does. What you can do is find her and tell her you're sorry, as you clearly are. That's where you begin afresh . . . with the ellipsis at the end of an unfinished sentence."

Meg gets up, shakes herself as one might shake off a chill. She walks again to the window and pulls back a faded, dusty curtain. The thunderstorm has washed the heat away and left the garden sparkling in lamplight. She opens a window and hears a frog croaking below from the edge of some swampy puddle.

The Messenger, grateful perhaps for having been given a message by the life in front of him, continues. "Or you can sit here devouring yourself from the inside like a lobster in a tank."

She puts both hands to her temples and shakes her head again. "I'm definitely going mad! It always was going to drive me mad." Looking out again, she speaks through clenched teeth, "These are the cloisters of hell."

The disembodied voice goes on, unrelenting, "For the dead there is no escape. To let things pass is to live. For one who's willing to learn, it's the potential not-to continue repeating the past by covering it over."

As though her protests don't matter, he repeats, "Let go!"

Meg, looking at no one, but at the place from which the voice emanates, seems to stagger. Suddenly her eyes dilate into great circles filled with something like terror. She strikes her forehead hard with both fists.

"My God!" she cries. "My God! I understand that! You son-of-a-bitch demon from hell! You're trying to take my Lisa away from me and I will not have it. I will not let you!" She screams hysterically to quash the last decibel of proffered hope. "No! No! No! No! I will not!"

Meg sinks to the floor in a flood of tears that have been dry for decades. Sometime later she pulls up the shirt and wipes her face. In the course of a few hours, the face has aged. Not new lines but old lines still more deeply engraved, misery incarnated in chiseled marks of woe.

She stalks angrily to the kitchen and pours more whiskey. Returning to the living room haggard, distracted, she sets the drink down, puts her hands over her ears, and again cries out violently, "No! No! No! No!"

Then, bending down to gather the chaos of pages at her chair, with trembling hands she takes them to the fireplace, opens the glass doors, and turns on the gas. The past goes into the fire a few sheets at a time until it's consumed. The notebooks by the chair first, then the stacks at the front closet, all ritually consigned to the flames of revenge. Nothing purgative here. No new beginning. Nor does she stop with the diaries. Other boxes are pulled from the shelf—class notes from years in the lecture hall, research notes from toil in a dozen libraries—the record and residue of life. Coldly, systematically. Like a dead soul, she feeds the inferno until the past has become ash.

The Priest
Pride

"Things that are not, bring to nought those that are."
I Corinthians 1:29

"Come have a glass of wine, Father."

The little white-haired Irishman looked slightly amused as he ambled around to the opposite side of the cloister and sat down.

The invitation was startling, coming from Joseph Barthes. They had only met twice, and both times the latter had felt little more than scorn for his brother priest. This drizzly afternoon Joseph was sitting in the cloister, waiting by design as Mark Maloney emerged from his pastoral call on Mr. Bourdieu. Why Joseph might have wanted to cross paths again is a mystery with no immediate solution. That the two men, who should have had much in common, differed radically made the invitation the more incongruous.

When Mary orchestrated their first meeting, Joseph appeared as a man of dignity and authority: neatly groomed and tastefully dressed, early grey hair parted almost in the middle, face charged with the alertness of an incisive mind. His whole body radiated intellectual energy. Though he said little on that occasion, the eloquent voice, when it spoke, did so in rounded sentences, head leaning this way and that, hands in motion gesturing for emphasis, fingers rubbing restively meanwhile against the thumbs. The piercing eyes shone outward like a beam into the world, accustomed to missing nothing, yet opposing what they gazed upon—as though in fixing on one thing, he let another pass.

That was his usual bearing. But not today. Today he had lost his center. The concentration of mind had failed. The sharp eyes appeared remote and preoccupied behind the scholarly glasses. His authority was weakened by an increase of nervous fidgeting in the hands and by a tendency to rearrange his body, as though, standing or sitting, he couldn't settle comfortably into the space provided.

Everything about the simple priest annoyed the distinguished man of science: the square body and craggy face of a farmer, the black shirt and pants smudged with cigarette ash, the heavy walking shoes with thick rubber soles worn at the heels. Even the beatific smile and the quietude of a contented mind annoyed him for what he took to be blindness to the hazards of the world. Yet Joseph had planned this encounter and even been inspired—secretly, no doubt—by some mischievous spirit of irony to provide a bottle of wine and a baguette!

Observing him thus distraught and derelict, Fr. Mark lit a cigarette and sat for a time smoking quietly. Maloney was no visionary, but these ambiguous signs in his companion were easy to read. Years in the confessional had developed sensitivities that might seem like unique powers to the uninitiated. But he had only enlarged a gift accessible to anyone, but which, not being cultivated, remains nascent. Just by breathing the same air and loving enough to listen without searching and probing, he recognized the temper of other minds and felt their dispositions.

At their first meeting, he had picked up Joseph's tone as he might have followed a familiar melody or the flow of a mountain stream, though in those few minutes sitting together in the garden, Joseph had made little effort to converse beyond some enthusiastic remarks on the geology of Louisiana and the river. In their subsequent conversation, Mark had been compelled to fill the vacuum by describing The Valmont as it had been in the days when he was confessor to the nuns.

Why Joseph should have been annoyed by comments that were neither banal nor self-serving is hard to say, but while the one contrasted the effects of the old garden with the modern spirit of the "Quad," the other sat attentive but aloof. Yet something essential must have passed in their first encounter, some authority perhaps that the proud Jesuit hadn't been able to dismiss as "mysticism." In any event, here Joseph was, having reached the limit of his capacity to deal with his own malaise, resorting to the humble parish priest and feeling contempt for himself for doing so. As he poured the wine and brought himself sufficiently under control to make conversation, Mark sat serenely waiting.

"When we met before," Fr. Joe casually began, "you spoke of the ancient mood of the monastery. Since then, I have occasionally compared the Spanish Virgin in the cloister with the statue of the Roman goddess of agriculture that Mary picked up in the Quarter and planted among the flowers."

As he paused, Fr. Mark replied. "The secular sensibility misses the difference, doesn't it?" These words were accompanied by a chuckle more compassionate than critical, for this was not at all what he had been invited to hear.

With a touch of awkwardness and condescension, Joseph continued. "You probably see The Valmont as haunted by the Mother of the nuns' dying God, decorated by the pagan Ceres, and consecrated to the modern god Real Estate."

As soon as it was out of his mouth, he hated himself for stooping to such observations. His private distress, the cause of his having sought out this superstitious old Dominican, made him incapable of sitting still or maintaining the facade of sociability where so much was at stake.

Maloney responded in a Celtic lilt that lent an oracular nuance to words at once detached and immersed in the nearness of things. "What the new pagans miss in the garden is the emptiness of the divine. Unaware of the spirits that possess them, they want all spaces filled with what's 'real.' Remember Augustine? 'The new is hidden in the old; the old is revealed in the new.' The garden is a voice of promise for the multitudes of the unborn."

Joseph groaned scornfully and writhed in his chair as Mark sipped the wine and nibbled at the bread. "No need to fill the world with imaginary beings. Simple emotions suffice." The remark came with willed politeness in a voice that oozed contempt.

"We're not speaking of occult powers, you know. When the world is captivated by consumer greed and love-starved sex, those are realities. Surely we need names to set these obsessions at a distance and make them communicable to ourselves and to others."

"Are you imagining diabolical possession or the spirits of the nuns still haunting the garden?"

Mark smiled benignly. "Something as ordinary as the mood of a room or the spirit of a friendship. If we weren't responsive to spirits, we'd be neuter and *care* for nothing." Before continuing, he snuffed out his cigarette and, not to litter the garden, deposited the butt in his match box.

"The ancients recognized nonobjective phenomena and gave them names. Remember Siddhartha, before becoming the Buddha, defeating the temptations of Mara's vicious spirits? Or the Holy Spirit as the vehicle of love for the whole of things set against the spirits of division and negation? Such commonplace non-things still let themselves be seen by the mind's eye when we care enough to look. Probably *felt* whether we look or not."

Joseph wasn't looking or listening. He was covering the words over by wondering instead how in mid-twentieth century a reasonably intelligent man could be such a credulous simpleton. One priest, loving but a part, had contempt for the other, who, loving all, recognized the pain of the first with charitable detachment.

It was inevitable that these two should seem half-lunatic to each other. The sane man of science who denied what couldn't be defined, counted, and managed would feel contempt for the madman who could love a mystery-filled and evil-stained world. But to understand why in his darkest moment Joseph should have sought out the very one whose "medieval irrationality" he disdained—*had* sought him out for the very reason he disdained him—for all that we must go back a bit.

—

One September evening during his first month at The Valmont, Joseph sat at the small desk that faced the French doors of his sister's living room. As a crimson and gold evening gave way to deepening shadows over the garden, he got up for a glass of wine and, on the way to the kitchen, passed a mirror on the wall where his own image startled him. He backed up and looked for himself in the image, not finding it.

What he *did* find was the face of a stranger lit from behind by the dying light. The usually neat hair was greasy and unkempt as from nervous fingers passing through it. The unshaven face had become rough, impatient, and suspicious. Intelligent still, but intelligent with cleverness rather than understanding, curious without care for patient thinking.

The agitated face bore no resemblance to his old ideal of the priest as a soul at rest. The stranger in the glass was a cold, self-absorbed man, convinced on the inside that he was exceptional but exposed by the mirror as a poseur who concealed the truth from himself. He reached out to touch the image, but it seemed to splinter as a reflection in water breaks at the touch of a finger.

Seated again before the window, he ate his biscuits and drank his wine, musing on that image of an erect spirit battling against itself, the husk of a wasted heart trying to comprehend its secret affliction. Was it possible that as learning deepened, the spirit could become a wilderness? He had no morbid religious conscience tormented by sin, no neurotic constitution troubled by the baying of the hounds of hell. Yet briefly he wondered if the soul could atrophy from neglect and finally vanish altogether.

It was not so much that he had lost the Christian fable of life as a pilgrimage. Only that he had let it wither, a treasure still—if it ever was a treasure—but mislaid long ago like a compass no longer consulted in navigating life because its precision can be doubted. He got up from the desk and paced the room. Up and down, far into the night, excavating layer after layer of a forgotten past, cutting with analytic skill into the quick of a being unvisited till now, collecting the facts, ignoring the connections. The doubting rationalist who carries no umbrella until he sees the rain.

Among the few instances of moral failure that rose before him to humiliate his pride, a recent one stood out above the rest. He had overheard his neighbor George Basson on the next balcony talking about the futility of prosecuting crime in the city. The tone of an angry man on, or beyond, the verge of despair. Then one afternoon he and Basson had crossed paths in the Quad. They exchanged a casual greeting and passed on until he was startled by a call from behind:

"Do you think I might have a word with you sometime?"

The question presumed a degree of familiarity for which there was no precedent, but Joseph turned back.

The voice was sardonic. "I'm Jewish, not Catholic. Not religious at all, but maybe I need a priest . . . or an analyst." Then with a dry chuckle, "With a priest and a stranger I'm safer from the press."

As the corners of Basson's mouth turned up in a spiritless grin, Joseph recognized the signs of misery. Possessed by his own pain, he had no time just then for the distress of another, but dutifully he consented, without mentioning a time, and they walked on. From that moment he avoided the Quad at the hour when they might meet, so that now, considering Basson's death, he accused himself of having neglected a priestly duty, with unforeseen consequences. More than neglect, he had put his own interests and state of mind ahead of service to another.

It is said truly that the inexistent past is never simply past, and, just so, the existent present is never simply present. Even as mind strains forward into the dark, it remembers foundations that lie all around in artifacts that tell other stories. That's why, if we would understand the malaise of Joseph Barthes, we must go still farther back.

He had descended from simple uneducated people who lived on the edge of necessity. His father was a hard-drinking steel worker in Pennsylvania and not a good husband or father. His mother had been a cook in a public-school lunchroom but, being devoutly Catholic, she sent his sister to the nuns for school and him first to the Christian Brothers for primary and later to the Jesuits for high school. Instead of his father's brawn and unreflective bonhomie, he had inherited his mother's fine features and reserved sensibility.

The tall, perceptive boy, predisposed by social inferiority, used his quick intelligence to distinguish himself scholastically. He read voraciously and became a model of academic discipline and devout obedience. Because languages, literature, and history came more easily than mathematics and science, he forced himself to excel in the sciences. When the stresses of molting adolescence took the shape of piety and the only avenue in sight for making his mark in the world was the religious life, he settled on the Society of Jesus. With attention fixed on the distant goal of becoming a Jesuit, he remained irreproachable in character, a hard worker, and exemplary in the public obligations of piety. In due course he was admitted to the order as a novice, and during the ensuing years of study, was much admired for his achievements in philosophy and theology.

However, there being no one near him with the penetration of a Mark Maloney, there was no one to guide his reflections. The result was that he neglected the difference between learning as mastery and learning as gratitude. Likewise insensitive to how intellectual growth might differ from moral growth, he pressed ahead, raising himself from obscurity by austere discipline like a sculptor carving an ideal from his own flesh and bone. Nimbly avoiding self-examination and interpreting the evasion as humility, he selected which motives to admit and which to ignore, then persuaded himself that ambition was vocation. Not that he was acting with an intention to deceive others. If there was falsehood, it was lived falsehood, conscientious and determined.

In due course he took orders and faithfully executed his priestly obligations with a scrupulousness that sought, rather than neglected, duty. In some secret corner of his soul, he may have known that it was policy without reflection, but he compensated by imposing hardships on himself. He fasted and observed voluntary silences, accepted eagerly the humblest duties of charity, all to reassure himself of his virtue. Occasionally the idea flashed across his mind that he did not believe or, if he did, believed with reservations, but that impression was quelled by the notion that one who acts as if he believes will end up believing.

In fact the reverse happened. Far from resolving the matter, his future studies confirmed a gradual drift into unbelief. For several years he taught natural science in a Jesuit high school where his province also had a college. When the order needed to replace an aging priest whose field on the college faculty was geology, the provincial sent Joseph back to graduate school to prepare for the appointment.

Thus began a new phase of life. Recognizing no division in himself and acknowledging no want of devotion, he plunged into a new study that exposed fissures in his intellectual rather than his moral life.

What captivated him was a fashionable evolutionary view of theology that squared with scientific progress. As a result, and without rigorous inquiry into the matter, he came to regard the doctrines and practices of the traditional Church as vaguely primitive and needing to be updated. It was this unexamined disposition that opened the first cracks in his defenses. Taken together they provided an intimation of what is generally known as the Crisis of Reason, except that, for him, in place of a choice of diverging roads, there was only drift.

He had always loved the myths and tales handed down by tradition and appreciated their power to give imaginative shape to collective experience. But love wasn't truth, and so, without examining the question closely, he took it for granted that these noble stories were mere fables: *his* in an aesthetic sense but inconsistent and fanciful, hence untrustworthy. The endless traditions of interpretation—of the Bible, Midrash, Dante, or the Battle at Waterloo—what did they show if not the impossibility of verification? Poetry, not truth. However subtle and useful as parables for life, fiction produced doubt rather than certainty and made no personal claim on him. And so he found himself home at last in the clarity and precision of science.

✗ Different orders of truth, joy excluded? Becoming incomprehensible to himself by ignoring his own fable?

Joseph's passion for what was present, measurable, and "real" did not set him in open opposition to the Jesuit order or to the teachings of the Church. Rather, piety became sentiment and was nearly forgotten even as he preserved the order of his life. By a process of fragmentation sometimes called "compartmentalizing," he kept his intellectual projects in one room of his mind, his obligations as priest in another, and congratulated himself on his skill in negotiating both.

So it went for years: esteemed by students and faculty at the college, increasingly distinguished in research, respected as an authority in his field, and regarded by his brothers as a model of the devout life. In short, success. Except for a quietly growing sense of weariness and aridity, as though down the corridors of the years he had gradually lost touch with something essential.

It may be an odd thing to say of a priest but, knowing so little about himself, he habitually ignored symptoms that might have been warnings. In confession he acknowledged petty lapses and used that sincerity to disguise a pride that passed unobserved into self-deception. By holding just out of mind the conviction of his own exemplary worthiness, he acquired the vanity that first consoled and later defeated him. Slowly he lost touch and slipped into darkness, though not the darkness of death—unless it was a different death. By using research as a means of not-searching his own predispositions, he had become a problem to himself until even research began to suffer. Then, on pragmatic grounds, he determined to hunt down the "mistake" in his life and bring it to light.

Thus his inquiry began with diminished resources. A search for intellectual clarity and "truth" in place of fables of history, character, and destiny—the very uncertainties that haunted him and made him human. Unaware that for one who dwells willy-nilly in possibility, the truth about everything from the big bang (or not) to cosmic expansion (or collapse) might leave him asking "So what?" What one of his discredited fictions calls *vanitas*.

By just such stealth of deception, accepting his own consciousness as the guarantor of truth, he tried to measure his malaise by lining up the achievements of his life and comparing them with the recent image in the dining room mirror of a man who had lost his soul. Against this vision, he conjured as a point of reference a fantasy of himself as a young novitiate. The point was, by comparing the two and without serious risk to his pride, to discover any mistakes he might have made along the way. So, like the return of the repressed, the imaginary novice became an intimate spirit who, from that moment, waylaid him, tracked him down as though daring him at every turn to know himself.

This was his condition when he sought permission of his superior to spend his sabbatical in New Orleans, ostensibly for assembling his research into a book.

—

Before Fr. Mark turned up on that chilly and rainy afternoon in the cloister, Joseph had lingered, haggard and unshaven, waiting. The wine and baguette sat on the small iron table, while a few feet away rain pattered gently on the walks, making the late-fall flowers quiver and the hedges glisten.

After the first awkward gestures of conversation had renewed his contempt for the older priest, he changed the subject by remarking gloomily, "One day this rain is going to start and not stop."

Instead of meeting the other priest's eyes, he shifted his gaze from one nearby object to another, all equally uninteresting. "New Orleans is doomed to sink into the primal muck or return to the sea like Atlantis."

His voice surged with an energy out of tune with the setting and out of proportion to the mood in the air. A malicious laugh implied that it served them right for building here, though the laugh was not quite his. "When it happens, there'll be no Noah, I can tell you."

"Can you? Won't there? I wonder." Mark winked with amusement, sitting at his ease, legs stretched out before him, hands locked behind his head. He looked at Joseph curiously and smiled, not repeating his earlier remark that human building was always precarious and possibilities unforeseeable. No point, since Joseph's words didn't say what he meant. They, those words, weren't about the threat to the city, universally recognized and universally disregarded. And his eyes, usually alive with consciousness, remained opaque as if trying—and finding—no place to hide.

For his part, Mark preferred to enjoy a quiet mind and the peaceful afternoon. Yet whenever empty words poured from a troubled soul, they imposed an obligation and inspired another idea that he was careful not to express: "The pride of life blocks vision and leaves him baffled."

The parish priest, Fr. Maloney, accustomed to searching for the center of gravity in words, to listening to the timbre of a voice and the rhythm of words, to watching the movement of eyes and the muscles of a face, recognized the effort it cost the man of science to set his pride aside and speak openly to one so much his inferior. Such a man would come to resent being in this position, and the informal confession—for it was sure to be that—would be unpleasant for them both.

With nothing to do but wait—enjoy the garden and the rain and wait—Mark rearranged himself on his chair, legs apart, feet flat on the flagstones, hands palm down on his thighs. In another man the posture might have looked aggressive, but in him it was composure as he took a crust of bread and another sip of wine.

Then, sudden as a thunderbolt: "I no longer believe!"

The words exploded as Joseph sprang from his chair and crossed to the edge of the cloister, where the rain continued to patter gently on the shrubs. He leaned his head and shoulder sideways against one of the arches with his back to the table. It was a gesture of disconnection from this man, who had gained a mortifying but irresistible power over him. As he turned around and resumed his chair, he imagined that his outburst had shocked the older priest and was glad.

But he was not shocked. He appeared only half to hear as a benign smile took Joseph in whole. He had heard it all before, many times. What he heard was less the repetition than a familiar impulse behind the words. He leaned his head back in a big, comfortable yawn then lit another cigarette. When eventually he responded, the Irish brogue added to his casualness. "Ah, not believing with your mind perhaps. We all have times like that. Belief in that sense is a red herring, don't you think? Unbelief is not about the mind; it's about the spirit."

Joseph aggressively, "I only know bodies and minds. What do you mean, 'the spirit?'" This came with flaring nostrils and a dragon snort.

He did not have to listen to this ignorant old man, superstitious as a loon, cuddling up to his folksy God. He moved as though to walk away from the encounter he had so foolishly arranged.

Mark took no notice. Just smoked quietly, watching the rain drip from the deck above their cozy nook. Eventually the lilting voice said, "You needn't believe in spirits either. Neither do I . . . probably. Not if we mean voodoo and magic. Spooks hovering in empty space. Lurking behind walls. Still, we're immersed in relations and dispositions. Are those unreal too? Don't they need names?"

He had a habit of making two or three short remarks then breaking off while they sank in. Again, he waited.

Joseph sat down once more then jumped up again and crossed the few feet to the cloister arch, where again he stood with his back turned as though he had lost interest.

Fr. Mark knew better. A man who takes the trouble to arrange such a meeting only pretends to himself that he isn't listening. Speaking to Joseph's back, "I leave it to you to decide what's real and what's not. I can never quite tell. But I need the word 'spirit' when I feel a spring of sorrow over a dying parishioner or joy in children's voices at play. Such things have an irresistible influence on how I think and act."

The remarks were oddly impersonal as, not facing each other, the two looked outward into the rain-soaked garden, separated "in spirit." Another benign, almost idle remark invited Joseph to treat himself more kindly: "When I get up on the wrong side of the bed and face the world through a veil of anxiety and resentment, I live less agreeably—for myself and for others—than when I bless the day."

Mark stopped again as if considering the matter for the first time. "Yes, I think I need the word spirit. Else I wouldn't be able to make an 'it' of my anguish or my lust or my pride—mark it by a name so I can get up and walk away from it. Just as I need to name the abundance of being—not a thing, mind you!—if I'm to love it faithfully and keep myself in good working order."

Out of all proportion to the occasion, Joseph's passion surged. "Once you imagine that these feelings are independent beings, you're just a step away from finding spooks behind the door. Or an imaginary Lucifer gaining possession of people and making them do what they otherwise wouldn't. 'The devil made me do it.' That superstition just gets us off the hook. It's madness," said the rational man who was slowly going mad.

"I'm not saying they're 'independent beings.' It's much simpler than that. I just welcome whatever moods and insights come to me and help me cope. It helps me to have names for the beneficial states of mind and to give the slip to the bleaker ones. Like the keys of E-sharp major and C-minor."

"Madness!"

Again the response was light, as though the subject were not of great importance. "Madness? Perhaps. I'm not sure of that difference either." He paused and poured himself a little more wine.

"This is what Father Jean-Paul Bienvenue used to say. He was an old Dominican I knew when I was young. He had been trained as a philosopher but, by the time I knew him, all that had mellowed into a quiet, homespun wisdom. He used to say that our sunlit consciousness is surrounded by a dark field of blind impulses. They push and pull us every which way. Not just spooks behind the door but old stories, a turn of phrase, the lilt of a friendly voice. They, this rich heritage, shape our desires, and the possibilities for making good use of ourselves. We can cooperate or resist, but there they are."

"You're only describing moods. The unconscious."

"Call them what you want. So long as the names you give don't hide the real effects."

The older priest let silence have its way for another few moments before adding, "In a simpler, more human world, there were angels to bless and demons to pounce in the dark. Now we use a different fable and imagine that these airborne influenzas all start with us. Even—God help us!—the true, the good, and the beautiful."

Joseph, eager to debunk this priest and the historical religion of his—their—Church, snarled.

"I suppose you imagine these fixations can be exorcised by priests! You must think we've learned nothing in all these centuries! Do you even believe in progress?" Not a real question. He knew very well that progress in one region is blindness in another, but he was talking for victory now, not truth: But victory over whom and to what end? That remained to be seen.

Fr. Mark sat a long time, smoking, weighing a mood that concealed unasked questions. When he spoke again, it was not to the doubting priest who hated spirits but obliquely to doubt itself. "Unbelief comes laden with affects. We love explanation and hate the inexplicable. Yet there would be no explanation if we weren't stricken by wonder and the desire to explore the unknown. And what else is love?"

Even in the dim light, his face had the radiance of a man at peace as he added an afterthought: "Unless we love *all*, we love the parts poorly."

The unbeliever, scandalized by superstition yet possessed by demons of his own that, being "unreal," went unnamed, pulled his body upright, bit his tongue to control his anger, and scoffed. "So knowledge is the enemy!" Then resumed his chair at the table, looking away still.

Fr. Mark rejoined, "The enemy is hate. If I hate ignorance or folly or superstition, isn't it because I fear the bit of inconvenient truth that may be hiding in them? The alternative is to let myself respond to the infinite 'beyond' that I face daily. Even things that aren't quite things."

He smiled benignly for an instant before his voice brightened. "Why don't you come and see? You can assist me next week."

Joseph spun around and banged his knee against the table, upsetting the wine bottle and spilling the contents so that it ran through the wrought iron onto Fr. Mark's cassock and the stones below. Ignoring the wine bottle, he stared, mouth open, speechless. When he had recovered somewhat, he responded with incredulity, his first true feeling of the day. "You're an exorcist?"

"Yes. For years. Not something to be proud of. These days it's regarded as little better than witchcraft."

"Then you believe in the apparitions and ventriloquisms, the moving furniture and splintering glass?" The details piled up with the passion and he groaned: "The year of our Lord 1978, and we've gotten as far as the dunking stool!"

What might have been taken as insulting wasn't. The expression on Mark's face was relaxed and generous. "It's not about what I believe, you know. I don't have the secrets of the real. My task is to respond to the person in front of me who's in need. Not in the name of the true. In the name of charity."

"So, you encourage a person who may be a psychiatric case to believe in spooks!" Even Joseph knew this was just grumbling.

"I'm not trying to convince anyone of anything, just to help a helpless soul go on."

Relenting, without crediting a word of it, "And how do you do that?"

"By showing him that he's loved."

"By whom?"

"It's not a matter of someone. The evidence lies elsewhere. The evidence is *made evident* in the fact that he *is* when he might not have been!"

Joseph lifted a hand, dismissing it all. "How did you get caught up in this stuff?"

"The old priest I mentioned, Fr. Bienvenue, asked me to assist him. I don't know why, maybe because others didn't want anything to do with it. I'd say anyone who *can* in charity avoid it *should* avoid it. But occasionally people hear—or think they hear—voices speaking to them, or spirits that take over their 'will,' as in crimes of passion."

"And when there are medical causes?"

"That's a difficult question, but we're careful about it. Our task is not to persuade the victim that he doesn't hear what he hears. Nor to persuade the lover that he's not in love. No. We only give names to nameless things so he is free to decide. You see, we're still speaking of names—prescriptions before the script can be written."

"So you're going to call up and expel the evil spirit in the name of Jesus! If there were a God, he'd strike you with a thunderbolt for the sheer presumption!"

Fr. Mark smiled and continued undeterred. "Translate the command to 'drive out devils' in whatever way makes sense to you. For me it's enough that a fixation on one thing can gain dominion over a life—money, sex, addictions, even obviously good things like knowledge or family. All such slavery can be replaced by gratitude for all and lead to a consistent and healthy way of life. I don't have a theory for it, but I've seen it many times."

Then aside lightly, amused, "Did you know such things still existed? We're an embarrassment to the Church. They may officially deny the myth of progress, but they tacitly accept control over 'evil' nature for the 'good' of human advancement."

"Humph!" Joseph muttered, tuning out what he didn't want to hear. Except that, oddly, he *did* want to hear exactly what he refused to listen to. Somewhere behind the fortress of his convictions he knew all this and was in revolt against that knowledge. He straightened in his chair and resumed the semblance of authority. "I've been trying all my life to see the world clearly. Why should I court bedazzlement?"

Fr. Mark omitted the irrelevant. "Leaving aside the difficulty of giving proper names for dark things, we'll just try to help people who have run out of options. Your role will be to assist me by reading the responses and an occasional Psalm or passage from the Gospels."

Ignoring Joseph's resistance and taking consent for granted, he described the "possessed," a young man of placid disposition named David Larkin, who had been popular, even charming, until he dropped out of college and cut himself off from everyone because of his "voices." Apparently he had a will of his own, except when the voices commanded him to rid the world of filthy people—prostitutes, drug addicts, and the like—to go into the streets at night, quietly kill them, and dump the bodies in a particular remote place in a swamp where he had never been. The familiar spirit seemed to want a clean, orderly world.

"You see?" Fr. Mark added with a chuckle. "A world without people! David's actual temptation isn't to *obey* the voice but to *kill* himself instead."

Joseph, repelled by the subject, squirmed in his chair and repeatedly cleared his throat. Maloney might *say* he didn't believe in specters, but action is what matters. Comes to the same thing. He ends up believing. It's embarrassing in an enlightened age to come across a brother priest who countenances such nonsense. The backward-looking moralism of it! Who is he, this priest, to decide good and evil? Certainly not to accept the word of ancient and inconsistent traditions.

Fr. Mark concluded with a smile as at a childish witticism. "By David's own account, he lost his faith several years ago," without adding that Joseph had said the same a few moments ago. Then gently, in parody, "I've lost my shoes. Now where could I have left them?" Then sadly, "Neglected, more like. It takes practice and good habits to keep up with one's shoes. Maybe neglect has left him with no resources for resisting The Tempter."

He leaned forward and clapped his hands on his knees as though to get up. "So, you come, and we'll see what happens. There'll be others there: the family doctor, David's brother, and his oldest friend. You understand that people sometimes have to be restrained, and we are all likely to be abused verbally, especially the priests. So you'll need to steel yourself. Remember that David himself wishes us no harm. Sometimes these poor souls get violent. Exorcism can be horrible, but it isn't about horror. It's about love."

———

Even a neo-pagan like me, Alex Dupin, can see that in a world rife with compulsive behavior, Joseph's accusing the exorcist of moralism makes no sense. It is *he* who is cutting reality into pieces, deciding which to keep and which to throw out. First by deciding what's real and what's not and then by legislating what *should be* accepted as true. It's what, all along, my tutelary spirit has been trying to get me to recognize in myself. In essence, that the disposition to cover-over amounts to absconding from the potential fully to-be.

But here is what's still not clear to me: If, for example, the spirit of consumerism becomes commonplace by naming it, might the naming itself not encourage that life-diminishing mode of being? What makes the apple from the tree of knowledge irresistible, if not the prohibition against eating it? Or does the warning sign on a dark night that a bridge is out just ahead provide essential information for making a right choice? As if to say, "Here you have slavery and freedom, so why not choose freedom?"

In any event, on the day specified for the exorcism, Joseph, haggard and worn from sleepless nights and an unquiet spirit, puts on his vestments and, without trying to imagine what awaits him, makes his way to an address provided. As anticipation inevitably rises from the prospect of unrealities on such a scale, so does visceral resistance.

The ritual is to begin in the evening at an address in the Irish Channel, where one would expect to meet ordinary working-class people. A stout, middle-aged woman, David Larkin's mother, admits Joseph to a venerable Victorian house where floors and walls and windows, as well as lives, are a bit askew. As he follows the somber Mrs. Larkin up the stairs and down a dimly lit back hall, he has to conceal trembling hands and an uncanny sense of alarm.

Some indistinct physical force pushes against his arms and chest and legs, making his progress laborious. Dreading disaster and humiliation in equal proportions, he checks a barely resistible urge to turn and run from the house by posing the question why a man of the world, a man of science should stoop to enter the haunt of imaginary demons or, if necessary, hesitate to do so. Shouldn't such a man snuff out feelings unworthy of a rational being?

The second-floor corridor leads to a back bedroom, where he's hit in the face by a rush of hot, stale air that smells vaguely of sweat. The shades, drawn over the two windows, leave it dark and desolate. A single bed and one table with a heavily shaded lamp are the only furnishings.

Fr. Mark, in surplice and purple stole, introduces the other persons present, while David, the one allegedly possessed, sits quietly in a chair beside the bed. He's college age, slender, blond, nice looking, perhaps a little shy, but apparently normal. No sign of the raving maniac in a straitjacket that Joseph had imagined. Just a bit disheveled; a bit subdued. The other attendants are also present as promised: the older brother, the friend, and the family doctor, armed with stethoscope and blood pressure sleeve.

Joseph knows the ritual and the stories of exorcisms lasting for days, of violent assaults and physical injuries, of flying furniture, and people physically constrained. All nonsense, of course. And yet anxiety grows.

As Fr. Mark lays out candlesticks, a crucifix, and the prayer book, Joseph recoils from a wave of revulsion that grips his entire body. David, now on the bed, is asked if he is ready and, as he nods assent, the exorcist lights the candles and kneels for the invocation:

"Do not remember, O Lord, our sins or those of our forefathers."

Joseph and the others read the response: "And do not punish us for our offences."

The rite proceeds slowly, and Joseph performs the assigned texts even as his thoughts wander along paths that don't coincide with the scene.

Eventually Fr. Mark rises from the floor, moves to the side of the bed, and calls in a commanding voice: "Snatch from damnation and from this Devil of our times this man who was created in your image and likeness . . . Force the Serpent to let go of your servant."

To hold his attention elsewhere than in the dark room and this outmoded language, the geologist silently fortifies himself against this wicked mythologizing by invoking the names of great anthropologists—Boas among the Kwakiutl, Malinowski in the Trobriand Islands, and Mead in Samoa. Any historical substitute rather than this odious unreality!

Meanwhile, the exorcist, standing now above David, continues reading. "Throw your terror, Lord, over the Beast who is destroying what belongs to you."

David, on his back on the bed, eyes closed, face composed, remains calm until Fr. Mark, still at his side, commands the spirit to reveal himself: "Tell me, with some sign, your name, the day, and the hour of your damnation."

At the command, David writhes as though under attack by a swarm of wasps. His arms appear confined by an unseen force, and his face contorts in pain as of severe toothache. The brother and friend move closer to the bed as the doctor captures one arm to check the pulse.

Holding the crucifix before his face, Fr. Mark commands, "Obey me in everything, although I am an unworthy servant of God."

At that moment a shudder passes through David's body, feet to head. He lurches, convulsive as an epileptic, so that the two muscular men have difficulty pinning him to the bed until the fit passes and leaves him limp and exhausted.

The image of a person stretched on a dark-age rack fills Joseph with pity for the victim and loathing toward the priest who continues issuing commands in a voice not his own. *He's* the one possessed! Glorying in his power to torment this lad. Proof if proof be needed, that his demonic notions about evil spirits open the way for the sadistic witch-hunter and this latter-day Dominican inquisition.

When Fr. Mark again commands the spirit to reveal himself, David half rises from the pillow. In a span of minutes the corpse-white face has been reduced to the bone structure of a death's head, and the voice emanating from the ruined face is no longer David's quiet tenor. It's a deeper, gruff, and mocking voice that hurls accusations of "Deceiver," "Turncoat," "Apostate," "Traitor"—not at the exorcist this time but at Joseph Barthes!

The unrecognizable face turns on the Jesuit with the bared teeth of a snarling beast and eyes that glare with fury. An inhuman voice flings accusing questions at him as though the demon knows him intimately. "Why do you stand by while this ignorant ass torments us with his gibberish? You don't believe this shit. Do you see any spirits in the room? You know there is no such thing as Evil Spirit. This unwashed old fraud is the one possessed."

As the voice snarls with a bestiality not unfamiliar in asylums for the insane, Joseph staggers back against the wall, unaided by his dogma that everything real is objective. Overcome by the alien being on the bed that rails with tongues of fire, he searches the other faces in the room checking for hallucination, but they respond with horror to the same voice and the same face.

"You don't believe in that charlatan Jesus. You're one of us! You sold Christ!" From behind, a voice that Joseph cannot locate in the room,

"Sell him, sell him!" And a choral response: "Wanting to be God, you sold Christ for an idea! You belong to us! You trust power, not love!"

Shock passes into fear and fear into anger as Joseph takes a step forward to meet the accuser, but as he opens his mouth to speak, Fr. Mark lays a restraining hand gently on his arm. The unnatural force of that hand startles him. It's more electric jolt than human touch. The current seems to pass up his arm, through his chest and neck, and glow hot around his head as he breaks into a heavy sweat and remains fixed to the spot, mouth open but voiceless.

Mark had said in advance, "We must not deny whatever we are accused of. To argue is to lose. This is not about truth. It's about the power of love to redeem hate."

At the time Joseph had marveled at such credulity. Now, bereft of power to act otherwise, he stands exposed and dumb, restrained still by the weak but irresistible force of the parish priest.

Again Mark's voice rises with an authority beyond any character attributable to him. "I command you in the name of Jesus to reveal your name. What do we call you?"

David's back arches and he tears himself from the restraints of his hands and feet as though to attack his tormentor. The brother and the friend leap forward, catch him in their arms, and force him back on the bed. They bind the legs and hold the arms, while Mark shouts in an ever-stronger voice: "How many of you are there and how do you call yourself? I command you in the name of Jesus to give your name."

The response to the command "Reveal your name!" comes in another barely articulate snarl: "Ask him!" pointing to Joseph. "He knows us!" Then, without a pause, a wild and hungry howl: "We are The Dragon. And you, you prayer-groaning, cock-sucking, hypocrite priest, why do you lick the dust under the feet of your crucified despot? Think of your little boys in the dark corners of the vestry!"

David tears his arms free and reaches for his genitals. "Come here you psalm-droning slave! I know what you really want, you pious quack!"

Then impossible multiple voices derisively laughing in chorus. "Ha-ha-ha! Ha-hee!"

Though the raillery is directed toward the exorcist, it's Joseph who falls back against the wall farthest from the bed, doubled over as from a body blow. His mouth stretches into a thin, frothy horizontal line against his teeth. Great drops blister his forehead and run down his face, heavy as tears. Under his arms wet circles grow until his cassock is saturated to the waist. The assaulting laughter becomes deafening, and he covers his ears to protect against it. Not the obscenity of words only, but the music of debauchery, the animal gurgles and groans issuing in a foul breath that infects the already polluted air.

Joseph doubles over with pain in the pit of his stomach and falls forward almost to the floor as David grows calm. Something substantial seems to pass from the one to the other, as laughter or tears pass among the people in a room.

Forcing himself into an erect position, filled with the same resentment they have come to purge, Joseph confronts each person in turn for having witnessed his own humiliation. First David, then Mark Maloney, the brother, the doctor, David's friend—exposing each to the pride he has jealously hidden for a lifetime behind the habit of humility. Then he returns to Maloney, shakes an angry finger in his face, and cries, "Don't you dare judge me, you superstitious old charlatan!"

Under the sway of this great negation, his body mutinies and he lurches forward again. Nausea rises from the knot in his stomach into his throat and turns to bile in his mouth.

Father Mark makes the sign of the cross: "Behold the Cross of the Lord."

Joseph retches violently. Lurching forward, vomit running down his cassock onto the floor. He seizes the door handle and rushes out just as Mark, undistracted and undisturbed, commands, "Depart, Enemies! I exorcise you . . . in the name of Our Lord Jesus Christ."

—

Having pursued the history of pride to this point, I must confess that I, too, may be a member of Joseph's party. I feel a strong urge to explain this spook story away. If this is Mark's antidote to Joseph's pride, then is the cure not as bad as the disease itself? At a minimum the supernatural mystery-mongering is disgusting to the habits of the modern mind.

✗ That's what Joseph says repeatedly! Why are you, Scribe, lapsing into instinctive opinions where rigorous thinking is most needed?

I do see darkly. You mean, I suppose, how does the exorcism differ from my taking to heart what an inexistent muse says in the night? Or from the thinker who converses with imaginary interlocutors? Or the poet who insists that his words are not his own? Don't "normal people" respond internally or aloud to unfinished conversations with friends who are not present? As in, "What I should have said was . . ." or "I wonder what answer she would give to the question . . ."

—

After slamming the door, Joseph did not escape the danger. He was followed—or felt he was—down the stairs and into the street where he paused only for a moment as though making a choice. Then without noticing that it had begun to rain, he rushed ahead, the skirt of his stained cassock trailing behind in the mud. Had there been pedestrians on those rainy neighborhood streets, they would have stopped to stare at the figure in the flying black cassock, blotched and rain soaked. A mad priest fleeing demons!

He lost his way and wandered in circles for some time until he emerged at Coliseum Square, not a mile from where he had begun. When eventually he reached The Valmont, he let himself in and felt a surge of comfort at being locked away behind its fortress walls.

Upstairs, he stripped off the clothes that smelled of corruption and dropped them on the floor by the front door. What the rain could not wash off was purged by a long shower. Then, dressed in street clothes, he pushed the abandoned clerical robes, shoes and all, down the garbage chute.

Ordinarily he drank only wine and that sparingly, but not this night. He found a bottle of scotch in his brother-in-law's liquor cabinet and filled a highball glass, straight. The object was oblivion, to exorcise the exorcism by "spirits." He took the glass to the window, where he stared vacantly for a while through the rain into the blind and empty garden.

The events of the last few hours have left him empty and lost. So, to protect against contaminating influences, he pulls a veil of heavy drapery across the glass doors and begins shuffling absentmindedly through research notes. But the geology of the Mississippi Valley has little power over a mind breaking up. As though passing judgment on all knowledge, and on life itself, he tries to cover it over by repeating an old mantra: "'Vanity of vanities. All is vanity.' Especially the thought of vanity."

Eventually he collects himself and drags his travel bags from a closet. He piles all his belongings into the bags indiscriminately—clothes, books, research notes—then pours more scotch and sits down again in the living room just as the lights go out. Searching for the switch box, he loses his way and paces the room in the dark, playing and replaying the scene of his humiliation and cowardly retreat, calling on his no-god to damn this vile city.

Despite the storm, or because of it, he carries his self-contempt downstairs where, shielded from the rain, he feverishly paces the narrow corridors once trod by the feet of the nuns in peace and gratitude for being given. Restlessly he moves up and down the cloister, grateful only for the anonymity of the dark, muttering to himself, trying to justify a life rather than to know himself.

A voice walking beside him, invisible, yet distinctly "there," counters: "Still looking behind for causes? Pride of a knowledge bereft of meaning? Missing the moment and the time that remains!"

Joseph turns around. "Who's there?" Looking uneasily behind, then toward the other wings of the cloister, he reverses his steps. "Someone's here!"

The voice continues: "Loving an opinion because it is *yours*, not because it's true?"

Alarmed, Joseph turns and searches in all directions for a speaker. "This is not in my head. I know I heard a voice."

He makes a full circle, finding nothing but the palpable darkness. "There's someone here," he insists. "I heard it as clearly as my own. Someone is following me, trying to make me listen. But there is no one!"

He searches again. "I won't accept voices speaking from holes in the world!" Wheeling around, "Where are you?"

"In eternity."

"Of course you are!" he scoffs. "And where is that?"

"Between the throbs of a tortured heart. In the moment where the courageous are free to start over."

Confused, Joseph demands, "Show yourself!"

Silence, except for the swirling wind that lashes the garden from every direction. Bent over in frustration and grief, Joseph flees the shelter of the cloister by plunging like mad Lear into the storm.

The water contained by the four wings of The Valmont is ankle deep, obscuring the paths so that his shoes make holes in the mud. Even in the storm he's not alone. He feels—and rejects—the other, the secret agent stalking the sophist who seeks justification rather than clarity.

An impalpable hand touches his shoulder. To a deranged mind it registers as the restraining hand of the exorcist on his arm and momentarily restores his focus.

He straightens, listens, then emits an inaudible groan in protest against inexistent companions. "Demonic! No other name for it. You should have heard that voice!"

"I heard."

"You were there? Then you are real!"

"The question about *is*, is only a way of not-listening. Follow the words."

"Then say what you have to say. Show yourself!"

"Things may be revealed otherwise than to the eye. *You* accept what you can measure and leave out the rest. Thus you miss yourself and the opening into a livable world. Even the singular blade of grass and the pool under your feet."

"No! You've got it all wrong!"

"Be careful: Debate with spirits, and you give them a dwelling place."
"Spirits have minds of their own, do they?"
"Yes. When you lend them yours."
"Ah, you think I'm possessed!"
"To love or not to love is the guiding question."
"Sentimental ass! Away with you!"

More than one and fewer-than-two are standing in a shallow lake, once a lawn, when, suddenly, Joseph spins around as though to throw off the hand on his shoulder, then trips and ends on his back in the mud.

What happens next happens somewhere between the visible and the invisible where no one sees. At least no one is seen seeing, though a candle shines dimly in a third-floor window. The garden has disappeared and left a void, except when a flash of lightning reveals a storm-battered world. Each crash of light gives a black and white snapshot of the scene where plants thrust upward from the rain-soaked earth, thrashed by swirling winds. And two things beside: In the far corner, two indifferent piles of marble and, in the middle, two figures wrestling in the mud. Then the light goes out.

The next flash restores the garden and reveals two adversaries on the ground: Joseph with an opponent in a headlock, face down in the mud. One figure, sometimes two, as each burst of light tears open a place in the visible dark and produces another ruined garden. In one flash, the nameless one has escaped Joseph's hold and sits upright in the mud, while Joseph, on his knees, glares into the face as the light goes out, leaving only voices.

"I will have your name!"

The answer comes in a still, small voice making itself heard through the din of the storm as on a different frequency.

"You may call me Nuntius."

"That's not a name! You think I don't know Latin? Nuntius is messenger. What's your message?"

"Beware, priest. Knowing misses the wisdom of desire and the knowledge of unknowing."

"What I know is that Maloney is an ass, you are an ass, and your god is an ass. I will not be duped! I know truth when I see it, and I don't see you."

—

Joseph taped a note to the condo door, gathered his bags, and called a cab.

To anyone or no one:

Fr. Barthes has been called away suddenly and will
not return.

At the train station there was just time to buy a ticket for New York and points beyond, then rush for the quay. At the waiting-room door, a man approached and offered to carry his bag. Not a red cap. An unshaven and derelict old porter in muddy shoes and an open trench coat. Something in the face was arresting, something more than incongruity or blurred recognition. The effect on Joseph was of seeing himself being seen and being known through and through. The porter reached for the bags, and he surrendered them without protest.

Side by side they walked down the platform without speaking until they reached a sleeping car. The porter handed him the bags, smiled into the wide-open eyes: "Farewell, traveler. Adieu."

Joseph climbed the steps then turned back for another view of the strange little man, but he wasn't there.

www.ingramcontent.com/pod-product-compliance
Lightning Source LLC
Chambersburg PA
CBHW051224210726
48290CB00003B/794